His greeting was brutal.

"You look overtired, Miss Temple. Haven't you slept?"

"I have not," Elinor told him tartly. "Your welcome did not encourage me to spend a restful night."

"I wonder why it should surprise you? To have some chit of a girl dumped on me in the middle of the night—it would try the patience of a saint."

"And you are no saint, my lord. That much is abundantly clear..."

MEG ALEXANDER

HIS LORDSHIP'S DILEMMA

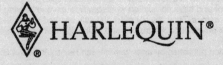

TORONTO • NEW YORK • LONDON
AMSTERDAM • PARIS • SYDNEY • HAMBURG
STOCKHOLM • ATHENS • TOKYO • MILAN • MADRID
PRAGUE • WARSAW • BUDAPEST • AUCKLAND

ISBN 0-373-30316-5

HIS LORDSHIP'S DILEMMA

First North American Publication 1998

MEG ALEXANDER

After living in southern Spain for many years, Meg Alexander now lives in Kent, although, having been born in Lancashire, she feels that her roots are in the north of England. Meg's career has encompassed a wide variety of roles, from professional cook to assistant director of a conference center. She has always been a voracious reader, and loves to write. Other loves include history, cats, gardening, cooking and travel. She has a son and two grandchildren.

Chapter One

They were on the last stage of their journey, but the girl huddled in a corner of the carriage appeared to find no comfort in the thought.

"We should not have come," she whispered in a voice little more than a croak. "His lordship did not reply to your letter. Suppose he should turn us away?"

"At this time of night, my dear? Lord Rokeby will do no such thing. As your guardian he must know his duty."

"I'm sure he does, Miss Temple, but he need not make us welcome. Oh, if only I did not feel so wretched..." She was seized with a fit of coughing.

Elinor quashed her own misgivings. It had been a blow to find his lordship's London mansion closed, with the knocker removed from the door. This told her at once that the owner was not in residence, but a servant had given her the direction of his estate in Kent.

Stiff and tired after the journey on the public coach from Bath, she had considered putting up at an hotel, but her funds were low, and Hester's chill was growing worse.

Even had she known of a respectable place to stay in the city, she could well imagine the reception which would be accorded to two females, one of them unwell, who were travelling with a minimum of luggage, and without an abigail.

By morning, if she were any judge, Hester would be unfit to travel further. She made her decision quickly. They must go on. The public coach had brought them as far as Tunbridge Wells, and there she had used her last few guineas to hire a private carriage for the journey out to Merton Place. She prayed heaven that Lord Rokeby might be at home. If not, she would insist that they were given shelter for the night.

Now she peered into the darkness as they turned through a pair of tall iron gates. At least there was a light in the lodge-keeper's cottage. Relief swept over her as the man confirmed that his lordship had not left the house that day. She turned and put an arm about her weary charge.

"We are there, my love," she said softly. "You will soon be tucked up in your bed."

As they swept along the drive, she thrust her head through the window. Ahead of her the great house was ablaze with light; as they drew up at an imposing flight of steps, the door opened and a figure hurried towards them.

Elinor stepped down from the coach with Hester close behind her. Glad to be rid of his passengers, the coachman dumped their bags beside them and set off again at speed. Elinor looked at the man who came to greet them. He was in livery, and was clearly a servant of some kind.

"Will you please inform Lord Rokeby that his ward is here?" she said pleasantly.

The man looked startled. "Ma'am, his lordship did not say... I mean, he was not expecting..."

"I am aware of that." Elinor began to mount the steps. "I wrote to Lord Rokeby but my letter must have gone astray. Please do as I ask. Miss Hester Winton is not well. She should retire at once."

"But, ma'am, his lordship has given strict instructions. He is entertaining, and may not be disturbed."

Elinor strolled into a lofty hall. There she turned and looked at the agitated man.

"I will take the responsibility," she announced. "Hester, do rest upon this settle for the moment. I shall not be long..."

A loud burst of cheering drowned the rest of her words as a door opened at the far end of the hall. Through it appeared a half-clad maiden with a young man in hot pursuit. Shrieking with laughter, the girl fled towards the staircase. She hadn't reached it before her cavalier caught up with her and kissed her soundly, stripping the remaining draperies from her shoulders as he did so. Then he swept her off her feet and ran lightly up the stairs, still carrying his fair burden.

Elinor glanced at Hester, to find that the girl's eyes were wide with astonishment and dismay.

"Ma'am, I'm sorry..." The servant looked uncomfortable. "If the young lady would care to wait in the library...?"

"That might be best," Elinor agreed. "You need

not announce me…'' Without waiting for a reply she walked towards the open door and entered the room.

A scene of chaos greeted her. On either side of a long dining-table a dozen men lounged, coatless and clearly the worse for wine. From the number of bottles on the table Elinor was unsurprised. What did astonish her was the sight of a woman standing on the table, her skirts drawn up about her waist. It was abundantly clear that this houri had no use for undergarments. All eyes were on her as she took careful aim and kicked at a row of oranges in line before her. Her expertise was undeniable. She did not miss, and grabbed eagerly at the bag of gold which was handed to her as she was lifted down.

''My turn next…'' A red-haired woman disengaged herself from the clutches of the man who had been fondling her breasts, and attempted to climb up on the table.

For a few moments Elinor's presence went undetected. She looked quickly around the table. Surely the fat man slobbering over a voluptuous blonde at the far end of the table could not—must not—be Rokeby. If so, she would remove Hester at once. Then one of the men looked up.

''What's this?'' He held up a hand for silence.

''A Puritan…a virgin? Marcus, you've done it again. I knew we could rely on you for something different. You haven't failed us yet…''

Elinor heard the scrape of a chair drawn aside. She had overlooked the man who was sitting at the head of the table with his back to her. Gently he disengaged the girl who was clinging to his neck and rose to his feet.

When he turned to face her she felt an uncomfortable churning in the pit of her stomach.

This was Rokeby, there could be no doubt of it. So dark as to be gypsy-like and swarthy in appearance, his eyes were extraordinary. In that tanned face they were of the palest blue. She had seen eyes like that in seamen, or those who had travelled to the furthest corners of the earth. She knew at once that he would make an implacable enemy.

Now they roved over her from head to toe, and she coloured, feeling naked beneath his gaze.

"You do me too much honour," he said to the company at large. "I do not know this lady. Bates, I had not understood you to be hard of hearing. Did I not make it clear that all visitors were to be denied?"

Elinor looked at the dejected expression of the servant who had followed her into the room and her temper rose.

"You will please not to blame your man, Lord Rokeby. I insisted upon seeing you." Though her voice was low and musical it reached clearly into every corner of the room. The result of her words was another burst of shouts and cheering.

"Marcus, I never thought I'd live to see the day. Have your chickens come home to roost at last?" The fat man at the far end of the table rose unsteadily to his feet. It was the signal for an outburst of coarse chaffing and cries of "Shame!"

Their meaning was unmistakable. Elinor had no intention of being taken for a wronged woman. She withdrew her gaze from Rokeby and bent it upon the unruly crowd.

That look had served to quell the spirits of many

a class of undisciplined sixteen-year-olds, and it did not fail her now. An uneasy silence fell.

Elinor turned back to Rokeby to see an expression of astonishment mingled with admiration in those curious eyes.

"I have something to say to you, my lord," she announced in a crisp voice. "May we speak in private?"

"Certainly, madam. I am quite at your disposal." The ironic tone did not escape her, but she suffered him to lead her from the room.

Elinor did not waste words. "Your ward is here, Lord Rokeby. I have accompanied her from Bath."

Rokeby's composure vanished, and when he spoke she noted with amusement that his fashionable drawl had disappeared.

"My ward? Good God, woman, what can you be thinking of? This is no place for a child. What right had you to remove her from her school?"

"The school is closed, due to the death of the owner. And Hester is no longer a child. She is seventeen."

"Why bring her to me?"

"You are her legal guardian, sir, and we... Hester had nowhere else to go."

His lordship took a turn about the hall, running his fingers through his tousled hair.

"You can't stay here," he said at last. "Your coach shall take you back to Tunbridge Wells. I will call upon you in the morning."

"Our carriage is gone, my lord."

"I see." His anger flared. "Did you hope to present me with a fait accompli? It will not serve, Miss...?"

"My name is Elinor Temple."

"Well then, Miss Temple, my own carriage shall convey you back to the town."

"That will not be possible. Hester is unwell. She is not fit to travel further."

"I don't believe you!"

"Then you had best see for yourself." Elinor made her way to the library. "This, my love, is Lord Rokeby." She tried to keep her voice impersonal, but even to herself the note of contempt was apparent.

Hester was unaware of it. As she looked up at her guardian with pain-filled eyes she was seized with a fit of coughing. She tried to rise to make her curtsy. Then she fell back with a groan. Elinor laid a cool hand on her brow to find it burning with fever.

His lordship snapped his fingers for his servant. "Bates, you will accommodate these ladies in the west wing. See to their needs." He turned on his heel, clearly in a towering rage, and was about to leave them without another word.

"Lord Rokeby?"

"Miss Temple, I beg you will not address me again until tomorrow. For sheer irresponsibility your actions are difficult to credit. To bring a sick girl halfway across the country on what might well have been a wild-goose chase? It is unbelievable..."

"Hester was quite well when we started out this morning, and had you answered my letter..."

"I received no letter from you. Had I done so, I should have made more suitable arrangements."

"The letter was sent to your home in London."

"Miss Temple, I have been out of the country. I have seen no letters for many months. The lack of a reply makes your actions even less excusable. What, may I ask, would you have done if you had not found me here?''

''We should have stayed to await your return.''

''Without my permission?''

''Without your permission,'' she agreed sweetly.

Rokeby muttered something beneath his breath. It sounded suspiciously like a curse. He strode away without another word.

Glad to be rid of his presence, Elinor turned to Bates.

''Will you show me to our rooms at once?'' she said. ''Miss Winton has a fever. Then, perhaps, a cold drink? Some lemonade, if you would be so kind?''

Bates looked startled. Lemonade was not a beverage which was normally to be found in any of his lordship's establishments, but he nodded.

''Shall I help you with the young lady, miss?''

''No, do you lead the way. We shall manage the stairs.''

She slipped an arm about Hester's waist, and lifted the girl to her feet.

''If you will put your arm about my neck, Hester? Just a few steps, and then you will be comfortable in your bed.''

It was a vain hope. Despite the luxury of down pillows and cool linen sheets Hester coughed continually throughout the hours of darkness. As the first pale light of dawn was streaking the night sky, she fell asleep at last.

Elinor had not undressed, though she had asked for a cot to be brought into Hester's room. She lay down for a time, but could not rest. What a coil she had made of the whole business! Her cheeks flamed as she remembered Rokeby's cutting words, even though his accusations were unjust.

She could not have known that Hester would be taken ill, nor had she imagined that they would arrive at Merton Place to find his lordship indulging in an orgy. Doubtless he was annoyed to be caught at a disadvantage by his two unexpected visitors.

She heard the revellers leaving in the early hours, although the sound of their carousing had not reached the west wing. Even so, she had taken the precaution of locking the doors of their apartments against the possibility of some drunkard bursting in on them.

If this was Rokeby's usual way of life, he was no fit guardian for her charge, but where else could Hester go? Her parents were long dead, carried off seven years ago in a smallpox epidemic. And at seventeen she could not be sent back to school. Elinor herself could not offer the girl a home. The eldest of eight children, she had taken a teaching post to relieve the burden on her family, thankful that her scholarly father had insisted on a classical education for his girls. She could not return to Derbyshire, to become just one more mouth to feed.

She must find another post, but it would not be easy. Most of the girls in her care had been sent away from home to get them out of the way until they had reached marriageable age. They learned deportment, a little painting, embroidery and how to play a musical instrument.

Parents were inclined to frown on too much "bookwork" as they termed it. When Elinor remonstrated with her pupils, she had been assured on more than one occasion that mammas did not believe that gentlemen would offer for any girl regarded as "too clever".

Hester was different. Elinor regarded the flushed face on the pillow with affection. From their first meeting Hester had enjoyed her studies, and for Elinor it had been a joy to watch that young mind unfold.

No beauty, Hester was inclined to plumpness. Her neck was too short, and she had never had the semblance of a waist. Her fine straight hair would not stay in place, and for a time she had been the butt of the other girls. Even her academic brilliance had been greeted with contempt.

Elinor's heart went out to the shy, plain child.

"You have a good brain," she had said. "Remember, Hester, no one can take that away from you. There is no substitute for a keen intelligence."

To her surprise the girl's face had crumpled. "I hate my face," she had sobbed. "If only I were pretty... I wish I looked like you..."

Elinor had stroked her hair. "You would like to be tall and thin?" she'd teased.

"You aren't thin, Miss Temple. Emma Tarrant said that you were willowy..."

"That is a poetic thought." Elinor had eyed her champion with some amusement. "Now go and wash your face, my dear. As you get older you will grow taller and lose your puppy fat, believe me."

But Hester had not done so, and her confidence was fragile. Her puckish sense of humour appeared only in the company of friends. With strangers she was nervous and ill at ease.

Elinor sighed. The girl would never be likely to feel at ease with the sophisticated rake who was her guardian. She found herself wondering why he had undertaken such a charge…a charge for which he was clearly unsuited. There had been some mention of distant kinship, but in all the years that Hester had been away at school he had not troubled to visit her. She must make it her business to find out more about him.

She began to examine the few garments which the maid had hung in the cupboard. They were sadly crumpled, but it was no matter. Hester would not rise that day. Her own grey woollen morning-dress had suffered less. She was about to change when she heard a knock at the door.

The arrival of a chambermaid with coffee, fruit and rolls was more than welcome. Elinor had not eaten since noon on the previous day, and her stomach was protesting.

She smiled at the girl as she searched for a shawl to throw about her shoulders.

"Why, miss, the fire is almost out. You'll catch your death. I'll send the footman up to you."

"Thank you." Elinor gave her a grateful look. She did feel cold, but she had put it down to weariness. "I'd like some hot water, if you please."

"Yes, Miss, at once. Bates says that you are to ask for anything you need. Must I take your gowns away for pressing?"

"That would be kind." For some unaccountable reason Elinor was glad to realise that she would not need to face his lordship in clothing which might cause a sneer, though naturally it did not matter what he thought, either of her or her attire.

Hester was still asleep, and there was no point in wakening her, so Elinor settled down to eat her breakfast. With the arrival of hot water, a footman to mend the fire, and the return of her neatly pressed gowns she began to feel more hopeful.

By now Lord Rokeby must have had time to consider his position. Surely he would think of a solution to their problems. It could not be denied that Hester was his responsibility but, try as she might Elinor could not imagine what he would suggest. She prayed that his decision might be satisfactory.

Fond as she was of Hester her own position must be considered. The journey from Bath had made serious inroads into her few savings, and it was imperative that she find another post without delay. And, to be honest, she had no wish to remain at Merton Place. A few minutes conversation with Lord Rokeby had convinced her that he and she would quickly be at odds.

At all costs she must keep her temper during the coming interview. No purpose could possibly be served by telling his lordship what she had thought of his behaviour on the previous evening. Whatever provocation he might offer, she must hold her tongue.

That was easier said than done. When Bates arrived at her door, he bore a message from his master. Lord Rokeby presented his compliments and would like to see Miss Temple in the library without delay.

Crushing down the flutter of anxiety in the pit of her stomach, Elinor went down to meet him. His greeting was brutal.

"You look fagged to death, Miss Temple. Haven't you slept?"

Elinor forgot her noble resolutions.

"I have not," she told him tartly. "Your welcome did not encourage me to spend a restful night."

"I wonder why it should surprise you? To have some chit of a girl dumped on me in the middle of the night, together with her duenna—it would try the patience of a saint."

"And you are no saint, my lord. That much is abundantly clear..."

"Shocked, my dear? A man must take his pleasures where he may. Doubtless you found the display of carnal instincts a little disturbing. Lack of experience, Miss Temple? I wonder now that I did not ask you to join us."

It was a calculated insult, but Elinor did not rise to the bait.

"Sir, we have much to discuss. May I ask what plans you have for Hester?"

His lordship strolled over to a chair, sank into it, and stretched out his long legs.

"None whatever, Miss Temple. You appear to have a managing disposition. Will you not give me the benefit of your advice?"

"You have not asked me how she is today," Elinor said sharply.

"I know how she is. She is suffering from a severe chill. She will be confined to her bed for several days, and then she is like to need a period of convalescence."

Elinor stared at him. She was surprised to find that his diagnosis matched her own.

"I was not referring to Hester's physical condition," she said with dignity. "I am concerned about her future."

"Are you indeed? May I ask the reason for your interest in my ward?"

"Your ward?" Elinor did not trouble to hide her contempt. "If I am not mistaken, sir, you had forgot that she existed. I wonder that you should have undertaken the charge since you have had so little interest in her."

For a heart-stopping moment, she wondered if she had gone too far. A muscle in his lordship's jaw had tightened. Then he glanced at her through lowered lids.

"How well you understand me," he said softly. "Shall I satisfy your curiosity? You are right, of course. I was motivated by no moral arguments. My purpose was to thwart the ambitions of my late aunt's husband."

"Your uncle?" Elinor was puzzled. "I do not understand you."

"Lord Dacre is my uncle by marriage only, Miss Temple. I claim him as no relative of mine. My aunt suffered much at his hands." His face darkened.

"Might it not have been better to allow her to take charge of Hester?"

"She died in child-bed within a year of her marriage. She had no wish to live, you see." His face was oddly twisted.

"And the child?"

"A whey-faced stripling in his twenties, so I hear. I have not met him, and have no desire to do so."

"You would judge him unseen and unheard? Does anyone meet with your approval, sir?"

He was out of his chair in a single lithe movement. Two steps brought him to her side and he gripped her lightly by the shoulders.

"Why, yes," he said lightly. "I had ever a softness for a slender form and large grey eyes. This morning I fancy they are flecked with amber. May I satisfy my curiosity?''

Elinor turned her head away as she strove to free herself. He was much too close and she found that her heart was pounding, partly from the shock of his behaviour and partly from a deeper, more disturbing feeling. She could feel the warmth of his fingers through the fabric of her gown, and it caused an unaccustomed flutter in the pit of her stomach.

"Look at me," he said softly. Lean fingers cupped her chin and he raised her face to his.

"Yes," he murmured. "It is as I thought. There are sparks of magical colour against the grey..."

Elinor stood stiff and silent within his grasp, as anger threatened to overwhelm her. How dared he insult her so? Did he hope to drive her away?

Rokeby bent closer, and she was strongly aware of a male scent of fine tobacco, soap, leather and broadcloth, mixed with a faint aroma of the outdoors. For an awful moment she suspected that he intended to kiss her. If he did so she could no longer stay beneath his roof. Squarely she held his gaze.

"Sir, we are wasting time. We were discussing Hester."

"So we were." He turned away with a glint of amusement in his eyes. "May I compliment you, Miss Temple? My manners do not frighten you, I think."

Elinor was tempted to ask if he could lay claim to any manners, but she did not. "Why should I fear you?" she demanded coldly. "We fear only those who are able to do us harm."

"And you are inviolate? A charming notion, but

misplaced. You will not tell me that no man has succumbed to your evident charms?''

"I shall not tell you anything of my life. I wish to know what is to become of Hester."

"You have no suggestions, ma'am, as to what I am to do with her?"

"None, my lord. The decision must be yours..."

"Then naturally you will agree with whatever course of action I suggest?"

Elinor saw the glint of mischief in his eyes and knew at once that she must tread carefully if she were not to find herself embroiled in some scheme which she could not countenance.

"I can have nothing to say in the matter," she announced in a colourless tone.

Rokeby threw back his head and laughed aloud. "Come Miss Temple, you shall not take me for a fool. Since your arrival we have conversed for less than an hour. It has been long enough to convince me that you will fight me tooth and nail if you disapprove of my decision."

"And that is?"

"I'll give the girl a season. It may be enough to allow her to find a suitable husband."

"To take her off your hands? Hester is young, my lord. She is no judge of character..."

"I can lay claim to neither of those interesting attributes. You may rest assured that I shall choose her husband with great care. There is, however, one condition..."

"Which is?"

"That you stay with her for the next few months at least. If she is as green as you say...and I believe you...she will need the support of all your self-assurance. You, I am convinced, will find no difficulty in hinting away all the gazetted fortune-hunters…''

''Fortune-hunters?'' Elinor gazed at him in astonishment.

''You did not know? Hester is a considerable heiress, ma'am, and for that we must be thankful. You will be working with unpromising material, I fear. I had not thought it possible for any girl to be so plain.''

''That is both unkind and unfair.'' Elinor fired up at once in defence of her charge. ''She was feeling wretched when you saw her.''

''And looked it.'' Rokeby's reply was unfeeling. ''Still, her wealth will serve to cast a veil over her shortcomings…''

Elinor was speechless with indignation. She was strongly tempted to strike his snuff-box from his hand. Instead, she turned away in an effort to control her rage.

''Well, Miss Temple, do you agree with my suggestion?''

''I cannot, sir.'' Elinor flushed. ''I must find another post without delay.'' She had no wish to discuss her poverty-stricken state with Rokeby, or to explain that each quarter she sent back to Derbyshire what little she could spare.

''I have just offered you a post,'' he told her quietly. ''Your allowance would be generous…'' He mentioned a sum which caused her eyes to widen. ''I must also reimburse you for the cost of your journey here.''

He walked over to his desk, unlocked the middle drawer, and handed her a small leather bag. The weight told her at once that it was gold.

"This is too much, my lord. I will write down the details of our travelling expenses."

"Take it!" he commanded. "Today I leave for London, but before I go I must have your decision."

"Not today, Lord Rokeby. I must have time to consider." Every instinct warned her against acceptance. True, she could watch over Hester, and her financial worries would be over, but she did not underestimate the danger.

Rokeby represented everything she disliked most in a man. Not only was he steeped in vice, but he was arrogant and unfeeling—the perfect example of one who had inherited wealth at an early age and grown to manhood with no curb upon his morals.

"You have ten days," he announced. "After that I shall be forced to make other plans for my ward." His tone left her in no doubt that they would be far from pleasant.

Rokeby strode towards the door. "Merton Place is yours until my return," he told her. "I beg that you will not terrorise my servants in my absence, Miss Temple. Hurling unruly servitors from the battlements is quite out of fashion."

"I had not noticed any battlements," Elinor replied demurely.

"Perhaps not, but the same applies to the use of boiling oil."

Elinor was tempted. She raised her eyes to his, and again he seemed to read her mind.

"Ah, I understand," he said with a slight smile. "The boiling oil is to be reserved for me."

He was gone before she could think of a suitably cutting retort, and the door had closed behind him before she realised that she had failed to discover his exact relationship to Hester.

Chapter Two

As Elinor returned to her patient, her mind was deeply troubled. Had his lordship's offer come from anyone else she might have welcomed it, though she considered Hester too young for marriage. The girl was barely out of the schoolroom, and knew nothing of the world. She doubted if her charge had ever held a conversation with a man.

Yet it might be the answer. Girls as young as Hester were betrothed and wed each season, to the satisfaction of their parents and themselves.

But Rokeby had made it clear that the choice of a suitable husband would be his alone. Elinor shuddered at the thought of the crowd of roisterers about his dining-table. Would Hester be given in marriage to some creature such as the fat man who had shared his board? That would not happen if she could prevent it.

Perhaps Rokeby intended Hester for himself? No... She dismissed the idea at once. It was preposterous. Rokeby was a wealthy man. He had no need of Hester's fortune. Yet, had he been penniless, she doubted if he would have offered for the girl. Even on short acquaintance she had become aware that his lordship's taste in females was that of a connoisseur. She had been well conscious of the dismay in his expression as he looked at Hester.

She had no patience with such arrogance, and she despised him for his lack of charity. As for herself...he had tried hard enough to put her out of countenance.

The low murmur of his voice as he'd gazed into her eyes had been almost a promise of seduction.

And those cheap compliments had been insulting, she decided with a sudden spurt of anger. She, no more than Hester, could have no appeal for a rake. A vivid memory of the raven-haired beauty, white fingers caressing the nape of Rokeby's neck, who had been seated on his lap the night before, returned to taunt her.

Did the man feel obliged to challenge the sexuality of every woman he met? If so, she was not mistaken in her judgment of his character. She would not leave Hester in the care of such a man without as much protection as she could give.

Once her decision had been made, Elinor began to consider practicalities. The difficulties of her own situation must be set aside for the moment. She would save what money she could from the generous sum which Rokeby had suggested as her allowance. Then, if Hester did eventually marry, she would be independent.

Her thoughts returned to Hester. When she entered the bedroom she found that her patient was awake, though still feverish. As Elinor moved towards the bed she tried to struggle upright against her pillows.

"No, my dear, stay where you are. You shall not

leave your bed today. Will you take a little nourishment?''

''I...I cannot. My throat feels as if I have swallowed thorns...''

''Then perhaps a cooling drink?'' Elinor tugged at the bell-pull to summon the maid.

It was his lordship's housekeeper who came into the room.

''My name is Onslow, miss.'' The plump little woman gave her a cheerful smile. ''Is the young lady better?''

''Her throat is painful, Mrs Onslow. She cannot eat, but if she might have some more of your excellent lemonade...?''

''She shall take it mixed with honey. Now, don't you go worrying, Miss Temple. As a boy his lordship never got through the winter without a putrid throat. Rest and warmth is the best cure. She'll feel more herself tomorrow.''

Elinor smiled at her. ''Have you served Lord Rokeby for long?''

''For all his life, and his father before him.'' There was a note of pride in Mrs Onslow's voice. ''Now then, ma'am, shall you wish to take your nuncheon in the dining-room, or shall Robert set up a table here?''

''In here, if you please...and just a tray with something light...'' The thought of eating alone in that enormous dining-room held no appeal for Elinor, and her appetite had deserted her.

She managed to eat a wing of chicken and some Italian salad, but she felt utterly weary. Hester had fallen asleep again, so she stretched out on her cot, vowing to close her eyes for no more than a few minutes.

When she awoke she found that the curtains had been drawn against the early darkness of a winter afternoon, and the fire was burning merrily in the grate.

Elinor glanced at the ornate clock upon the mantelshelf and was surprised to find that she had slept for several hours.

"Miss Temple?"

"Yes, my dear?" Elinor was on her feet at once. "How are you feeling now?"

"My throat is better, but I'm sorry to be a trouble to you, and to Lord Rokeby."

"You did not fall sick on purpose," Elinor said reasonably. "And Mrs Onslow tells me that, as a boy, his lordship suffered often from the same complaint."

"But what must he think of me? I did not even make my curtsy to him. In fact, I can't remember much about him, except that I thought him a black-looking man."

"You were tired and ill," Elinor soothed. "As you learn to know him better, you will grow fond of him." She kept her fingers firmly crossed behind her back.

"Shall I?" Hester put a hand up to her head. "It all seemed so strange last night. There was so much noise...and a girl ran across the hall...and then a man. Was I dreaming?"

"Lord Rokeby was entertaining his friends," Elinor told her smoothly. "They are gone away, and so is he...to London, for a time. We have the house to ourselves."

"Then I need not see him again just yet." Hester gave a perceptible sigh of relief. "I thought he seemed...formidable."

"That was your imagination. Now let me help you out of bed. You shall sit by the fire and bathe your face and hands whilst the bed is made for you. Then I shall go down to the library and find a book. We'll have our supper up here, and spend a cosy evening together."

The girl looked up at her with a sigh of gratitude. "I wish it could always be like this...with just the two of us."

"You would soon tire of that, my dear. Now that you are a woman grown, you must take your rightful place in society."

"Must I? I had much rather not." Hester wore a hunted expression. "Miss Temple, I don't know what to say to people...to strangers, I mean."

"Young ladies making their come-out are not required to be brilliant conversationalists, Hester. In any case, you will find that most of the people you meet prefer to talk about themselves. It is a common human frailty." Elinor rang for the maid. Then she made her way down to the library.

She was amazed by the range of books she found there. For a time she lingered over the beautifully bound volumes of Greek philosophy and ancient history, eyeing them with appreciation. Then she turned to more modern works.

Evelina, or a Young Lady's Entrance into the World looked promising. She had heard of the book, which was by a female author—a Miss Burney. The subject, she hoped, would interest Hester.

She returned to find her patient looking more comfortable in a clean bed-gown, and propped up against her pillows. A tantalising smell arose from the table which had been set beside the bed, but Hester would not eat.

"Now, Miss Temple, don't you fret yourself." Mrs Onslow stood beside the steaming dishes. "The young lady has flesh upon her bones. 'Twill do her no harm to fast for a day or two."

Elinor managed a faint smile. "I don't feel very hungry myself," she confessed.

"You are tired, miss, that's all. Now do you try a little of cook's cream soup. 'Tis made with leeks and potatoes and is very nourishing…" She removed the lid from a great tureen and served Elinor without more ado.

Elinor refused the timbale of macaroni which followed, but she accepted a little of the fish.

"That was delicious," she said at last. "We seldom saw fish at Bath…being so far from the sea. You will give my compliments to his lordship's cook?"

"Chef will be disappointed, Miss. You ain't touched his glazed beef, or the orange jelly."

"Perhaps tomorrow," Elinor promised. "Then we shall both enjoy the jelly. Hester, won't you try a little now? It will slip down easily."

Hester shook her head. "Just a drink," she croaked.

When the dishes had been removed, Elinor began to read aloud, but the story which had kept Sir Joshua Reynolds awake all night failed to do the same for Hester. In a very few moments she was asleep.

Elinor laid the book aside. She had much to think about. It was a blessing that Rokeby had decided to return to London for the time being, but she would have given much to know his plans. Did he do much entertaining at Merton Place? She would try to learn more from Mrs Onslow. Hester could not stay in her room for ever, but she must not be exposed to the rackety company of his lordship's friends. An heiress would be an obvious target for such men.

Still, Rokeby had spoken of giving Hester a season, and that meant London. But how was he to launch her into society? He would need the good offices of some lady who had the entrée into the highest circles to act as chaperone to Hester.

A lady? Elinor's lips twisted in scorn. She doubted if he were acquainted with a respectable woman. And, even if he should succeed in finding such a person, what would be her own position? Most probably little more than a lady's-maid.

There was another consideration. Where were they to live? Rokeby's bachelor establishment could not be considered suitable as a home for two unmarried females. If only the wretched creature had a wife! She sighed in despair. Whatever her worries, she could could not wish that fate upon some unfortunate girl.

She undressed slowly, still searching for some solution to her problems, but exhaustion overtook her. Within minutes she was sound asleep.

By the following day Hester's throat was much improved though she still felt unwell. Her cough had given way to fits of sneezing and her eyes were streaming.

"'Tis the usual course of a chill," Mrs Onslow

had announced. "Miss Temple, you are looking pale. Will you not step out for a breath of air?"

Elinor welcomed the suggestion. She had hardly left Hester's sick room since their arrival, and she prayed that she, too, would not catch the infection. She would need all her wits about her if she were to deal with Rokeby.

The air was still as she left the house in the cold of a December morning. Frost rimed the grass and, though she was wearing pattens, she kept to the gravel paths as she walked through the parterre. Locked in their winter sleep, the gardens appeared as desolate as her mood, but when she reached the height of an elevated knoll and turned to look back her spirits lifted.

The old stone house was beautifully sited in a fold of the Kentish hills. It looked as if it had been a part of that rolling countryside for centuries. No battlements, she noted with amusement, though the frontage had been embellished with colonnades, which she guessed were of more recent origin.

It looked what it was—a comfortable country mansion eminently suitable for a gentleman of means, surrounded by parkland designed in the modern taste. Capability Brown? She thought not. There was no lake, and no sign of a river with its course altered to improve the landscape, or evidence of a hill being raised and planted with an artful arrangement of trees. This was the work of a gifted amateur.

She had wandered further than she had intended; when she consulted her watch, she was surprised to find that it was already noon. She turned and hastened back towards the house. It would not do to upset Chef.

Bates met her in the doorway.

"Miss Temple, you have a visitor. It is Mr Charlbury—one of his lordship's friends. I have put him in the library."

Elinor's heart sank. She had no wish to meet any of the men who had so disgusted her on the night of her arrival.

"You did not tell him that Lord Rokeby was away from home?"

"I did, miss, but he said that he would wait."

Elinor straightened her shoulders. Her unwelcome visitor should be sent about his business without delay.

Mr Charlbury's appearance came as a shock to her. Tall and thin, she guessed him to be in his early thirties, about the same age as Lord Rokeby. What disarmed her was the sweetness of his smile.

"You must forgive me, Miss Temple," he said quietly. "I had no notion that Marcus was to be away. We meet each week, you see, for a wrangle on questions of philosophy." He gestured vaguely in the direction of the books.

Elinor looked her astonishment. "You surprise me, sir. I had not thought his lordship interested..."

"Have you known him long?"

"We met but a day ago, Mr Charlbury. I have accompanied his ward to Merton Place."

It was Charlbury's turn to look astonished. "His ward? He said nothing of her to me."

"I believe he had forgotten she existed." Elinor's tone was dry. "At present she is suffering from a chill, and is confined to her room."

"I am sorry to hear it, ma'am, and trust that the

young lady will soon be recovered. If there is anything I can do in Rokeby's absence…?''

"Perhaps you would care to stay for a light nuncheon?'' Elinor had taken a liking to this shy creature. She could not imagine him in the company of Rokeby, but clearly he was one of his lordship's closest friends, and an ally would be useful.

Charlbury took little persuasion, and they were enjoying a dish of oyster patties when Elinor broached the subject of his friend.

"You have known Lord Rokeby for long?'' she asked.

"Since boyhood, ma'am. We have always been close. He is the best of men.''

Elinor looked her astonishment, and he hid a smile.

"You must not let Marcus tease you,'' he said gently. "His manner can be provoking, but you will admit that the sudden arrival of his ward must have been a shock.''

"It was indeed!'' Elinor could not let this masterpiece of understatement pass. "I fear too that we appeared at an inopportune moment. His lordship was entertaining…''

"The hunting fraternity? They are a high-spirited crowd.'' He was careful not to elaborate. "I do not care for the sport myself, so my acquaintance among them is slight.'' He avoided Elinor's eye, and she made haste to change the subject.

There was no point in mentioning the ladies of questionable virtue who had shared the gentlemen's board that night, and later, no doubt, their beds.

"I had not thought of Lord Rokeby as a philosopher," she said with a smile. "Yet you tell me that you and he enjoy the subject..."

Charlbury waxed enthusiastic, and in the next hour Elinor learned much about her enigmatic host. Rokeby's interests were evidently wider than she had imagined.

"We are both members of the Royal Society," he continued. "We study matters of scientific interest."

Elinor nodded, though she was convinced that Rokeby's scientific interest lay more in the study of the female sex.

"I see that you are surprised, Miss Temple. It is not to be wondered at. Marcus likes to give the impression that he lives for pleasure alone. Nothing could be further from the truth. You will not find a better-run estate than this in the length of England."

"Doubtless his lordship is able to rely upon the experience of his bailiffs and his steward..."

"That's true, but the men who served his father are no longer young. They are inclined to be set in their ways. It has been no easy task for him to persuade them to adopt new methods of farming the land, but he has done it."

"I don't doubt it," Elinor said tartly. "He does not strike me as a man who would brook opposition."

Charlbury looked at her, his head on one side. "He believes in persuasion. Should it surprise you to learn that the welfare of his people here is foremost in his mind? At Merton you will find no wretched hovels and starving labourers. When you drive out, you will see that each man has a patch of ground beside his home, where he may keep a pig or some chickens, and grow enough food to feed his family."

Elinor smiled. "I begin to see why you think so well of Lord Rokeby. Do you farm yourself?"

"In a much smaller way. Marcus allows me to borrow all his works upon the subject. I believe he has every modern treatise that is published." He looked at the clock and jumped to his feet. "Do forgive me. I have outstayed my welcome."

"Not at all. I have enjoyed your company."

"Then I may come again? You have caused me to forget the main purpose of my visit. Marcus gives a Yuletide feast for friends and tenantry each year, and my family shares it with him. There were some small matters to discuss."

"Then you are our neighbour, Sir Charlbury?"

"I live just beyond the hill. When Marcus returns, he shall bring you and Miss Winton to visit us."

It was not until he had ridden away that Elinor thought to question the propriety of dining alone with a total stranger. True, Rokeby had assured her that in his absence she was to be sole mistress of Merton Place, but... She frowned. In future, perhaps she should be more circumspect, but she could not regret the time spent in John Charlbury's company.

He had given her much food for thought. Perhaps she had judged Lord Rokeby too hastily. Clearly there was another side to his character, yet she distrusted him.

It was some days before Hester felt able to leave her room, and Elinor found that time hung heavily on her hands. She had explored his lordship's library and found that Charlbury had not exaggerated the breadth of her employer's interests. The man was an enigma, and he intrigued her.

She looked across at Hester as they sat together by a roaring fire in a small withdrawing-room. A week of voluntary fasting had resulted in a spectacular loss of weight, and the girl's blue eyes now looked enormous in her pale face. Yet she was smiling as she read aloud from the *Spectator*.

The smile vanished quickly as a visitor was announced and Hester jumped to her feet. Elinor stayed her with an outstretched hand.

"You shall not run away," she said gently. "Mr Charlbury is no ogre. I liked him very much, and so will you."

Hester looked unconvinced. Her hunted expression had returned, and after the first conventional greetings she was silent.

Wisely, Charlbury addressed most of his words to Elinor, giving Hester time to recover her composure.

"No sign of Marcus yet?" he asked.

"We expect Lord Rokeby daily," Elinor assured him. "I hope that your arrangements may then go ahead."

"There is plenty of time, Miss Temple." Charlbury picked up the copy of the *Spectator* which Hester had laid aside. "Are you enjoying this excellent paper, Miss Winton?"

"Very much, I thank you, sir." Hester blushed to find herself at the centre of attention.

"You have read the essay on Sir Roger de Coverley?"

"Not yet."

"Then you must do so." He began to quote and soon had his listeners laughing so heartily that they did not hear the bustle in the hall.

Then the door opened and Rokeby strolled towards them, snuff-box in hand.

"I must congratulate you, John," his lordship murmured smoothly. "You have succeeded where I could not. You have made Miss Temple smile."

"Marcus, behave yourself! You shall not put the ladies out of countenance, especially when we are having such a famous time…"

"So I see." Rokeby looked at Hester. "I trust you are much recovered, my dear."

Hester jumped to her feet and sank into a clumsy curtsy, wobbling uncertainly as she did so.

Rokeby put out a hand to steady her.

"Still a little lightheaded, I see." He assisted her to her chair, and looked across at Elinor. "All is well here, Miss Temple?"

"You will find no broken bodies, my lord."

Charlbury and Hester looked mystified, but Rokeby's lips twitched.

"I am glad to hear it. John, you will dine with us, I hope?"

"A pleasure!" Charlbury smiled at his companions. During their nuncheon, he set himself to put Hester at her ease, and succeeded so well that the girl was soon absorbed in his conversation.

Elinor heaved an inward sigh of relief.

"A charmer, is he not?" Rokebury murmured in her ear.

"He does not strive to be so, which makes his kindness all the more endearing."

Rokeby smiled. "So he has become a favourite with you? I am happy to see that at least one of my friends meets with your approval."

Elinor ignored his reference to the night of their arrival. She changed the subject.

"Mr Charlbury called upon us last week," she said. "I believe that you entertain your tenants during the Christmas season. He wished to discuss the arrangements."

"Ah, yes." An imp of mischief lurked in his eyes as he looked at her. "Yet another orgy, I fear, Miss Temple, but this one you will be required to attend."

Elinor refused to be drawn. Her chin went up.

"I look forward to it, sir."

"To an orgy? Come, come, Miss Temple, I had supposed you to be set against such frivolity. There will be feasting, dancing, kissing beneath the mistletoe... Are you quite sure that you approve?"

"You are pleased to joke, my lord. I can assure you that I am not—"

"Quite the strait-laced miss that I suggest? I know that well, Miss Temple. Your expression can be severe, but your mouth gives you away. Those full lips...the curve when you smile..."

"Lord Rokeby, this is nonsense! At our first meeting you described me as the duenna of your ward. That is my position, and so it shall remain. If you wish me to undertake her charge as you suggested, I trust that you will treat me—"

"With proper respect? You have my word on it." He laid a hand over his heart.

To her fury Elinor realised that he was laughing at her.

"You have made arrangements for our stay in London?" she demanded.

"I have. We shall discuss them later. Am I to understand that we are in agreement? You will stay with Hester?"

"I will...for the time being—"

"Dependent upon my good behaviour? You drive a hard bargain, Miss Temple. Think what it means for a man of my unbridled appetites to be forced to tread the path of virtue." The blue eyes sparkled in his dark face.

Elinor turned to Charlbury, who was engrossed in a discussion about the recent Treaty of Amiens.

"Will the peace with Napoleon last?" she asked. It was enough to draw the four of them into an animated discussion, and Hester so far forgot her shyness as to give a good account of herself in the general conversation.

Rokeby was surprised, but he withheld his comments until later in the day.

He had summoned Elinor to the library.

"You have done well with the girl," he said without preamble. "She appears to have a mind of her own."

"She has. I wonder why it should surprise you."

"It is not usual, Miss Temple. You will not tell me that all the girls in your charge had similar interests?"

"No, they had not," Elinor admitted. "Hester was outstanding, no matter what you may think of her appearance."

"That is no matter," Rokeby mused. "It can be improved, and she has lost flesh since her illness." For some moments he was silent, lost in thought. "There will be much work to do," he said at last.

"We shall spend Christmas here, and then we shall go to London."

"My lord, where are we to live?"

"Well, hardly beneath my own roof." He was laughing at her again. "I have made some arrangements with a lady of my acquaintance, Miss Temple—" He raised a hand to forestall Elinor's objections.

"You will find the lady beyond reproach," he assured her. "My aunt has entrée to the highest circles. Even you may feel that she is a little...shall we say...high in the instep."

"Sir, I should like to be quite clear... What is my own position to be?"

"My dear Miss Temple, you are to be the equal of my ward, of course. You will be her friend and mentor."

"You forget my situation, your lordship."

"Just as you forgot to mention your distinguished connections? Your maternal grandfather is General Marchington, is he not? I wonder that you did not tell me of the relationship."

"It did not seem appropriate or necessary." Elinor was startled. It was clear that her future employer had taken the trouble to make inquiries about her.

"Then let us have no more of this nonsense. If you will guide my ward I shall be grateful. This charge is a trouble to me. I shall be happy to be free of it."

"I wonder that you should have undertaken it in the first place," Elinor flung at him. The words were out before she had time to consider their effect.

Rokeby's face darkened, and when he spoke his

voice was icy. "I thought I had explained," he gritted out.

"A disagreement with your uncle? It seems little enough reason to wish to gain control of another person's life..."

He gave her a sardonic smile. "I did not wish it, ma'am. The charge was laid upon me by a distant cousin."

"You might have refused it," she pointed out.

"True, but I did not. Hester might have found herself in very different circumstances."

"I don't understand you."

"Then let me explain." The grim smile had returned. "This may come as a shock to you, Miss Temple, but the courts do not require kinship when determining the disposition of an orphan. Anyone may apply to be a guardian."

"Surely not? What possible motive could there be?"

"The answer is not far to seek when the orphan in question is an heir or heiress. A guardian has full control of their fortunes at least until they reach majority, or, in the case of a girl, until she marries. There are rich pickings to be had."

"I find it difficult to believe that anyone would abuse such a trust."

"Do you? Then I fear I must disillusion you. Hester might easily have fallen into unscrupulous hands."

Elinor stared at him. "Then you do care about her?"

"I do not know the girl. How should I care about her?" His face was a mask of indifference. "As you so rightly guessed, I had almost forgot her existence.

Her fees were paid through my man of business…and I had no news of her.''

Elinor gazed at him in disbelief. "You did not think to seek her out…to comfort her in her loss?" She turned away before he could reply and was about to leave the room.

"One moment, please. Charlbury has suggested that we visit him on Thursday. This meets with your approval?"

"It will be a pleasure," Elinor said with feeling. At least in Charlbury's company she was spared the verbal sparring which seemed to be her lot whenever she met Lord Rokeby.

She heard what sounded suspiciously like a chuckle, but when she glanced up Rokeby's expression was bland.

"There is one other point," he murmured smoothly. "You will find some boxes in your room—trifles of dress and so on. I hope you will find them to your taste. I was…er…forced to guess at the sizes."

"The sizes? Sir, I hope this does not mean that you have taken the liberty of choosing a garment for me." Her voice was warm with indignation.

"Garments, Miss Temple…garments. Now do not fire up at me. We shall be entertaining over the festive season, and you have had no opportunity for shopping. If your virtue is outraged you may reimburse me as you think fit. Look at the gowns…you may not like them." His eyes were veiled, and she could not see his expression, but she guessed that he was laughing at her again. She flounced out of the room.

How dared he presume to choose her clothes? She

could well imagine his idea of a suitable gown for
evening wear. If he hoped to present her to his
friends in the type of finery worn by the half-naked
strumpet she had last seen upon his lap, he was mistaken. She would not even look at the gowns.

She was too late. When she reached her room, she
found that the boxes had been unpacked and Hester
was in raptures.

"Miss Temple, do but look at this! It's mine…my
name was on the box." Hester held up a gown of
cream silk tobine. The short puffed sleeves were
trimmed with self-coloured ribbon delicately embroidered with pale blue flowers.

Even to herself, Elinor was forced to admit that it
was an ideal choice for a young girl's first ball-gown.
And cream was, for Hester, a more becoming shade
than white. It warmed her pale skin, and made a perfect background for the small string of river pearls
which she wore about her neck.

"The pearls?" Elinor questioned.

"They are a present too, and so is this, and this."
She pointed to a morning dress made up to the throat,
with sleeves buttoned tightly at the wrists in a deeper
blue. Beside it lay another morning gown in
lavender.

Elinor hugged her, disarmed by the girl's excitement.

"You will be very fine," she announced. "Which
shall you wear when we visit Mr Charlbury on
Thursday?"

Elinor had half expected protestations of dismay
at the prospect of their outing, but none were forthcoming.

"The blue, I think. Miss Temple, the gowns on the other bed are yours. Won't you look at them?"

Elinor hesitated. Would it be possible to explain to Hester that, whilst her guardian had the right to buy whatever he wished for her, there was a question of propriety where Elinor was concerned?

"Do hold them up," Hester urged. "The colours are so lovely…"

A glance at the girl's bright face decided her. It would be churlish to rob the child of so much pleasure. After all, Rokeby had promised that she could pay for the gowns, and her allowance was more than generous. It was just that she disliked the notion of wearing anything which might be his lordship's choice.

It could do no harm to look at the garments. Doubtless they would be quite unsuitable, or at best they would not fit her. Then it would be a simple matter to return them to him.

Pleasure mingled with exasperation as her eye fell upon a half-gown of amber-figured silk with a treble pleating of lace falling off the neck. It was so exactly what she would have chosen for herself, had she the means. It was beautifully cut, but she fingered the fine material with a sigh, guessing rightly that her allowance would not begin to pay for it.

A charming day-dress of dark green challis was accompanied by a small matching spencer for extra warmth, and she could see at a glance that both gowns would fit her to perfection.

Her cheeks burned. What more could one expect from a rake? Doubtless he kept half the mantua-makers in London in business.

"Miss Temple, don't you like them? You are very quiet."

"Hester, they are quite beautiful. Lord Rokeby has excellent taste." And his expertise was no credit to him, she thought fiercely.

"But he did not give you a necklace..."

"Of course not, Hester. You are his ward. He may give you whatever he wishes. With me it is a different matter."

"You don't like him, do you?"

Elinor had forgotten Hester's quickness of intelligence. Shy and self-effacing, the girl was a shrewd observer, and Elinor had often marvelled at the way in which she picked up the smallest nuance of feeling. Poor child! That sensitive character had learned early to be aware of snubs and humiliations.

"Did you not say yourself that he was a fearsome character?" Elinor chaffed. "He makes me quake in my boots."

Hester threw back her head and laughed. "You are making gammon of me, Miss Temple. I know you aren't afraid of anyone."

"Well then, let us be in charity with Lord Rokeby, Hester. Mr Charlbury speaks so highly of him, and he has known his lordship for many years."

It would serve no purpose to explain her own misgivings. For the next few months they must both be dependent upon the master of Merton Place. It was no pleasant prospect, but it must be endured. Elinor found herself wondering where they would be a year from now.

Chapter Three

By the following Thursday the light covering of snow had melted, but the day was dank and cold. Seated in a corner of the comfortable carriage, with a fur rug about her knees and a hot brick at her feet, Elinor prepared to enjoy her first look at the Kentish countryside.

They had not far to go, but she delighted in the vista of rolling hills, and the tracery of leafless branches against the leaden sky.

"You do not know this part of England?" Rokeby lounged opposite the ladies, scorning the comfort of a rug.

"This is all new to me, my lord. My home is in Derbyshire." Elinor had determined to be civil.

"Ah yes...a sterner countryside, is it not? I have been to Matlock and found it impressive."

"Parts of Derbyshire are wild and beautiful," she agreed.

"Like their inhabitants?" he said in a teasing tone.

"I doubt it, sir." Elinor gave him a repressive look. "The natives of Derbyshire are hard-working. Their main concern is to earn a living."

"Very worthy! Am I permitted to hope that some of them find time for more frivolous pursuits?"

"One may always hope." Elinor turned away from him to gaze through the carriage window.

Rokeby turned his attention to Hester. "I must compliment you, my dear. You are in looks today."

Hester stroked the fabric of her new blue gown. Over it she wore a matching fur-trimmed pelisse.

"This is so pretty," she said softly. "I have not worn such dress before."

"It is vastly becoming." He smiled at her, and his face was transformed. "You shall have many more such gowns, Hester. Do you look forward to a London season?"

The question reduced Hester to confusion. She gave Elinor a pleading glance.

"Hester will enjoy it," Elinor said firmly. "There is so much to see and do. We intend to visit the Tower of London and St Paul's Cathedral..."

"Sparing some little time for a visit to the theatre, and to Almack's, with possibly a rout or two, I hope." The blue eyes twinkled.

Elinor was strongly disposed to strike him. Why did he always bring out the worst in her? She wasn't priggish, she told herself. Nor did she despise dancing, or a visit to the theatre. Why then did she feel obliged to behave like a staid schoolmarm?

Perversity was her besetting sin, or so her mamma had proclaimed on more than one occasion. Yet this time it was justified. Lord Rokeby must be kept firmly in his place if he were not to... Not to what? Disturb her peace of mind? No, that was ridiculous.

She stole a glance at him. Resplendent in a perfectly fitting coat of fine blue Melton, and immaculate from his beige pantaloons to the tips of his mirror-like Hessians, he was every inch the gentleman of fashion. Yet there was something else about him…some quality which she could not quite define. Was it his vitality? That was certainly overwhelming. Or perhaps it was those curious eyes, so light in that dark face? They seemed to see everything with remarkable clarity.

As if aware of her scrutiny, he turned to her.

"I dine from home tonight, Miss Temple. I trust you will excuse my absence?"

Elinor felt tempted to observe that she could bear the prospect with equanimity. Instead she held her tongue, merely inclining her head in acknowledgment of his words.

Better to have him pursue his questionable interests elsewhere than to invite his rackety friends to Merton Place. Though in fairness, and much to her relief, there had been no repetition of the evening party which had so disturbed her.

She looked out of the window once more to find that they were approaching a long, low, rambling house set in grassland beside a lake. The central portion, she guessed, was Elizabethan, but successive owners had added a wing at each end of the building, each in a different style of architecture. It was not in the classical mode, but even on that damp December morning it looked both comfortable and welcoming.

Her first impressions were not mistaken. As the carriage drew to a halt, Charlbury appeared on the steps, surrounded by a number of young people. Two of the boys ran towards the carriage, flinging open the door before the coachman could alight.

Rokeby jumped down, laughing at the barrage of questions which awaited him.

"Monsters!" he announced. "What will the ladies think of you?" He turned to assist Elinor to the ground, but Charlbury was before him, and it was Hester who took her guardian's hand.

"Miss Temple, may I present my eldest sister, Anne?" Charlbury led her towards a slender girl who was trying vainly to hold the younger ones in check. Anne was a beauty, with a cloud of chestnut hair framing a piquant little heart-shaped face. Her eyes, so like her brother's, were smiling, and Elinor warmed to her at once.

"Then you must meet Celia and Judith, and these two obnoxious creatures are Sebastian and Crispin."

As Charlbury's brothers and sisters surrounded her, Elinor looked across at Hester, who wore a wistful expression. She is thinking of the family she never had, Elinor thought to herself. Then Anne took Hester's arm and drew her into the house.

"Mamma will not forgive us if we keep you standing here," she murmured. "She is in the salon."

Elinor was surprised to find that the mother of this attractive brood was homely in the extreme. Small and plump, she looked like some little downy bird, but her eyes were quick and bright.

"My dears, you must be frozen with the cold. Do you sit by the fire. Then you shall take some mulled wine." She tugged at the bell-pull. "Miss Temple, I cannot tell you what a pleasure it is to meet you. John has spoken of nothing else for the past weeks and of Miss Winton too."

Elinor was quick to notice that Charlbury, with his customary courtesy, had taken his place by Hester's side, and was fielding the questions which his sisters asked of her. She gave him a grateful smile. He was kindness itself.

She turned to find that Mrs Charlbury was looking up at Rokeby.

"Marcus, you have given us a pleasant surprise. Two more ladies in the neighbourhood will be a positive boon if they will agree to give us their company often."

Rokeby dropped into a chair beside his hostess and kissed her hand.

"I can claim no credit, ma'am. We must all be grateful to Miss Temple." The irony in his tone was not lost on Elinor, but Mrs Charlbury picked him up at once.

"Don't try to gammon me, my dear boy. The responsibility will do you the world of good. You look a different person already."

"Are my grey hairs showing?" He grinned at her with affection. "Ma'am, if you must know it, I am bowed down with care."

Mrs Charlbury turned to Elinor. "Marcus likes to tease, as I'm sure you have discovered."

"Indeed, ma'am." Elinor managed a faint smile, but her back had stiffened, and the tension in the air was palpable. The older woman glanced at the faces of her two companions, but she made no further comment.

"Anne," she commanded, "do beg your papa to join us. It is now past the hour for nuncheon." She turned to Elinor with a rueful smile. "When my husband is working on his book he would starve, if we did not remind him of the time."

"It is kind of you to ask us here today," Elinor

said with feeling. "Hester, as you must know, has not been well since we arrived. This outing will give her so much pleasure."

"I hope it will be the first of many visits, Miss Temple. Your charge is a little shy, I think. To be thrust among so many strangers must be somewhat daunting."

"In your family one could not be ill at ease," Elinor assured her. "They seem to have such a gift for friendship."

"You have family of your own?"

"I have three brothers and four sisters, Ma'am. I am the eldest. Our home is in Derbyshire."

"You must miss them, my dear."

Rokeby was fondling the ears of a fat spaniel sitting at his feet, but Elinor was aware that he was listening.

"I visit them whenever possible," she replied. "And at Bath there was little time for moping."

"John tells me that you taught at the school there. My husband will be interested. He has strong views on education."

It was at that moment that the subject of her conversation entered the room. Henry Charlbury was an older version of his eldest son, and as Elinor gave him her hand she found herself looking up into the same brown eyes.

Seated beside him at the dining-table, she found him remote, but she guessed that he was still preoccupied with the latest chapter of his book. It was when Mrs Charlbury remarked on Elinor's teaching post that he looked at her with interest.

From then on she was the sole object of her host's

attention until Mrs Charlbury was forced to intervene
again.

"Charlbury, pray do not monopolise Miss Temple.
She is to visit us again, you know." Her smile
robbed her words of all offence. "Now tell me, my
dear, how do you celebrate the Yuletide season in
Derbyshire?"

"Much as you do here, I imagine, Mrs Charlbury.
We burn the great Yule log, and decorate the house
with greenery."

"And do you have presents? You must have presents." Crispin's question was urgent.

"We do...and games such as bobbing for apples."

"With prizes?" asked Sebastian.

"These two are a mercenary pair," John
Charlbury told her with a smile. "Miss Winton is
like to believe them capable of holding up the mail
coach."

"No, she won't." The boys had been quick to
seize upon Hester as an ally. "We're going to show
her our new kittens."

They led her away as soon as the meal was over.

"Now you shall not let the boys be a trouble to
you," Mrs Charlbury told her. "You must be firm
with them."

"They won't be a trouble," Hester said shyly.
"And I should like to see the kittens." It was clear
that she felt more at ease with the casual cameraderie
of the children.

Elinor glanced across the table. It had come as no
surprise to find that Rokeby had seated himself beside the beauteous Anne. The girl gazed up at him,
oblivious of the others.

It was only too clear that she was in love with

him. Elinor wondered why the knowledge should depress her so. In the eyes of society it would be an ideal match. The wealthy Lord Rokeby would be allied to the daughter of one of his oldest friends. But had those friends any idea of the depths of his depravity?

Elinor tried to suppress the emotions which filled her mind. It was nothing to do with her, but Anne was a sweet girl. Would she find happiness with a heartless rake? Even on short acquaintance she had realised that Mrs Charlbury would brook no ill behaviour on the part of a prospective son-in-law but, once married, even she would be powerless to control Rokeby.

She glanced at his smiling face in profile. She was aware of the clean lines of his jaw, and the straight, classical perfection of his nose. Swarthy though he was, he was still an attractive creature.

Had she not known his character as she did, she too might have found him pleasing. Yet still there was something about him which eluded her. Hester had described him as fearsome, but what was her other term? Piratical? Yes, that was it! There was somehow an underlying sense of recklessness...of fierce energies held in check by the thinnest of threads. This was a man who would be capable of anything.

And was she the only person who could see it? She glanced about her, and was aware only of the casual conversation of old friends. Could she possibly be mistaken in her judgement of Rokeby's character? Mr and Mrs Charlbury were not fools, and neither was their son, yet they seemed to hold his lordship in high regard.

Elinor's lip curled. Rokeby was clever, she must give him that. Whatever his motive for wishing to be accepted in this household, he played the part of a charming neighbour to perfection.

"Until next week then?" He bowed over the hand of his hostess as they prepared to take their leave.

"Oh, Marcus, we can't wait." The boys were racing round him as he handed the ladies into the carriage.

"Patience, my friends. It is the best of all virtues, together with perseverance." Rokeby was laughing as he took Elinor's hand.

She pulled away as if she had been stung. The touch of that warm flesh against her own had caused an unaccustomed flutter in the pit of her stomach. If he was aware of it, he gave no sign. On the way back to Merton Place he chatted to Hester about her new acquaintances, and chaffed her about her friendship with the boys.

"Take care or they will have you climbing trees and swimming in the lake," he teased.

Hester looked at him uncertainly. "Is it not too cold to swim?" she ventured.

"It is, indeed. Far better take a trip into Tunbridge Wells with Miss Temple. You will wish to purchase one or two small trifles...and you must see the Pantiles, and the church of King Charles the Martyr." He caught Elinor's eye, and she was quick to thank him.

The mention of presents had troubled her a little. She of course, would neither give them nor receive them, but Hester should have some small gifts by her to reciprocate any unexpected offerings which might be made by Anne and her sisters.

And his lordship had thought of everything. That evening he came to them attired in formal dress. He made no mention of his proposed destination. Instead, he asked what time they would wish to order the carriage for the following day. It was only when he had gone that Elinor found a small leather bag of guineas beside her place in the dining-room. Hester too had been amply provided with funds.

Elinor laid the bag aside. If Rokeby hoped to bribe her into lowering her guard, he would find himself mistaken. Her appetite seemed to have vanished. As she toyed with a slice of glazed ham and an Italian salad, she found herself wondering what his lordship was doing at that moment. Better not to think of it. She forced herself to attend to Hester who had discovered a book on the history of Tunbridge Wells.

"I hope we shall not be disappointed, Miss Temple." Hester's eyes were shining.

"I doubt it, my dear, though the place was in its heyday some fifty years ago, when it rivalled Bath as a watering place. I believe they still have balls in the Assembly Rooms."

"Shall we need to attend them?" Her voice was shaking with anxiety.

"Of course not, Hester. You are not yet out. Now pray do not trouble yourself with needless worries. You did so well today. Is it not pleasant to make new friends?"

"I liked the Charlburys," Hester said simply. "They make me feel so easy and comfortable...but..."

"What is it then?"

The girl hesitated. "You will think me ungrateful, but I cannot like Lord Rokeby. I don't understand why he became my guardian. I know he thinks me dull and plain...'' Her eyes filled with tears.

"Hester dearest, will you not try to understand? Lord Rokeby undertook the charge of a young child who was away at school. He has not seen you in all these years, and thought most probably that you were still in pinafores. It was unfortunate that he had no warning of our arrival. Then he was presented with a young lady and her companion, come to live with him. He has had a shock.'' Her lips twitched in spite of herself. "I shall not soon forget his face that night. I might have had horns and a tail...''

"I believe he wishes us far away.'' Hester could not manage an answering smile. "He makes jokes which I do not understand and, when he looks at me with that curious smile I can find nothing to say to him.''

"I doubt if we shall see much of him when we are in London,'' Elinor soothed. "We are not to live with him, you know, and I doubt if he would care to appear at Almack's or such places.''

"Emma told me that Almack's was a marriage mart. Does his lordship wish me to be wed? I suppose I should then be off his hands...'' Her look of desolation wrung Elinor's heart.

"You shall do nothing which you do not like,'' she promised. "And there is plenty of time before you make your come-out. Now tell me about the chalybeate spring at Tunbridge Wells. Is not the water said to cure all ills?''

The question served to divert Hester's attention and she went to bed in a happier frame of mind. Elinor was not so fortunate. She could not be easy when she considered Rokeby's plans for Hester's future. Any other girl would have welcomed the prospect of a London season, with balls, parties and routs, and a wardrobe of new clothes to set her off to the best advantage, but she was well aware that Hester dreaded it. Yet there seemed to be no alternative.

After hours of fruitless speculation she fell asleep at last, still with no other solution in mind.

Much to Hester's disappointment, the chalybeate spring at Tunbridge Wells was closed on the following day.

"I doubt if we should have liked the taste, though," she admitted. "The water is full of iron and must be bitter."

Elinor shivered in the keen wind. "The church of King Charles the Martyr is quite close, I believe. It is just a few yards across the highway. Let us go there quickly, Hester. We have not yet done our shopping and we should strive to return to Merton Place before it grows dark."

They hurried towards the plain red-brick building, built by subscriptions from supporters of the Stuart cause. The somewhat nondescript exterior gave no hint of the beauty within, but Hester was soon in raptures over the splendid plaster ceiling and the unusual wooden gallery.

Elinor dragged her away at last to walk back through the colonnaded Pantiles. The cold had sent the usual crowd of pedestrians to seek the comfort of their firesides, and the place was almost deserted.

Elinor turned into a draper's shop, and though she was appalled by the prices in that fashionable watering-place, she purchased ribbons and a number of lace-trimmed handkerchiefs, as well as a charming pin-cushion and some needle-cases, all with Hester's enthusiastic agreement.

"And the boys? Shall we take them some sweet-meats?"

"A good idea, Hester. Do you choose those from the shop next door whilst I am paying for these."

She came out to find Hester laden with small packages.

"Heavens!" she cried. "Are those all for Crispin and Sebastian? You will spoil them."

"It is not so very much," Hester murmured. "But, Miss Temple, I have nothing to give Lord Rokeby…"

"Don't worry about it, Hester. His lordship will not expect a gift from you. In any case, I should be at a loss to know what would please him."

The girl looked downcast, and Elinor had an inspiration.

"Let us go into this bookshop," she said. "We may find something…"

It was by happy chance that they came across the essays of Montaigne, translated from the original French.

"This is ideal!" Elinor turned the pages with a loving hand. Montaigne was one of her favourites. The pungent wit would appeal to Rokeby's mordant sense of humour, she hoped, as would the Frenchman's cool intellect.

Rokeby had returned to Merton Place before them, and Elinor sought him out. In her hand she carried the bag of guineas which he had left beside her plate that morning.

His lordship was looking jaded. It was not, perhaps, the ideal time to confront him, but Elinor plunged ahead.

"This belongs to you, sir." She laid the bag on the table by his hand.

"You are mistaken, Miss Temple. It belongs to you. It is an advance upon your allowance."

"I prefer to earn my salary before I am paid," Elinor said stiffly.

"You will earn it, my dear. Nothing is more certain."

Elinor eyed him with dislike. Even by candlelight she could see that the lines beneath his eyes were more pronounced.

"Do you feel quite well, my lord?" she asked sweetly.

"Self-inflicted wounds, Miss Temple. I expect no sympathy, and will get none, I imagine."

Elinor ignored the sally. She guessed that his head was pounding after a convivial evening with his friends. She turned to go.

"Miss Temple, you will please to obey my wishes." He picked up the small leather bag and came towards her, holding it out.

"I cannot, sir."

Rokeby made as if to seize her hand, but she moved away. She had no wish for a humiliating struggle which she had no hope of winning. Then a thought struck her.

"Will you hold the money against the cost of my gowns?" she said quickly. "Until I have paid for them, at least in part, I shall feel unable to wear them."

Rokeby sighed in exasperation, but he set the bag aside.

"Miss Temple, you are something new in my experience," he announced. "Obstinate...provoking...and determined to have your way."

"I am not alone in that," she told him sharply.

His firm mouth curved into a reluctant smile. "No, you are not, my dear. But I wonder if you have the least notion..." He caught himself in time. He had been about to tell her that most of the women of his acquaintance would have been happy to accept whatever he chose to give them. Her fierce independence both piqued and intrigued him. She was totally without means. He knew that. Yet it did not stop her from clinging to her pride and her own notions of honour.

"You enjoyed your day at the Wells?" he asked.

"Very much, my lord. With your permission we shall visit the town again. There is so much to see..."

"I hope you spared the time to do your shopping." He was laughing at her again, making her feel like some dowdy schoolmarm who thought only of antiquities and such. She would show him.

She dressed with extra care that night. The new green gown became her to perfection, and in a moment of madness she released her curls from their constricting band and allowed them to fall about her face.

"Miss Temple, you look different," Hester murmured shyly.

"I will quote the old saw to you, my dear, 'Fine feathers make fine birds.' You look quite charming yourself."

It was true. The dusky pink of Hester's modest half-dress gave her pale skin a glow. She looked almost pretty, though her hair, as always, showed a tendency to hang limp about her face. That must be altered when we reach London, Elinor vowed to herself. She took Hester's hand and led her into the salon.

Rokeby must have taken some remedy to clear his head, Elinor decided. He looked himself again, and was, as always, a credit to the attentions of his valet.

As they entered the room he walked towards them with his customary bow.

"I am dazzled," he said lightly. "Hester, how much that shade of pink becomes you! You shall wear it more often. And Miss Temple, what can I say?"

Elinor longed to beg him to say as little as possible, but he was determined to torment her.

"A vision!" he announced. "May I be permitted to hope that you are pleased with my choice of gown?"

"It is delightful," Elinor told him with a stony look.

For some reason this bald statement sent him into whoops of laughter.

"I cannot bear these transports," he announced at last. "Miss Temple, I beg that you will try to control your enthusiasm."

At that precise moment dinner was announced, much to Elinor's relief. Whenever she was in his lordship's company, her self-control was sorely tested. How she longed to give him a crushing setdown, but it would not do. No matter how provoking he might be, she would not abandon Hester to his tender mercies.

As the soup was served Rokeby began to discuss

the forthcoming festivities, and Elinor felt obliged to offer her assistance, if it should be needed.

"No, no!" He brushed the suggestion aside. "I thank you, but all is well in hand. I advise you to get plenty of rest beforehand. My tenants invariably make the most of this annual feast."

He did not exaggerate. For the next week Merton Place hummed with activity as green boughs were brought indoors, together with gaily berried holly. The Great Hall was transformed, but it was not until the eve of Christmas when the long trestle tables were set out that Elinor realised just how large a celebration it would be.

"Surprised, Miss Temple?" Rokeby stood by her side. "We shall not be dull this Yuletide, I can promise you."

"Do you plan to roast an ox, my lord? I cannot think how else you might feed such numbers." She smiled, feeling more in charity with him for his generosity to his dependants.

He laughed as he shook his head. "I believe you will find that no one will suffer from lack of either food or drink," he assured her. Then he tilted his head. "Listen!"

Elinor could hear the sound of singing from outdoors, and she looked at him in surprise.

"We are being serenaded. Let me send for your cloak. The night air is cold, but you shall not venture beyond the open doorway."

As Bates threw wide the great oak door, Elinor gasped with pleasure. By the light of lanterns held aloft she could see a circle of men, women and children with their voices raised in song. As the old hymns followed one another she felt a sense of peace.

"Later they will go in procession to the church," Rokeby told her. "It is an old tradition here, though I believe the custom originated on the continent of Europe."

As the music died away Rokeby stepped forward and she heard the clink of coins. Then, as she turned to move back into the hall, he laid a hand upon her arm.

"Are you cold?" he asked.

Elinor shook her head. The music had lulled her into a dreamlike state. "Thank you," she said impulsively. "I enjoyed that so very much."

"You are fond of music?"

"I love it. It is one of my greatest pleasures."

"Then you will enjoy yourself in London. There are many concerts, or perhaps you prefer the opera." He drew her arm through his. "Shall we take a turn about the terrace? The night is so fine that it seems a pity to retire just yet."

Unresisting, Elinor allowed him to lead her out of doors. Still in a trance, she seemed to have no will of her own. Overhead the moon shone full, bathing lawns, trees and shrubberies in its silver light. The stars in their vast canopy seemed low enough to touch. She caught her breath at the sheer beauty of the scene before her.

"You sense the magic, too?" Rokeby's lips were close to her ear.

"There is something mysterious about the eve of Christmas, above all nights in the year for me," she murmured in reply. "I cannot quite say why."

"Tonight I think I have the answer, for myself at

least.'' Rokeby turned to face her. "Have you any idea how beautiful you are, Miss Temple? Here, with the moonlight on your face you might be Aphrodite, the Greek goddess of love.''

Elinor moved away from him at once. There was a low caressing note in his deep voice which she found disturbing. They had moved some distance from the doorway leading to the Great Hall, but she forced herself to resist the temptation to flee indoors as fast as she could run.

"I fear your imagination rivals Hester's, sir,'' she told him stiffly. "I do not care to listen to such nonsensical ideas. May we return to the house? I find it colder than I thought.''

She heard a cynical laugh.

"I suspected that we should have a frost before morning,'' he chuckled. "Allow me to lead you back to safety.'' He took her hand and tucked it into his pocket, keeping her fingers entwined in his. "Better?'' he asked smoothly. "It distresses me to find you cold.''

Elinor was furious, both with him and with herself. She had been lured into dropping her guard for the briefest of moments, only to find herself the object of his lordship's unwelcome attentions.

She could think of no set-down crushing enough to express her feelings. As they reached the hallway she tore her fingers from his grasp and hurried to her room.

Chapter Four

By the following morning Elinor had come to a decision. If she and Lord Rokeby were to continue to deal together she must take good care never to be left alone with him.

His attitude towards her was impossible to understand, though she suspected that it amused him to attempt to put her out of countenance with his advances.

Such behaviour was unworthy of a gentleman, she thought bitterly. Her affection for Hester had made it impossible for her to leave the girl, and well he knew it. It was cruel of him to use that knowledge to pay her out for her evident dislike of him. She clenched her fists. It would take a stronger man than Rokeby to break her.

Feeling as she did, it went much against the grain to wear the amber gown that he had chosen, but the feast that day was clearly the occasion of the year for the staff and tenants of Merton Place and the Charlbury estate. Some effort would be expected of her, and of Hester too. She was being well paid for her services, though Rokeby had assured her that she would earn every penny of her allowance. She was beginning to believe him.

And the gown itself was beautiful, she could not deny it. Caught high beneath her bosom with a self-coloured satin ribbon, it fitted her to perfection, and the glowing colour emphasised the whiteness of her skin. She glanced at herself in the long dressing mirror, fearing that she might be over-dressed for what was, after all, a country gathering.

She could not think it so. Though the fabric was rich, the style was simple and she gave a wry smile. Such classic elegance came at a high price. She turned to Hester.

"Ready, my dear?"

"Miss Temple, do I look...?"

"Hester, you look charmingly."

It was not quite true, though Hester's gown became her as nothing she had yet worn. Sadly it could not disguise the look of terror in her eyes. Her hunted expression had returned.

"I...I don't know... There will be so many people and I do not know them..."

"You know some of them," Elinor encouraged. "The Charlburys are to bring Sebastian and Crispin, and the girls were kind to you... You will not tell me that you are afraid of their mamma, or of John Charlbury?"

"No..." It was a reluctant admission. "But, Miss Temple, did you see the tables? There will be hundreds come to dine."

"All you need do is to smile and bid them welcome. Some may be shy and ill at ease. We should think of them. Now let us go down before the guests arrive."

Hester was thoughtful as she moved towards the door. It had not occurred to her that others might feel as timid as she did herself. As she stepped on to the landing her foot caught a small package.

"Oh, look!" she cried. "This is for me and there is another for you."

Hester tore at the wrapping and drew out a small pearl bracelet, clearly chosen to match her necklace. It came with his lordship's good wishes at the festive season.

Elinor opened her own gift with misgiving. She had not expected it and would prefer to have returned it unopened, but with Hester's eager gaze upon her she could not ignore it.

"Oh, Miss Temple!" Hester caught her breath. "That is exquisite…"

Elinor looked down at the fine Kashmir shawl which nestled in its wrapping. Hester had not exaggerated. It was the loveliest thing she had ever seen. Fine and warm, the rich colours were an excellent choice to complement her gown.

"See, there is a note for you." Chester handed her a card.

As Elinor read it she felt her colour rising. "I would not have you cold" was the message. It was unsigned.

She laid both card and shawl upon her bed and turned away.

"Will you not wear it?" Hester questioned in surprise.

"I have no need of it at present." Elinor tried to keep her tone impersonal. It would not do to give vent to her true feelings. "In a large gathering I am like to feel overheated."

That was no lie. She felt ready to explode with rage. How like Rokeby to accompany his gift with a clear reference to their conversation on the terrace. He was a master of innuendo, but she would ignore it.

"I must not forget my present for his lordship." Hester picked up the neatly wrapped book. "I think I had best give it to him now."

Elinor felt incapable of further speech as she followed her charge downstairs. She longed to run away, to hide, anything to avoid all further contact with her lascivious employer. Instead, she accompanied Hester to the library.

Rokeby gave her a quizzing look as Hester handed him the package. Then, as he opened it, his expression changed.

"Montaigne?" he said. "How clever of you, Hester! I have searched for a copy of this book."

"Miss Temple chose it," Hester told him shyly.

"Did she, indeed? Then it is a joint gift, though I see that she scorns to wear my own..."

"I am not cold," Elinor said shortly, then bit her tongue.

"Really?" His eyes were dancing. "I am delighted to hear it. In the meantime, I must thank both of you for this kind thought."

Elinor felt anything but kind. She had not thanked him for the shawl, which she had every intention of returning to him, but she could not express her displeasure in front of Hester.

At that moment the Charlburys were announced, followed by a long procession of tenants, and Elinor took her place in the receiving line, with Rokeby by her side.

To her surprise he had dropped his provoking manner. He welcomed each family with enthusiasm, remembering the names of all their children without apparent effort, and urging them all to eat and drink their fill. As forelocks were tugged and curtsies dropped Elinor felt that the line would never end, but finally all were seated.

The tables were a splendid sight. Great glazed hams lay side by side with roasted geese and turkeys. Pies and pasties in abundance filled the gaps between, whilst creams and syllabus and jellies stood in waiting on the side. Barrels of ale had been broached and were in readiness, but the bowls of punch were universal favourites.

Elinor watched in awe as the food began to disappear. She had not thought it possible that the tables could be cleared so fast, but as the hams were reduced to a single bone, and the poultry to a few fragments, the dishes were replaced with joints of beef and mutton.

Beside her Henry Charlbury chuckled. "The English were ever the best of trenchermen, Miss Temple. Their meat consumption is the envy of Europe."

"They look well on it," she smiled.

"It gives them stamina, that is certain. We shall be longing for our beds before the night is ended, I assure you."

He was right. Toasts to their employers followed the end of the meal, and both Rokeby and Henry Charlbury responded with grace and humour. Then the tables were cleared away and the musicians struck up in the gallery.

"Shall you care to join in the country dance, Miss Temple?" John Charlbury was by her side.

"I think not, thank you. Perhaps Hester?" Elinor looked across the room, but Hester, regardless of her finery, was bobbing for apples, cheered on by Sebastian and Crispin.

"Oh, dear!" Elinor gave him a rueful look. "Her gown will be ruined, I fear."

"Is that so important?" He took her arm. "Miss Winton is at her ease with children. It is pleasant to see her enjoyment."

"You like her, don't you?" Elinor asked impulsively.

"I do indeed, Miss Temple. When she comes out of her shell she is a joy."

"Hester is underrated, but you, at least, seem to understand. Now as to your offer to join in with the dancing…?"

"A pleasure!" He gave her his arm and led her into the centre of the floor.

It was long since Elinor had enjoyed herself so much, and her delight increased at the sight of the smiling faces round her. Then, as she went through the figures of the dance, she glanced across the room. Rokeby was watching her intently. As she caught his eye he raised his glass to her in an ironic toast.

Elinor did not acknowledge it. When the music ended she pleaded lack of breath, and went to sit by Mrs Charlbury.

Rokeby, she noted, was now deep in conversation with Anne. The girl was looking up at him with what could only be described as adoration. Elinor looked at Mrs Charlbury, wondering if she too had seen the expression on her daughter's face. She was not left long in doubt. The older woman shook her head as she patted Elinor's hand.

"Don't trouble yourself, Miss Temple. Anne is suffering from hero-worship."

Elinor blushed as she made a hasty disclaimer.

"Ma'am, I hope you do not think... I meant no...criticism."

"Of course not. You are much too kind for that, but I believe you are a little disturbed. Marcus is a charming creature, isn't he? Yet Anne is not the wife for him."

Elinor was overcome with embarrassment. She had been indiscreet. In future, she must keep a closer guard upon her expression.

"First love can be an agony," the older woman continued. "Poor Anne is in the throes, but she will recover." She surprised a question in Elinor's eyes. "You are wondering, perhaps, why her father and I would never countenance such a match?"

"Ma'am, I beg of you... There is no need to explain." Elinor felt acutely uncomfortable. On the surface, Rokeby appeared to be a welcome visitor in the Charlburys' home, but perhaps his neighbours were well aware of the darker side of his character.

"Miss Temple, I hope that you do not mistake me. Marcus is like another son to Charlbury and myself. His weaknesses are far outweighed by his virtues, but Anne is too young for such a man as he. Nor has she the strength of character to match him. We are thinking of his happiness as well as Anne's."

"He is lucky in his friends," Elinor said with feeling. "You are very good to him."

"And he to us. He is a sensible man. To give him

credit, he does not encourage Anne above the common ties of friendship.''

Elinor's expression grew wooden, and her companion smiled.

''I see that you are not in charity with him, my dear. That is unfortunate, but you will grow to know him better. He can be the most provoking creature in the world, and he has a love of mischief.''

''I had noticed,'' Elinor said bitterly.

''But you will handle him. It is a blessing that you are here with Hester.''

''I could not leave her, ma'am.''

''Of course not. Marcus would be lost without your help, yet I believe that this business of his ward will be the making of him.''

''Ma'am?''

Mrs Charlbury chuckled. She seemed about to speak and then she changed her mind.

''You think the responsibility...?''

''Yes, my dear. Now let us rescue Hester before she is quite drowned in the apple barrel.''

As the ale flowed and the punch bowls emptied, the noise in the room increased. Rokeby, Elinor noted without surprise, was in the middle of a kissing ring, holding a sprig of mistletoe above his head. She skirted carefully past the group, hoping that he had not seen her. The prettiest of the village girls was in his arms, and he was saluting her with relish.

Elinor made her way to Hester's side.

''Are you quite soaked?'' She asked the kneeling girl.

Hester raised a glowing face. ''It is only water, Miss Temple. It won't stain.''

"But it is cold water, Hester. You must not catch another chill." Her smile belied her anxious look.

"Oh, don't take her away, Miss Temple. Hester is the winner." Sebastian, as always, was ready to champion his ally.

"She shall return directly," Elinor promised. "But, Hester, I believe you should change your gown. I will go with you."

Obediently, Hester rose to her feet. It was the work of a few moments to help her strip off the sodden garment, and once attired in lavender muslin Hester was anxious to be off again.

"May I go now?" she pleaded.

"Very well, my dear, but I believe you should suggest hunting the slipper, or some game which will keep you dry."

Hester nodded and ran out of the room.

There was no need to ask if she were enjoying herself, Elinor thought with relief. She had never seen Hester look so animated. Children's games were not, perhaps, an ideal preparation for her London season, but at least she had forgotten her shyness among strangers.

Elinor turned to the pier-glass. The energetic country dancing had loosened her piled-up hair. As she pinned it back into place, she noticed that it seemed almost chestnut in the candle-light. She pulled a face at her reflection. It was the effect of the amber gown again. She shrugged, and gathered up her reticule.

In the corridor outside her room the candles burned low in their sconces and the light was dim. In the distance she could hear continuing sounds of revelry, but the west wing was far from the Great Hall.

She caught up her skirt preparatory to descending the staircase. Then she jumped as a figure stepped from one of the embrasures.

"Did you think to escape me?" Rokeby had one hand beneath his back. "I am come to claim my due." He raised his hand above her head, and looking up she saw the pearly berries glistening.

Elinor stepped back in dismay. Her heart had begun to pound. There was no way she could escape him in the empty corridor.

"My lord, this is childish. Allow me to pass if you please." To her relief her voice was steady, and even cool.

"But this is the festive season," he protested in feigned indignation.

"I believe that you find all seasons festive, sir." Elinor moved as if to pass him, but he caught her by the waist.

"There is much to be said for festivity, or do you not find it so? I thought you enjoyed the dancing."

"I did, sir, because I was treated with courtesy by all."

"None would challenge the ice-maiden?"

"Lord Rokeby, you have a mistaken idea of my character. Is it too much to ask that you treat me with respect? That much, surely, is due to a woman in my position."

"But, my dear, I am your slave..."

Elinor lost her temper. "That is exactly what I mean," she cried hotly. "You persist in talking nonsense. I do not like it, sir."

"You find me repellent, Miss Temple?"

"I can have no opinion on that subject." Elinor stood rigid within his grasp.

"What a bouncer! And you a model of rectitude! Come now, admit it! You think me a loose fish?"

"I do not understand that expression."

"Then allow me to explain. It refers to one who has no moral principles."

Elinor was silent, though it cost her much to bite back her reply. She longed to tell him exactly what she thought of his behaviour from the moment of her arrival.

"Careful!" he advised. "I fear you will explode! Have you no urge to reform me?"

"None whatever, sir. In my opinion you are beyond reform..."

"Unkind!" he reproved. "Must I remind you that this is the season of good will to all men, including me?" There was no mistaking the glitter in his eyes.

"You will please to let me go," she said stiffly.

"Certainly, my dear, when we have observed this charming tradition..." He twirled the sprig of mistletoe between his fingers. "It is but once a year, you know. I may have long to wait before you grant me another kiss."

"You should save your kisses for those who may want them, Lord Rokeby. I'm sure there is no shortage of willing candidates." Her voice was icy.

"And you do not care to be one of many? That is understandable..." The amusement in his voice made her long to strike him.

"Miss Temple, delightful though I find this tryst, may I remind you that we should join the others. Our absence may give rise to comment." He was laughing at her again. She saw the gleam of white teeth against the tanned skin.

"The remedy is in your hands," she snapped.

Incautiously she lifted her chin, and he bent his face to hers. Elinor turned her head, and his lips merely grazed her cheek.

"Ungenerous!" he murmured. One hand came up to cup her face and his mouth came down on hers.

In that moment the world was forgotten. The touch of his warm flesh against her own caused a tide of fire to course through Elinor's blood. Unconsciously she clung to him. Her head was spinning and her legs refused to support her. She was suffocating... drowning in delight, and she seemed to have no will of her own.

He released her at last, and held her away from him.

Elinor opened her eyes to see a strange expression on his face. It was a mixture of shame and vulnerability.

"I'm sorry!" he said abruptly. "That was ill done of me. I should not have used you so." He turned on his heel and left her.

Elinor ran back to her room. She closed the door and stood with her back to it, trembling in every limb. Rokeby's kiss had shaken her to the very core of her being. For the first time she had beome aware of the true nature of passion. At last she could begin to understand his lordship's obsession with the opposite sex. Flesh against flesh, she thought in awe. She had not suspected that it could lead to such delight.

Her face burned at the direction her thoughts were taking. Could Rokeby possibly be right? He had accused her once of latent sensuality...something about her mouth, she recalled. She had proved him right, she realised to her own disgust. Her surrender to his lips had been that of a wanton.

The memory of her own behaviour made her squirm. She must have disgusted him, else he would not have apologised so quickly. How could she ever face him again? Yet she must do so, and the others too.

Slowly she bathed her face and hands. The cold water served to bring her to her senses, and some of her judgment returned. Was she not making a great piece of work about nothing? One kiss beneath the mistletoe at Christmastide? It was not so very wonderful to find herself enjoying it. And Rokeby was experienced with women...none more so. He had known how to give her pleasure, as he had done with countless others. He had spent much of the evening saluting every female in the room.

But had they felt as she did, or returned his kiss with such abandon? She could not think so. Some spark had flashed between herself and Rokeby in that tender moment, and she was too honest to deny it, though it was difficult to define. Was it simple lust? Her mind recoiled from the idea. Whatever that strange emotion was that disturbed her so must be crushed out of existence.

Her expression was wooden as she made her way downstairs. At that late hour the crowd of revellers was thinning fast.

At the far end of the hall she could see Rokeby's tall figure standing by the open doorway as he bade his guests farewell.

Elinor looked round for Hester. If she could find the girl they might retire before Rokeby came to join them.

"Over here, Miss Temple." John Charlbury's voice drew her towards a small knot of people who were chatting by the dying embers of the fire. Hester stood among them smiling, but clearly ready for her bed. Beside her Crispin and Sebastian were asleep on an oaken settle.

"A successful day, I think, my dear." Mrs Charlbury's bright eyes searched Elinor's face. "You have found it tiring?"

"I must confess that I envy Crispin and Sebastian." Elinor looked down at the sleeping boys. "But I believe that everyone has enjoyed the celebration."

"Indeed they have, and so have I. It is pleasant to see so many old friends...and our new ones..."

Elinor was quick to thank her.

"We shall be away as soon as my husband has bidden everyone goodbye. Meantime, my dear, will you sit with me for a moment? My spirit is willing to continue standing, but my feet are not."

Mrs Charlbury perched on the settle beside her boys and made a place for Elinor.

"I hope we shall see you soon," she said.

"I cannot promise, ma'am, much as it would please me. I believe Lord Rokeby intends us to move to London shortly. There is much to do before Hester makes her début."

"But you will not go before the start of the new year?"

"I cannot say. We are quite at his lordship's disposal."

Something in her voice caused the older woman to give her a sharp look, and Elinor was aware of it. She made an effort to retrieve her composure. "Shall we see you in London for the Season, ma'am?'' she asked.

Mrs Charlbury chuckled. ''I see you do not know my husband yet, Miss Temple. To suffer the rigours of a London season is his idea of purgatory. He finds that he cannot work upon his book, and he will not be parted from his library.''

''You do not mind, I think. You and he seem always to be in such accord...''

''Mind? I welcome his decision. Apart from the expense, I would not have my girls exposed to flattery and temptation.''

''I could wish that Lord Rokeby felt the same,'' Elinor mused. ''I cannot believe that Hester if ready for a season.''

''This case is different, Miss Temple. Hester is an heiress, and Marcus wishes to do his best by her.''

Elinor was silent. She could not bring herself to agree. Rokeby, she was certain, wished only to rid himself of all responsibility for his ward.

''And a season would not serve for Anne,'' Mrs Charlbury continued. ''She has not expressed the least desire for such a thing, which is a relief to her papa and myself.''

Anne had already found her love, Elinor thought in dismay. She had eyes for no one but Rokeby.

''Yet we are not to be quite unrepresented in the great world, so I hear.'' Mrs Charlbury did not trouble to hide her amusement. ''This is the first time that John has expressed a wish to visit London for the Season.''

''Oh, I am so pleased! At least we shall have one friend...''

"You will find another in Lady Hartfield, I believe. Are you not to stay with her?

"Do you know her, Mrs Charlbury? Lord Rokeby warned me. He described her as...er...top-lofty."

"Letitia brooks no nonsense from him. He has had the rough edge of her tongue. She believes him lacking in his duty to the family. He has no nursery yet, you see."

"Does she not find it strange to think of him as Hester's guardian?"

Mrs Charlbury crowed with laughter. "She insisted on it. Perhaps I should not mention it, but he did his best to persuade her to relieve him of the charge. She would have none of it."

"She sounds formidable," Elinor murmured.

"I doubt if you will find her so. You and she will deal together extremely, I imagine."

Elinor twinkled at the older woman. "Two managing creatures together, ma'am?"

"I believe you will always do what you feel to be right, my dear, and so does Letitia."

"Let us hope that our judgment of what is right happens to coincide..." Elinor rose to her feet as Henry Charlbury came towards his wife.

"Shall I ask Robert and Jem to carry the boys out to your coach, sir?" Elinor raised a hand to signal to the waiting footmen.

"No need, my dear. John and I will manage these sleeping beauties." Henry Charlbury lifted Crispin from the settle and smiled across at Hester. "My sons are in your debt, Miss Winton. They won't forget your kindness to them on this night."

Hester blushed and nodded. She was disconcerted

to be singled out for praise, but she thanked him with more assurance than Elinor had thought possible.

Elinor herself felt as shy as any school-miss as Rokeby came to join the group. She could not look at him, and was thankful when he addressed his words to Hester.

"Say your farewells, my dear. There is no necessity for you to wait up longer. Mrs Charlbury will excuse you."

It was a clear dismissal, and Elinor could only feel relieved. She needed time to think, and to recover her composure in his lordship's presence. She hurried her charge away.

Hester was too tired to talk. She was asleep almost before her head touched the pillow, leaving Elinor a prey to her own turbulent thoughts. Rokeby's kiss meant nothing, she decided. He was simply following the old Yuletide tradition. It was her own reaction to it which had disturbed her so. She, who had always been so sure that she knew herself well, knew now that she was mistaken, but those hitherto unsuspected yearnings must be crushed.

And Rokeby did not know of her dismay. She would take care to hide it from him, pretending that she had accepted his embrace in the spirit in which it was given.

It would not be easy to convince him of her indifference. Too distant a manner would suggest the matter of too much importance. Neither should she be too friendly, else he might imagine that she had mistaken his intentions.

Her face grew fiery. Now she regretted her decision to stay with Hester. The child would doubtless have done quite well in the care of Lady Hartfield.

A moment's reflection convinced her that she was being selfish. Bonds of affection tied her to Hester, and they could not be broken for her own convenience. She had given her word, and she must abide by it.

She would stay, but who knew at what cost?

Chapter Five

The baying of hounds aroused her on the following day. Throwing aside her coverlet, she hurried to the window to find the meet assembled on the gravel drive before the house.

Rokeby, resplendent in hunting pink, was prominent among them. Glass in hand, he was laughing with his friends, some of whom she recognised. As the last of the stragglers joined them, the hunt moved off.

Elinor sighed with relief, guessing that his lordship would be away for most of the day. After a disturbed night she was glad to return to her bed for another hour or so.

It was not until almost noon that she was roused again by the arrival of her breakfast tray. Absently she nibbled at a roll, only half attending to Hester's chatter.

"Miss Temple, was my guardian cross with me last night, do you suppose?"

"I doubt it, Hester. Why do you ask?"

"When he came to say goodnight, I thought he

seemed a little strange…I mean, he sent me off to bed so sharply…"

"He saw that you were tired, that is all."

"I thought he might be angry because I played games with the children instead of joining in the dancing."

"I don't believe he noticed. There were many people with claims upon his attention."

"Then that's all right." Hester's face cleared. "I should not care to make him angry, but I don't know how to dance."

"Hester, what a bouncer! Did you not take part with the others in the dancing classes at school?"

"No, I hid. No one wished to be my partner, you see."

"You will soon learn, my dear. You have such a love of music. That will set your toes tapping once you are shown the steps. Now let us dress. We are slug-a-beds today."

"May we go out for a walk?" Hester asked eagerly. "Sebastian says there is a grotto at the entrance to the wood. The inside is full of shining crystals and sometimes it is lit by candles when there is an evening party."

"It sounds delightful." Elinor glanced through the window at the lowering sky. "You must wear a warm pelisse and take your muff. I fear we shall have snow before the day is out."

The grotto was all that Sebastian had promised, but it was too cold to linger. Elinor drew her cloak about her as they began to walk back to the house. Then she heard the sound of a horseman at full gallop. At the sight of his strained face she broke into a run.

"Stop!" she cried. "What is it?"

"It's Rokeby, ma'am. He's injured."

"Go ahead and warn Bates. How bad is it?"

"His leg is broke, but that's not the worst of it. He is unconscious."

"Then will you ride on for the surgeon?"

The man nodded. He was away before Elinor and Hester reached the house. They found a scene of confusion, with the servants milling about.

Elinor dismissed the servants about their business except for Bates and Mrs Onslow.

"How will they bring Lord Rokeby home? she asked.

"The grooms have taken a gate. Oh, ma'am, it does sound very bad..." Mrs Onslow's face crumpled.

"Let us not imagine the worst until we know the extent of Lord Rokeby's injuries," Elinor comforted. "The surgeon will need hot water and clean cloths. Will you see to it?"

Wiping her eyes, the woman hurried away.

Bates looked very white. "His lordship's father was killed on the hunting field, Miss Temple. He, too, was brought home in the same way..."

"Lord Rokeby is still alive," Elinor said firmly, as she took a decanter from a side table. "Drink this, Bates, and remember that his lordship will have need of all your help." She forced the glass into his hand.

He downed the spirit quickly, and some of his colour returned. "I hear them coming, ma'am."

Elinor followed him to the door to see a small procession of men moving towards the house. At each end of the gate the grooms were sweating under their burden.

As they passed into the hall and she caught sight of Rokeby, Elinor's heart sank. Above the torn and muddied coat his face was ashen and there was no sign of life.

"Upstairs!" she ordered. "Lay him on his bed as gently as you can. Bates, when you and his lordship's man remove his clothing you must try not to move him more than is absolutely necessary. The surgeon will soon be here…"

She looked again at the inert figure. There was a huge lump on Rokeby's forehead, which was already turning blue. He must have fallen forward, she surmised. At least his neck did not appear to be broken.

"Ma'am?"

Elinor turned to stare into the eyes of a very young man. She had last seen him in the hall on the night of her arrival. Now he looked very different from the gay cavalier who had been intent on chasing his quarry up the stairs.

"Ma'am, if there is anything I can do to help…?"

"You might begin by telling me exactly what has happened, sir."

"I don't know." His face was miserable. "The hedge was high, and there is a ditch on the other side, but Rokeby knows it well. He could not have been attending… We heard a thud, and he was down with the horse on top of him."

Elinor laid a hand upon his arm. "If you care to wait the surgeon will tell us more…"

"Thank you. I confess I cannot understand it. Marcus is such a bruising rider…"

"Then you shall not tease him when you see him, else he will be badly mortified." Elinor forced a smile which belied her own misgivings.

She seized upon the arrival of the surgeon with relief, but it was a sombre crowd which gathered in the hall.

"I could tear up cloths for bandages," Hester whispered at her side.

"Will you do that, dearest? Mrs Onslow will be glad of your help." Elinor sensed that the girl was badly shaken by the accident. It would do her good to find some occupation.

"Bates, will you see to the gentlemen? You may fetch out more of the brandy."

Elinor walked slowly up the stairs and sank on to a seat outside his lordship's bedroom. All her antagonism towards him had vanished. She could think only of that broken body, lying helpless on the makeshift hurdle.

The next hour was the longest of her life. Then the door opened and the surgeon came towards her.

"I have set the leg," he said. "But I cannot like his lordship's condition. He has not regained his senses."

"His neck...his backbone...?"

"Nothing else is broken, ma'am, but he has taken a nasty blow to the head. I have made him as comfortable as possible...but only time will tell if he will make a full recovery."

"Shall you return today?"

"I cannot do more, I fear. I will see him in the morning. You will stay with him? If there is any change you may send for me at once. No visitors, mind! He must have rest and quiet."

Elinor nodded, stricken by his grave face.

When Elinor entered the room she found Bates bending over his master's unconscious form. The mud had been washed from Rokeby's face, but his pallor was intense, and the huge lump on his brow had swollen even further.

Bates looked at her with anguish in his eyes.

"He's uttered never a sound, ma'am. Not a murmur or a groan..."

"We must be thankful that he wasn't conscious when the surgeon set his leg," Elinor murmured gently. "Bates, do you go about your duties...I will stay with Lord Rokeby."

"Did the surgeon say...?" It was a plea for reassurance.

"He will return tomorrow. We are to send for him if there is any change... Meantime, his lordship is not to be disturbed."

Bates wiped his eyes. Then he turned to Rokeby's valet, who was gathering up a pair of bloodstained buckskins, a shirt which had clearly been cut from his master's person, and a pair of boots which had suffered the same fate.

"You heard Miss Temple, Jervis. Get you gone!" He pushed the man out of the room.

Elinor knelt down beside the bed, praying for some sign of returning consciousness. She took Rokeby's hand in hers and stroked it gently, murmuring to him as she did so, but there was no response. She kept on with her self-appointed task as the leaden hours crawled by. Then Hester crept into the room.

"Mrs Charlbury is here," she whispered. "Will you see her? I will stay here."

"You will call me if you see a change?"

Hester nodded, but she could not hide her agitation.

"Don't worry so, my dear." Elinor managed a faint smile. "Had there been any immediate danger the surgeon would have stayed. We can do naught but wait until his lordship recovers his senses."

Her comments to Mrs Charlbury were less sanguine.

"How is Marcus now?" the older woman asked.

"He looks ghastly, ma'am. The leg is set successfully, but it is his head…" Elinor sat down suddenly, and buried her face in her hands.

"Do not give way, Miss Temple. We are all relying upon you, my dear, but you are tired and shocked. Have you eaten?"

Elinor shook her head.

"Then you shall do so." Mrs Charlbury removed her cloak. "My family will spare me for tonight. John may bring my things…"

"Ma'am, you are very good, but I have promised to stay with his lordship."

"And so you shall, but first you must rest. When Marcus comes to himself, you are the person he will wish to see."

"I doubt it, ma'am." Slow tears rolled down Elinor's cheeks. "We do naught but quarrel. It may be that I am to blame for this accident. Last night, you see…" She could not go on.

"Such nonsense! You are overwrought, my dear. You shall take a little broth and go to bed."

It was useless to argue against such determination.

"You will tell Hester?" Elinor murmured in a low voice.

"Yes, yes…I am on my way." Without more ado Mrs Charlbury bustled towards the staircase, leaving Elinor a prey to a myriad of conflicting thoughts.

Of course, it was foolish to imagine that she could have caused Lord Rokeby's thoughts to wander. Hunting accidents happened all too often, even to the best of riders...but last night he had looked so strange. Even Hester had noticed it. There must be some other cause. Wearily she pushed her hair back from her brow and sought her room, leaving the tray of food untouched.

There was a hollow feeling in the pit of her stomach, and as she lay in her bed she was consumed by dread. Suppose the worst should happen, and Rokeby did not recover? No, she would not think of that. She pressed her hands against her brow as if by so doing she could dispel such a horrifying idea.

It was true that she had longed to get away from him, but she had never wished his death.

The full difficulty of her situation burst upon her then. With his lordship gone, what would become of Hester? Her tears were very near the surface. She bit her knuckle to force them back, and buried her face in her pillow.

The sound of her name roused her from an uneasy slumber. At first she thought that she was dreaming. Then a hand on her shoulder shook her awake. It was Mrs Charlbury.

"I think you should come at once," she said. "Marcus is in high fever."

Elinor threw a shawl about her shoulders and followed the older woman along the corridor.

Rokeby was no longer lying still and his face was flushed. Groaning, he tossed and turned about the bed, muttering unintelligibly. His dark curls were damp with sweat and when Elinor touched his skin she found it burning hot.

"Bates has sent Robert for the surgeon," Mrs Charlbury said. "Meantime, we must do what we can for him. Will you wipe his face whilst I soak more cloths?"

Elinor sponged away the sweat as best she could. "I wish we could keep him still," she cried. "If he thrashes about, the leg must needs be set again."

It took the combined strength of both women to prevent their patient from rolling on to the injured leg as his restlessness increased.

Elinor looked up with relief as the door opened. She was expecting to see the surgeon, but Robert brought bad news.

"I could not find him, ma'am. He's attending a confinement. I left a message…"

Elinor's heart sank. It might be many hours before the surgeon arrived.

"Do you get dressed, Miss Temple. Robert will help me hold his lordship. We can but keep him as cool as we may."

Elinor flew back to her room. It took but a few moments to bathe her hands and face. Then she threw on the first gown to hand, and dragged a comb through her hair, scarcely knowing what she was about.

When she returned to Rokeby's room, his struggles had abated. She threw a fearful look at Mrs Charlbury.

"No, he is no worse. In fact, I think his pulse is steadier. Take heart, my dear, we may be over the worst…"

Elinor bent her head to hide the tears which would not be denied. She sat beside the bed and again took his lordship's hand in hers.

"He is still unconscious," she choked out. "Oh, how I wish the surgeon would arrive..."

It was afternoon before her wish was granted, and still her patient seemed unaware of his surroundings.

"The only remedy is to bleed him, ma'am." The surgeon's face was grave.

"But he has lost so much blood already," Elinor protested.

A gesture of dismissal sent her out of the room. Perhaps the man was right, she thought in despair. Something must be done to rouse Rokeby from his coma.

She made her way downstairs to find John Charlbury sitting with Hester and his mother.

"Admirable woman!" Charlbury's eyes glowed with approval. "Thorne told us how you had taken charge when you heard news of the accident."

"Thorne?" Elinor was mystified.

"The young man who told you what had happened. From now on, ma'am, he is your devoted servant, as are we all."

"I didn't feel very brave," Elinor confessed. "But Hester has been of the greatest help."

"Miss Temple! All I did was to roll the bandages and sit with my guardian for a little while..." Hester had flushed at the words of praise.

"You kept your head," Elinor told her gravely. "No one can ask more." She turned to Mrs Charlbury. "Ma'am, I feel we cannot impose upon you further. Your husband and your family..."

"My dear Miss Temple, let us see what the surgeon has to say before I think of leaving you."

Four pairs of eyes looked up as the door to the salon opened.

"I have taken a pint of blood and I think his lordship is a little easier," the surgeon announced. "Keep him quiet—"

"He will live?" Elinor's voice was raw with emotion.

"He is holding his own at present. More I cannot say. Only time will tell." The man was clearly unwilling to commit himself.

"John shall stay with you for the present," Mrs Charlbury announced when the surgeon had gone. "I will return this evening." She took Elinor in her arms and kissed her cheek. "Be of good heart, my dear. Marcus is young and strong. He will come through this."

Elinor pressed her hand. Then she hurried away before her face betrayed her. The awful suspicion that Rokeby meant more to her than she dared to admit was uppermost in her mind. It was foolish in the extreme to feel as she did, just because her employer had been injured.

What had happened to the self-assured Miss Temple? In the aftermath of a single kiss she had been reduced to a quivering mass of nerves. She, who prided herself upon her common-sense and her ability to handle any situation? She was behaving like an idiot.

Her distress was due solely to the shock of the accident and its possibly appalling consequences, she told herself. Mrs Charlbury was right. Someone must keep up the spirits of the household at this anxious time. She would not fail.

Her resolution was sorely tested when she returned

to the sickroom. Rokeby lay still and silent, and his face had taken on a greyish hue. Elinor's heart sank. In profile, the aquiline nose looked sharp and the contusion on his brow seemed more prominent than before.

Elinor laid a hand upon his forehead. It was still hot to her touch, but he did not seem to be sweating quite so much. She sat down by his side and took his hand in hers.

She had heard somewhere that hearing was the last of the senses to fail, and the first to return. She began to speak to Rokebury in a low voice, telling him of her family, her work at the school in Bath, and the visit which she and Hester had paid to Tunbridge Wells.

The wry thought crossed her mind that had Rokeby been himself his eyes might have glazed with boredom at her chatter, but what she said was unimportant. A phrase or even a single word might penetrate his consciousness.

At length she fell silent. It was hopeless. She did not know how long she had been sitting by his lordship's bedside, but her efforts had been in vain.

She gazed in anguish at his face. If only he would speak or give some sign that he was aware of her presence, she would forgive him everything.

The door opened softly and Bates came into the room.

''Ma'am, will you not rest? His lordship must be washed and changed.''

Elinor nodded and attempted to withdraw her hand. A convulsive shudder ran through her patient as he gripped her fingers with surprising strength.

"My lord?" She was on her feet in a second to bend over him.

Rokeby's lips were moving, but she could not distinguish the words. She put her ear to his mouth.

"Don't go!" The blue eyes flickered open. "I want you here. I don't know why..."

"I won't leave you." Elinor found that she was shaking with relief. She looked across at Bates to find the tears coursing down his cheeks.

"He's come to his senses, ma'am?"

"I believe so." Elinor's smile was radiant. "Bates, will you tell the others? And a message should be sent to Mrs Charlbury..."

Rokeby's fingers squeezed her hand, and she turned back to him. His eyes were filled with pain, but a faint smile hovered about his lips.

"Still managing everyone?" he murmured. Then he fell into a deep sleep.

Elinor sat with him for the rest of that long night, but he did not wake again until the early hours.

Elinor was dozing by the light of a shaded candle, her hand still held in Rokeby's grasp when a small sound aroused her. She opened her eyes to find them held in Rokeby's blue gaze.

"Oh, thank God! You are awake! My lord, you should have told me..."

"I liked to look at you...so peaceful and defenceless."

"I am not in the least defenceless," Elinor began hotly. Then she heard a chuckle.

"I see that you are feeling better, sir," she said in a dry tone. "I will send for Bates."

The grip on her hand had tightened. "Wait! How long have you been sitting here, Miss Temple?"

"I can't recall...since some time yesterday, my lord."

He nodded. "I thought I sensed you near. What day is this?"

"It is the twenty-eighth day of December. Now, sir, you shall not talk. The surgeon insisted that you must have rest."

"Damned sawbones! He's naught but a blood-letting leech. No wonder that I feel like something the cat would not give her kittens..."

"He set your leg, sir." Elinor frowned at him. It was clear that his lordship was unlikely to be the best of patients.

Rokeby raised a hand to finger the lump upon his brow. Then he winced.

"Fool!" he cried impatiently.

"Sir?"

"Myself, not you. What of Beau, my horse?"

"He had to be put down, Lord Rokeby. I'm sorry."

"So am I...for my own folly." He reached out for the bell-rope.

"What are you doing?" Elinor cried in alarm.

"I want Jervis."

"For what purpose?" Elinor cried in alarm. She would not put it past him to insist on his valet dressing him and helping him out of bed.

"My dear Miss Temple!" Rokeby raised a quizzical eyebrow.

"Oh, I beg your pardon." Elinor blushed and fled as Jervis entered the room. There were the calls of nature to be considered. She should have thought of it before and sent for Jervis.

The great house was silent at that early hour as she crept back to her room. The fierce energy which had sustained her for so long had drained away and she felt utterly weary, but her mind was at rest.

She stripped off her clothing, lay down on her bed, and was asleep in seconds.

It was afternoon when she awoke to find Hester by her side.

"The surgeon is here again, Miss Temple. Shall you wish to see him?"

"I think so, Hester. He may tell us what treatment he recommends."

Hester giggled. "Lord Rokeby swore at him. He says that he will do exactly as he wishes."

"Did he indeed? I may have something to say about that. His lordship shall not give us another fright!"

She found the surgeon by his patient's bedside, engaged in fierce argument. Rokeby was refusing to be bled again. At length the man threw up his hands and turned to Elinor.

"I can do nothing more," he announced stiffly. "His lordship will not heed my advice."

"May I have a word in private?" Elinor led him from the room. "Let us see how he goes on," she pleaded. "His lordship is growing agitated. Did you not tell me that he must be quiet?"

"He was ever the worst of patients, I'm sorry to say." The surgeon would not be mollified. "I have changed his dressings and examined the leg, but other than that he will not allow of further treatment.''

"At least he is conscious again, and for that we must be thankful—"

"Ma'am, it was due entirely to the blood-letting."

"I am sure that you are right." Elinor's tone was conciliatory. "He looks so much better, sir. Will you not tell me how we should go on? I will see that he follows your instructions."

The man shot her a sharp look. "He will heed your advice no more than mine, I fear. When I arrived, he was attempting to persuade his man to help him into a chair."

"He shall do no such thing," Elinor said with decision. "I shall warn him that he may suffer a relapse."

"I wish you luck, ma'am. If he does so, you may send for me again. Otherwise there is no point in my returning." With a last angry look he stalked away.

"But, sir, you have not told me—?"

"Rest and quiet, ma'am," he barked the words over his shoulder. "That is all you can do."

When Elinor returned to the sick-room, her patient was unrepentant.

He grinned at her. "Did you get rid of him?"

"I did, my lord, but he is not best pleased. You were not over-civil…"

"Come now, you shall not scold me. I am a sick man…"

Elinor saw the gleam of mischief in the blue eyes.

"You will be much sicker if you persist in behaving foolishly," she retorted. "I hear that you were planning to leave your bed."

"Oh, I have no wish to do so if you will stay with me."

Elinor looked at him straightly. His splendid constitution had served him well. Newly shaven and in a clean night-shirt, he looked a different man from the broken creature of three days ago. His complexion was no longer grey, and the blue eyes were very bright.

Bates came into the room and busied himself in mixing something in a glass. Then he walked towards the bed.

"What's this?" Rokeby said suspiciously.

"You are to take this dose three times a day, my lord."

"Nonsense! Take it away!" He waved a hand in dismissal.

Elinor reached out for the glass. "Will you worry us all again?" she asked gently. "These last few days have not been easy..." She held the glass to his lips.

Rokeby swallowed the contents with ill grace. Then he leaned back against his pillows and closed his eyes.

Elinor signalled to Bates to leave them.

It was some moments before Rokeby spoke. "You must believe there is a curse on Merton Place," he murmured.

"How so, my lord?"

"Since your arrival you have spent all your time in sick-rooms... You must be tired of it."

"No, sir." Elinor sought for words. "I am content."

"You are easily contented, ma'am. I think you do not ask for much from life."

Elinor chuckled. "You are mistaken. I ask a lot."

"In what way? I have seen no evidence of it."

"Sir, you must not talk. You are to rest—"

"For God's sake, woman, what else have I been doing? You do not answer my question."

Elinor considered carefully before she spoke. "I value friendship and affection," she said quietly. "Those, to me, are all important."

"You do not seek the wilder shores of love?" The self-mockery in his voice surprised her.

"I...I do not understand you."

"Oh, I think you do, Miss Temple." The blue eyes opened and raked her face. "I am speaking of an overwhelming passion..."

"I know nothing of such things. Sir, shall I ring for Bates? I am sure you have not eaten—"

"Don't change the subject. How old are you, Miss Temple?"

"Sir?"

"I asked how old you were."

"I am twenty-three...though what that has to say to anything...?"

"What a waste! How long have you been teaching?"

"I went to Bath four years ago, through the good offices of a friend."

"You were not begged to stay in Derbyshire?"

"No, my lord. My father agreed that I should go to Bath."

"I was not speaking of your father, ma'am. You did not leave behind a lovesick swain or two? I can't believe it!"

Elinor smiled. "I had an offer, sir, but it would not serve."

"Why not?"

"My affections were not engaged."

"He was old and fat, and without means?"

Elinor bridled. "He was my own age, sir, and not ill looking. As to means, he was heir to his father's properties."

"Then I wonder that your parents did not insist upon your being safely settled."

"They would not force me," Elinor cried indignantly. "Their standards are not yours, my lord." She was about to say more, but caught herself in time. She must not irritate her patient.

Rokeby seemed untroubled. A mocking smile played about his lips. "At nineteen you could have been no judge of what was best for you."

"Perhaps not, but my father is not wanting in judgment. He was happy to allow me to do as I wished."

"And you have been doing so ever since?" Rokeby gave her a sly look. "You are young to have such self-command."

"I am able to look after myself."

"Indeed you are! It is a source of some disappointment to me, I confess." His mouth curved.

"Sir, you are making gammon of me, and tiring yourself at the same time. I will leave you now. Jervis will sit with you, but do not, I beg of you, persuade him into folly."

"I have not the least wish to persuade Jervis into folly, I assure you. Now, as to persuading you...?"

Elinor rose to her feet. "You are quite comfortable?" she asked.

"My pillows...they need re-arranging."

As Elinor bent over him a strong arm slid about her neck, and Rokeby drew her face to his.

As his mouth found hers, the same dizzying sensation assailed her as it had done on Christmas Eve. She struggled to free herself, but he would not release her. Then a tide of love swept over her as the pent-up emotion of the last few days found release. She gave herself up to the pleasure of that kiss with an abandon which shook her to the very core of her being.

Rokeby was murmuring endearments as he rained kisses on her eyelids, her brow, and the tip of her nose. At last she pulled away from him.

"I see that you are much recovered, sir," she gasped. "That was unfair! You tricked me!"

"I must be delirious," Rokeby murmured wickedly. He raised a hand to his head. "Yes, it is as I thought. I am on the verge of a relapse."

"Oh, you...you...you are impossible! Sir, you shall find another nurse—"

"How can you be so cruel? The agony!" Rokeby let out a counterfeit groan. "Send for the surgeon, I beg of you!" He opened one eye and looked at her.

"He will not come," Elinor said briskly. "Nor do I blame him. He is up to all your tricks, and I am learning them to my cost."

"My dear Miss Temple, how can you rail at a sick man? Please go! These strictures are too much for me. There is no need to summon Jervis. I shall rest now...alone in my bed of pain..."

Elinor began to laugh. She could not help herself.

"Heartless!" Rokeby murmured. "I knew it from the first moment I looked at you."

"And you may believe it, my lord!" Elinor fled.

Chapter Six

The Charlburys, she knew, were waiting in the salon. Since Rokeby's accident they had paid a daily visit, but she felt unable to face anyone in her present state of confusion.

She slipped along the corridor to the Long Gallery. There she began to pace the floor, striving to come to terms with her own emotions.

Lord Rokeby was becoming a serious threat to her peace of mind. Since Christmas Eve, she had managed to convince herself that she was making far too much of a single kiss, stolen beneath the mistletoe. Since the day of her arrival she had been so stiff and prim with him. For a man of his temperament it was only to be expected that he would try to tease her into losing her composure. And he had succeeded. The knowledge had angered and disturbed her.

Yet as she sat beside his bed, looking at his still unconscious form, she had vowed to forgive him anything if only he would speak. By now she knew every detail of that swarthy face, from the strong line of his jaw to the curving, mobile mouth. She had brushed away the damp curls which clustered on his brow as he lay in fever, and held his hand until her own had ached from the fierceness of his grip as he writhed in pain.

A wry smile played about her lips. She had prayed for his recovery, and today he had given her proof that he was on the mend.

She should have been furious, but she couldn't find it in her heart to censure him! It was a joy to see the twinkle once again in those blue eyes, but she was honest enough to admit that her own reaction to his kiss had not been one of unmixed relief at his recovery.

She had enjoyed it, and therein lay the danger. Bored and confined to his bed, Rokeby was merely amusing himself, but her own reaction had been far from casual. He now occupied her mind to the exclusion of all else, and the sensation was new to her.

She turned at the end of the gallery and glanced up at the portraits which lined the walls. Those same blue eyes had been in the Rokeby family for generations. Now they seemed to follow her as she moved past, some indifferent to her predicament, some disapproving, some amused, and some filled with the light of mischief which she had grown to know so well.

She stopped before a portrait of Rokeby's father and looked up at him.

"You have much to answer for, my lord," she scolded aloud. "The sooner your son is wed and settled down, the better for his family."

It was strange that the thought gave her no pleasure when it was clearly the sensible answer to her own problems. With Rokeby safely married to some charming girl, his suitability as guardian to his ward could no longer be in doubt. Rather than marrying off Hester, she might become a part of his household. Then she herself would be free to pick up the threads of her own life.

It was an oddly depressing idea. Elinor frowned. It was what she wanted; indeed, she had longed for the chance to do so, and the day must come when she would be forced to face her future alone. Better sooner rather than later, she thought to herself. She was becoming too involved with the inhabitants of Merton Place.

"Oh, here you are!" Hester walked towards her. "Are you not cold in here, Miss Temple?"

"No, I have been walking. I was stiff after sitting by his lordship's bedside for so long." Her excuse sounded reasonable enough. Apart from its function as a portrait gallery, the long chamber had been intended as a place for taking exercise in inclement weather.

"Mrs Charlbury would like to see you," Hester said shyly. "She is here with Mr John."

Elinor gathered her scattered thoughts. For the moment there was nothing she could do about the problems which faced her. Rokeby, as far as she knew, had, as yet, no thoughts of marriage. He would be incapacitated for some time, and might even be forced to put off Hester's début until the following year.

She was soon disillusioned. As she entered the salon Mrs Charlbury's quick eyes noted her heightened colour and her glowing looks but she made no comment.

"I have seen Marcus," she began. "He has written to Lady Hartfield explaining that your arrival in

London is like to be delayed. Meantime, he suggests that Hester takes dancing lessons from Monsieur Gaston in Tunbridge Wells.''

Elinor nodded her assent.

''I hope you don't think I was interfering,'' Mrs Charlbury added. ''Marcus asked me for the name of the man who taught my girls—''

''Not at all, ma'am,'' Elinor disclaimed quickly. ''I do not know the town. I could be of no help in such matters.''

''The town bronze must wait for Lady Hartfield's expert guidance, but Hester is a pretty-behaved girl. There will be no difficulty...''

''Then his lordship is determined?'' Hester looked alarmed.

''Come, Miss Winton, you will not deprive me of the pleasure of your company in London? Had we not decided to sail upon the river and visit the Tower?'' John Charlbury pleaded.

Hester nodded, but she was not altogether reassured.

''And, with Monsieur Gaston's permission, John shall come and partner you,'' Mrs Charlbury promised.

''Always providing that you do not mind a partner with two left feet.'' A chuckle accompanied John Charlbury's words.

''Marcus seems to be in spirits today.'' Mrs Charlbury looked at Elinor with affection. ''It is all due to your devoted nursing, my dear.''

Elinor blushed. ''His lordship has a splendid constitution... We are all so thankful that the worst is over.''

John Charlbury gave a shout of laughter.

"Optimist!" he cried. "Your troubles are just beginning, Miss Temple. He has just assured my mother that he is ready to come downstairs..."

"Oh, no!" Elinor rose to her feet in dismay. "Ma'am, I hope you advised him that it was out of the question?"

She moved to the door, intending to return to the sick-room. Then she remembered. She had made up her mind that she would not be left alone with Rokeby again.

"Will you not speak to him?" she asked John Charlbury.

"I will do my best, Miss Temple, but I fear that we shall lose this battle, at least within a day or two." Still laughing, he left the room.

"Now do not upset yourself, my dear." Mrs Charlbury patted her hand. "Marcus is impatient with his own weakness, but if we threaten him with a set-back..."

"Doubtless he will announce that we are talking nonsense," Elinor said ruefully. "Ma'am, he really is—!"

"Yes, he is, isn't he? But that is Marcus. Do your best with him, Miss Temple. He will not wish to distress you or add to your worries, I believe."

Elinor was not so sure.

By dint of summoning the younger Charlburys to play cards with his lordship, by persuading Hester to read to him, and allowing John to chat to him by the hour together she managed to confine her patient to his bed for the next few days.

Anne and her mother were with him, together with the younger Charlbury girls and Hester, as Elinor walked past his door. Gales of laughter sounded from the room, but Elinor did not enter. She felt oddly excluded from that merry crowd, but it was of her own doing.

Since the day he had slipped an arm about her neck and kissed her, Elinor had taken care never to be alone with Rokeby. That he was well aware of her decision she had no doubt.

She had seen the glint in his eyes as he looked at her, but he had not referred to the fact that when she entered his room she was not alone.

As the days passed and he grew stronger, she had cut down upon her visits to the sick-room, restricting them to a brief daily greeting, and an enquiry as to his health. Forestalling any remonstrations, she had pleaded the need to supervise Hester's dancing lessons and her deportment classes. Rokeby had nodded and made no comment.

Elinor felt guilty. After his daily visitors had left she had abandoned him to hours of boredom, but it must be for the best, though it wasn't easy. She had learned to look for the way his eyes lit up as she walked into the room, and she missed the banter which was common currency between them.

A week later she was in the salon, playing for the dancers, when the door opened and Rokeby was assisted into the room on the arm of a large footman.

Elinor rose to her feet with a gasp of dismay.

"No, no, don't get up, Miss Temple!" His lordship gave her a smile of charming innocence. "I heard the music and felt that it was time I bestirred myself to join you. Do please go on." He settled himself in a chair with the injured leg stretched out before him, and bent a benevolent look upon the startled dancers.

Elinor could have hit him. For one thing he should not be out of bed, and for another his presence was sure to undermine Hester's growing confidence in her ability to learn the complicated steps.

She was right. It was not many moments before Monsieur Gaston threw up his hands in despair.

"Mademoiselle Winton, I beg of you! Please to remember that here you must turn towards your partner..."

Hester made several more attempts to follow him, but all to no avail.

The little Frenchman had an inspiration. "Perhaps if Miss Temple would demonstrate...?"

It was the last thing Elinor wished. With Rokeby's cynical gaze upon her she would feel like some houri of the east, performing especially for his benefit.

"Miss Temple?" Monsieur Gaston looked anxious.

"Of course!" Elinor rose from the instrument and held out her hand to the dancing master. A coy refusal would give the matter far too much importance. She went through the dance as Hester watched. Then she returned to her seat, aware that Rokeby had enjoyed her discomfiture.

"Will you assist me, Miss Temple? If I might sit beside you, I could turn the pages of your music...?"

Elinor eyed him coldly. "I fear you might sustain a fall, my lord."

"I see. You feel perhaps that you are not strong enough to bear with me? Then John shall help me."

Unaware of the tension between Elinor and her tormentor, John Charlbury set a chair beside the music stool and lifted Rokeby to his feet. Ignoring his lordship's close proximity, Elinor began to play. At least with his attention diverted from herself Hester might recover her composure.

It did not serve, and at length, aware of Monsieur Gaston's increasing agitation, Elinor dismissed him until the following day.

"Miss Winton is a little tired, I fear," she told him with a smile. "She will be more herself tomorrow."

"You do look pale, my dear." Rokeby raised his quizzing glass to inspect his ward. "Fresh air is what you need. John shall take you for a turn about the grounds, if he will be so kind."

"I will go with you." Elinor stood up. It was a blatant attempt on his lordship's part to be left alone with her, and she would have none of it.

A strong hand closed about her wrist. "Will you not spare me a few moments of your time, Miss Temple? We must talk...I have some news for you."

Elinor threw a despairing glance at her companions, but they seemed unaware of the pleading in her eyes. She had no choice but to resume her place on the music stool.

"You should not be here, my lord," she announced stiffly. "You will give yourself a set-back."

"I thought I had already been given one." Rokeby grinned at her. He was not referring to his broken leg. "You have been avoiding me, Miss Temple. If Mahomet won't go to the mountain, you know...then the mountain must come to Mahomet."

"Your news, my lord?"

"Ah, yes. I have heard from Lady Hartfield. She

suggests that you bring Hester to London without delay.''

Elinor's heart sank. "Surely there can be no immediate hurry?'' she protested.

"I fear there is. You have heard the old saw about 'February fill-dyke'? It is only too true. When the spring rains come the roads in these parts will be among the worst in England. It is the Wealden clay, you see. It turns into a greasy mass which clogs the carriage wheels.''

"I see.'' Elinor was silent for a time. Then she decided on a last plea to Rokeby's better nature. "Sir, won't you re-consider your decision? Hester, as you see, is not ready for a season. Perhaps next year...?''

"Impossible!'' His face was implacable. "You know my reasons for a wish to see her wed.''

"I do indeed!'' she cried bitterly. "They are for your own convenience!''

"Must you always think so hardly of me?'' He lifted her hand and raised it to his lips. At the touch of his warm mouth against her skin, Elinor began to tremble. It took a great effort of self-control not to snatch her hand away. Instead, she allowed it to lie limp within his grasp.

"You give me no reason to think otherwise,'' she told him steadily. "You make every effort to put me out of countenance—''

"You!'' He threw back his head and laughed aloud. "I doubt if I, or any other man, would succeed in doing that. Come, my dear, you do not object to a little chaffing?''

"Sir, you are a trifler!'' she burst out in a rage. Disappointment was mixed with anger. She had

made a perfectly reasonable request on Hester's behalf, and he had refused it. Now he was back to his
old tricks, treating her as if she had been put on earth
merely to amuse him.

"A trifler? Surely not with your affections?" He
looked at her with half-closed eyes. "You cannot be
at risk from me, the invulnerable Miss Temple? No,
it is too much to hope."

With what dignity she could command, Elinor disengaged herself from his grasp. "When does Lady
Hartfield expect us?" she asked coldly.

"I believe the weather will hold until next week.
Shall we say Monday? You will need an escort, but
John assures me that he will be happy to oblige. It
is strange...this sudden desire of his to visit London
for the Season... I can't recall it happening before."

Elinor could not mistake the mockery in his eyes
and she blushed a fiery red. Surely he did not suspect
that John Charlbury hoped to capture her affections?
The idea was ridiculous.

"You think highly of him, do you not?" Rokeby's
question was apparently casual, but Elinor sensed the
tension in him as he waited for her answer. Doubtless
he thought her an unsuitable match for his friend.
Some imp of mischief prevented her from telling him
the truth.

"He is charming, sir. No one could fail to warm
to his delightful character."

She had the satisfaction of seeing Rokeby's expression change. A crease appeared between his
brows and his mouth set in a hard line.

"Shall I ring for Robert, my lord?" she asked
sweetly. "You will not wish to sit here alone."

"Your round, I think, Miss Temple." Rokeby

made a swift recovery, but a spasm of pain crossed his face as he shifted in his chair.

Elinor was beside him at once. "You will be more comfortable in your bed," she said more gently. "My lord, may I not persuade you to take more care, just for a little longer?"

A smile lit his eyes once more. "You could persuade me of anything, I believe. Well, I suppose it is bed again, but alone, alas!"

Elinor hid a smile. He was incorrigible. "Bear up, sir," she said with mock asperity. "It will not be many weeks before you are able to resume your normal way of life."

"I doubt it. I have suffered a severe blow to my self-esteem. I shall not be the same again. When you look at me so, I feel like some curious type of insect."

"What nonsense!" Elinor said robustly. "If you go on like this, I shall think you suffering from delirium."

"I have thought so myself, especially when the sun catches your hair as it is doing at this moment. You appear to have a halo, ma'am."

"That is an illusion, sir. Must you always have the last word?"

"It is some comfort to me," Rokeby admitted weakly. "For the moment it is all I have, but I promise you that when I am recovered..."

Elinor laughed and pulled the bell-rope. "Threats will not weigh with me, my lord. Nuncheon shall be sent up to your room. Then, I hope, you will rest."

"I am like to die of boredom," he told her with a grim smile. "I am tired of looking at those four walls."

"It is trying for you," Elinor admitted. Then she had an inspiration. "Sir, it cannot stop you making plans...for the estate, I mean. Your time need not be wasted. Only this morning there was some treatise arrived upon the latest seed-drills, and the use of seaweed for manuring land. I could make notes for you as you study it."

"You would find it a boring task, Miss Temple."

"Not at all, my lord." Elinor had noticed the change in his expression. "You forget that I was brought up in the country, and you are keen to improve the yield of all your crops, are you not?"

His face grew sombre. "It may be vital to our survival. This peace with Napoleon cannot hold. He intends to make himself master of Europe, including this country. The French will blockade our ports, to starve us into submission."

"Then there is no time to lose," Elinor told him briskly. "I will fetch the books, and my writing materials."

At that moment Mrs Charlbury came in through the garden door. "Marcus, what are you about?" she cried.

"Disobeying orders, ma'am." His lordship looked so guilty that Elinor was tempted to laugh.

"So I see!" Overriding all his protestations, Mrs Charlbury insisted that he returned to his room at once. Elinor gathered up a pile of books and pamphlets, found a notebook, and followed them.

"There, my lord!" She laid the pile of books beside his bed. "I shall return directly after nuncheon."

"I am glad to see that you intend to insist that Marcus does not overtax his strength," the older woman told her when they were alone. "I have told my girls that they may not visit him today."

Anne's reddened eyes told Elinor of her disappointment, and she was moved to pity. "Perhaps tomorrow?" she suggested.

As the girls departed, Elinor blushed. "Ma'am, I hope that I did not go against your wishes in suggesting that the girls might come tomorrow?"

"You are thinking of Anne, I believe? Miss Temple, I am much too old a hand to make the mistake of keeping Anne away from Marcus. Nothing is more likely to confirm her notion that she loves him than parental opposition."

Elinor was silent.

"You do not agree? My dear, Anne would become so obsessed with fighting us that she might forget to consider that she and Marcus are not suited to each other."

"How wise you are!" Elinor gave her a warm smile. "We shall miss you, ma'am. We are to leave for London on Monday. I confess, I cannot be easy about Hester's coming season. She is so shy, you see. It is a torment for her to mix in company and try to be what she is not."

"Then she should not do so," Mrs Charlbury said with conviction. "It is always a mistake to dissemble. Hester is quiet, but she is a charming girl with a loving heart."

"I know it, but Lord Rokeby is determined that she shall wed as soon as possible. I cannot think it right."

"Trust him!" her companion advised quietly. "Marcus is no ogre, my dear. Behind that teasing manner lies a cool head, and much kindness."

"I hope you may be right." Elinor felt a little happier. Mrs Charlbury had known Rokeby since he was a child, and she was shrewd. It was unlikely that she could be mistaken in him. Even so, she could not repress a twinge of doubt.

"Now, Miss Temple, you must be strong. Do not allow Marcus to repeat his folly of this morning, however much he tries to browbeat you."

"I think I have the solution, ma'am. I have offered to become his secretary. He is to give instructions, and I am to write them down." Elinor smiled in spite of her misgivings. Had she not vowed to avoid his lordship's company unless others were present? Hopefully, he would be too absorbed in his plans for the estate to persist in teasing her.

She was not mistaken. When she returned to his room that afternoon, he was lost in thought. A map of the estate and the open treatise on the new seed-drill lay across his knees.

"There you are!" he said impatiently. "I thought you were never coming." He began to dictate at speed.

Elinor was astonished by his quick grasp of the way in which the new methods could be used on his own land, and the clear way in which he defined his plans. Soon she found herself infected by his own enthusiasm, and she forgot the passage of time until it became too dark to see her paper.

"How thoughtless of me! You will ruin your eyes," Rokeby said suddenly. "Will you not ring for candles?"

Unthinking, she reached out for the rope which lay beside his bed-head, and was startled when his fingers closed about her wrist.

"No, don't pull away from me," he murmured in a low tone. "I wish only to thank you for your kindness. You have borne this dull discourse with a good grace."

"My lord, I have enjoyed it," she told him truthfully.

He gave her a smile of indefinable charm. "You are a woman of many parts, my dear. I confess that today I am more content than at any time since that stupid accident. Why did we not think of this before? It has been a productive afternoon, and I am grateful to you."

As always, she had found his touch disturbing. "That is because your mind was occupied with matters which are of use to you, sir."

"That as much as anything. May we do the same thing tomorrow?"

"Only if you promise to stay where you are, Lord Rokeby."

"Your wish is my command." He gave her a mock salute as she left him.

She went downstairs to find Hester in reflective mood.

"Is something wrong?" she asked.

"No, but I was wondering what Lady Hartfield will be like. She is my guardian's aunt, is she not?"

"She is, but that is no reason for you to be afraid of her. Lord Rokeby is a young man. His aunt's ideas are likely to be very different from his own."

"A young man?" Hester sounded astonished. "He seems old to me."

"As does anyone over the age of twenty, I make no doubt." Elinor's eyes began to twinkle.

"Oh no, you are not old," Hester disclaimed hastily. "Nor is Mr Charlbury."

"He is the same age as Lord Rokeby," Elinor teased. "He must be all of thirty-two, or so."

"No, he isn't. He's twenty-eight. He told me so himself..."

It was becoming clear that Hester's discussions with John Charlbury had progressed from learned matters to others of a more personal nature. A warning bell sounded in Elinor's mind. How stupid she had been in thinking of Hester as a child, not much older than Sebastian or Crispin. It was only to be expected that the girl would develop an affection for their gentle neighbour.

And what a solution that would be, Elinor thought wistfully. Hester would be welcomed into a loving family where she already felt at ease. She wondered that Rokeby had not thought of it. Perhaps he had, only to dismiss the idea out of hand.

For all she knew, he might have suggested the match to John Charlbury already. It seemed unlikely. His friend was no dissembler, and his manner towards Hester was that of an elder brother.

Her main concern was that Hester should not be hurt. The child had suffered enough rebuffs in her short life. She glanced across at her charge. Hester met her gaze with such a candid look that Elinor was satisfied. There was no harm done as yet, but she must be on her guard.

Mrs Charlbury might be right in supposing that Anne's passion for Lord Rokeby would fade with time, but Hester was of a very different temperament. Once she formed an attachment, she would not change.

Elinor sighed. She would feel the same herself, should she ever give her heart to another, but how was it possible to be sure of one's judgment?

On this very day, for example, she had seen another side of a man whose character she despised. They had sat together in pleasant amity for the whole of the afternoon, and she had liked him better than at any time since their first meeting. His quick mind had delighted her, and she had been as absorbed as he in his plans for the estate.

It did not alter the fact that she found him both exciting and disturbing. Even so, she found that she was looking forward to the following day, when she would be taken into his confidence again.

It was all so confusing, but their time together would be short. The knowledge should have cheered her, but she found it strangely depressing.

"We should make a start on our packing," she murmured. "The maid will wish to know what we are to take."

Hester was startled. "Shall we return to Merton Place?"

"I do not know...so much depends..." The look on Hester's face caused her to amend her words. "I mean that it will depend on Lady Hartfield's wishes," she said quickly.

"Or if I marry." Hester's face crumpled. "Oh, it is all so hateful. I wish that I were dead."

Elinor hugged her close. "Don't worry, my dearest. Let us pin our faith on Lady Hartfield. Mrs Charlbury thinks well of her..."

Hester would not be comforted. "She will be exactly like Lord Rokeby," she wept. "And I shall hate her."

Chapter Seven

In that she was mistaken. Lady Hartfield was a surprise to both Elinor and her charge. Tall and thin, she could never have been a beauty, but her elegance was unmistakable.

A pair of sharp black eyes inspected both ladies and their escort as they walked towards her. Then she smiled and Elinor saw something of her charm.

Her ladyship rose to greet them with an easy grace remarkable in one no longer young, and held out her hands to Hester.

"So you are Rokeby's ward? Welcome, my dear. Miss Temple, I have heard much about you. It is a pleasure to meet you." She looked enquiringly at the man beside them.

"Lady Hartfield, this is Mr Charlbury, a neighbour of Lord Rokeby. He was kind enough to accompany us."

"A friend of Marcus? You, sir, appear to have more sense than my great-nephew. At least you are in one piece... How is Rokeby? I trust you left him in better health?"

Charlbury chuckled. "You need have no worries

about him, ma'am. His health is improving, but not, I fear, his temper.''

"Fretting, is he? Serve him right! I take it he was riding *ventre à terre?*''

"It was unfortunate, ma'am—''

"So it was! Well, let us forget him for the moment.'' Her ladyship rang for refreshment, but Charlbury would not stay. He left with a promise to call upon them later in the week.

"A pleasant young man!'' Lady Hartfield's gaze rested upon the faces of her companions. Then, apparently satisfied, she began to pour the tea.

"Well, my dears, what are your plans?''

"Your ladyship, we are entirely in your hands.'' Elinor smiled at her. Beneath the brisk manner she sensed a kind heart, and she had warmed at once to this ugly woman who exuded such an air of self-confidence.

"What a responsibility!'' The older woman made a little moue of mock dismay, and even Hester smiled.

"Rokeby has explained his wishes to you, Hester?''

"Yes, ma'am.''

Lady Hartfield laughed. "My dear, I promise not to throw you to the lions. A season is not such a very dreadful thing, you know, and you will have Miss Temple with you, as well as myself, to frighten off anyone you may not care to meet.''

"You are very kind, your ladyship.'' Hester's voice was colourless and she kept her eyes upon the carpet.

Lady Hartfield shot a speaking glance at Elinor.

"You will have a full two months before you need

make your come-out," she went on. "We must buy some gowns for you, of course, but you will wish to see something of the London scene. Would Mr Charlbury consent to be our escort? I confess I should like to see more of him..."

"Oh, ma'am, would you? He is so kind. I am sure that you will like him." Hester brightened up at once. "I thought, you see, that you might not think it right for him to visit us."

"Great heavens, child! Whyever not? With that handsome creature by our side we shall be the envy of every woman in London."

Hester smiled her gratitude, but the strain of being thrust into a strange household had taken its toll. She looked very pale.

"Here I am chattering on," her ladyship announced. "You must both be tired after your journey. Royston shall show you to your rooms. Now you must forgive me. This evening I have an engagement which I cannot break. Shall you mind if I leave you to your own devices? Dinner will be served at eight, and you will be quite alone."

Silently Elinor blessed her for her thoughtfulness, guessing rightly that her ladyship's engagement was the result of some deliberation. She realised in surprise that Rokeby must have mentioned Hester's nervousness with strangers to this formidable woman. Whatever his reasons, it had resulted in an act of kindness.

"There now," she teased when she and Hester were alone. "Do you still plan to hate her ladyship?"

Hester blushed and shook her head. "I like her," she announced. "She is not in the least what I expected."

"Nor I," Elinor admitted. "I think we shall be happy here, don't you?"

"Oh, yes…" Hester considered for a moment. "She thinks Mr Charlbury handsome, doesn't she? I had not thought of it before."

"Well, Hester, he is not exactly ill looking. I mean he has neither horns, nor an extra eye in the middle of his forehead."

Hester began to laugh. "Miss Temple, you are making game of me," she reproached. "I mean…well…he is just our friend."

"And a good one. Hester, think of the fun we shall have. We shall drive in the park, and see the sights."

"And he says that there are balloon ascents." Hester sighed in ecstasy. "Of course they depend upon the weather, and it may be summer before we see them…"

Hester lay upon her bed. Her eyelids were drooping, and in minutes she was sound asleep.

Elinor heard a gentle tap upon the door, and opened it to find her ladyship standing in the corridor.

"She is asleep?"

Elinor nodded.

"I thought as much, poor child. Will you spare me a few moments of your time?"

Elinor followed her into a pretty boudoir at the end of the corridor.

"We have a task upon our hands, I think, Miss Temple." Her ladyship closed the door.

Elinor looked at her in some trepidation, but ready with a fierce defence of her charge.

"No, there will be no need to fire up at me," Lady

Hartfield gave her a faint smile. "I mean to do my best for Hester, but I should be glad of your advice."

Elinor was disarmed at once. "Hester is not at her best with strangers," she admitted slowly. "She had a bad time at school. She is reserved, you see...and then...she was never a pretty girl."

Her ladyship leaned back in her chair, her fingers toying with her fan. "That is what decided me to take her."

"Ma'am?" Elinor was startled.

"Ah, looking as you do you will never understand. Beauty is fleeting, so they say, but every woman longs for such a gift. Look at me, Miss Temple. As a child my nickname was 'The Maypole'."

"But, ma'am that cannot be... You are so—"

"Elegant, my dear? That is my answer to the world. The French term is *une jolie laide*, which is almost untranslatable, but I believe it to mean an ugly beauty."

Elinor was silent. There was nothing she could say.

"Rokeby was worried about Hester," the older woman continued. "He begged me to take over all responsibility for her, but that was not possible. I should have refused in any case. It will do my nephew no harm to have someone else to think of."

"His lordship is very good to his tenants, Lady Hartfield." To her own surprise Elinor found herself defending her employer.

"So I should hope. It is his duty. I hear too that his estate is something of a model, but it is not the same thing, you will agree? Marcus knows my views. It is high time he settled down and found himself a wife."

"Oh, ma'am, you do not think of Hester for him?" It was a tactless remark, but Lady Hartfield did not take it amiss.

"Of course not! Two people more ill suited would be difficult to find. Now you shall not worry about Hester, my dear. I know how fond you are of her, and she shall not be pressed against her will, but it can do her no harm to acquire a little self-confidence and acquire her own style during these next few months."

"Of course not. But, ma'am, with all respect, you cannot hope to transform her into a woman of fashion...I mean...she will never look as you do."

"I should hope not. The art is in being an original. A copy can be nothing but false coin. Now, Miss Temple, will you trust me?"

Elinor gave her a smile of purest gratitude. "I could wish that you were her guardian, Lady Hartfield."

"As a woman that would not be possible, my dear. For some reason best known to themselves, the courts believe that females are inferior creatures, incapable of handling either their own affairs or those of anyone else. It is only when one is widowed that one has a little freedom."

She looked so cheerful about her loss that the words of sympathy died upon Elinor's lips.

"You think me unfeeling? I was married against my will to a man much older than myself. I cannot grieve that that particular trial did not last for many years... Now, Miss Temple, you must excuse me. I shall see you in the morning."

As Elinor returned to her room her mind felt more at ease. Perhaps she had found an ally. Lady

Hartfield's experience of marriage might make her more sympathetic to Hester's cause. And at least she was not the dragon that she and Hester had expected.

She found herself wondering if Rokeby knew his aunt as well as he thought he did. Lady Hartfield's idea of a suitable match might not be his own. The ensuing contest was likely to be a battle of the Titans. She was smiling as she entered Hester's room.

Her ladyship was not an early riser and it was not until noon on the following day that they were summoned to her presence. She was sitting up in bed with a most becoming boudoir cap perched upon her head.

"You slept well?" she enquired. "You both look rested... Now Hester, let me look at you in daylight. Walk over to the window, my dear, then turn and come towards me."

In silence, Hester did as she was bidden.

"Yes, your carriage is good," the older woman mused. "It makes you look taller than you are. Your complexion, too, is excellent. Thank heavens that you are not covered in spots. I suffered from them mightily when I was a girl."

Hester managed a reluctant smile.

"Today I thought we might go shopping," Lady Hartfield continued. "We shall not wish to be abroad in the town when Mr Charlbury comes to call, but I believe he mentioned Thursday, did he not?"

"Yes, ma'am." Hester was all attention. "I should like to go shopping today, if you please."

"And tomorrow is Wednesday. Perhaps the hairdresser?"

Hester made no demur. She would have agreed to

anything if she might be free to greet their visitor on Thursday.

Elinor felt a twinge of alarm, but her ladyship's expression was bland, so she crushed her own misgivings. Hester was merely looking forward to seeing their friend again.

It was all too easy to grow accustomed to companionship when one was in daily contact with another person. Already she herself was missing Rokeby's easy banter and the rakish look which was a constant challenge.

Her thoughts were taking her in a dangerous direction and her face grew rosy. Glancing up, she found Lady Hartfield's eyes upon her and her blush deepened.

She must pull herself together, or her hostess might imagine that John Charlbury's proposed visit was of more than common interest to her. She stiffened, expecting a little gentle chaffing, but Lady Hartfield did not pursue the subject.

Later that day Elinor brought it up herself. She and Lady Hartfield were seated side by side, enjoying the refreshments which were offered only to Madame Germaine's most favoured customers. Madame herself was deeply sensible of the fact that she owed much of her success to her ladyship's patronage, and she welcomed her distinguished client accordingly.

Now they were surrounded by fabrics of every hue in fine wool, silks and muslins, together with the latest pattern books. Her ladyship wasted no time. She knew exactly what she wanted, having already discussed her requirements with the little Frenchwoman.

"Simplicity must be our choice for Miss Winton,"

she announced. "You have seen her, *madame*. Do you agree?"

"I cannot fault your taste, your ladyship. It is a mistake, I find, to gown the very young in too many frills and flounces."

Elinor felt relieved. Before meeting Lady Hartfield, she had been concerned lest Hester be dressed for the Season in garments chosen to proclaim her wealth. Her ladyship, she realised, would not be guilty of such vulgarity.

"Not white, I think," her ladyship mused. "Hester needs something to warm her skin... This shade of apricot bloom would be ideal, and also the coral. Hester, my dear, will you go with *madame?* She will take your measurements."

Hester's eyes were sparkling as she followed the mantua-maker, and she threw a look of gratitude at her two companions.

"Hester is in spirits today," her ladyship observed. "I think we may put it down to the prospect of some new gowns, as well as to the thought of seeing Mr Charlbury again..."

She had given Elinor the opening she needed.

"Ma'am, I hope you do not think that Hester regards John Charlbury as more than a friend...any more than I do myself..."

The black eyes rested on her face. Then Lady Hartfield smiled. "I have no worries about Hester...as to you, Miss Temple, whatever Rokeby may believe, I cannot think Charlbury the man for you."

Elinor blushed to the roots of her hair. "Lord Rokeby said...? Oh, ma'am, I cannot imagine how he came to think...Mr Charlbury has been kind to Hester and myself, but that is all.''

Her ladyship turned to finger a bolt of pale green silk. ''Rokeby is not always the wisest of men...at least, where emotions are concerned. Miss Temple, this shade of green would become you well. Do you like it?''

Elinor was too confused to do more than murmur her assent, and anger mingled with embarrassment. How dared Rokeby discuss her prospects with his aunt? It was the outside of enough.

At that moment Hester returned to them dressed in a classical gown which was the height of fashion for that season. The pale blue gauze was caught high beneath a fitted bodice with a velvet ribbon of deeper blue, and the short puffed sleeves were trimmed with the same fabric.

Lady Hartfield regarded her critically. ''Yes, that is the style for you for evening wear,'' she said.

''You do not find it too low at the front, ma'am?'' Hester tugged anxiously at the neckline.

''Not at all, my dear. Your skin is good, and you are without those ugly hollows at the neck. When one is too thin this style can be a disaster.''

Elinor blessed her silently. Hester had always hated her chubby figure, and even though she had lost weight she was still well rounded. To be told that this was an asset made her flush with pleasure.

With the preliminaries over, Lady Hartfield gave her order with dispatch. High-collared spencers with long sleeves to be worn over matching spring gowns were bespoken, together with several pelisses in wool.

''Those will serve for the present season,'' her ladyship announced. "Miss Temple, will you not choose something for yourself whilst *madame* and I decide upon a summer wardrobe for Hester?"

Elinor hesitated. She had guessed at once that anything ordered from Madame Germaine's establishment would be far beyond her means, and she had not yet paid in full for the gowns which Rokeby had brought back to Merton Place.

Yet her travelling cloak was shabby, and none of the garments she had worn in Bath would do for London. It would be impossible to wear her one good gown on a daily basis.

Lady Hartfield drew her to one side. "Miss Temple, pray do not worry about the cost," she murmured. "I have an arrangement with *madame*..."

Elinor's colour was high. "Ma'am, you will think me foolish, but I have not yet paid Lord Rokeby for the gowns he chose...not in full, I mean."

Lady Hartfield laughed. "You give Rokeby too much credit, my dear. He did not choose them. They came from here, and the same arrangement applied."

"You chose them?" Elinor stared at her. "But how did you know? They were just exactly right for me."

"I had a most excellent description of your height and your colouring, Miss Temple," her companion answered drily. "Now please, I beg of you, do make your choice." She turned her attention to the pile of muslins, lawns, cambrics and gauzes, both plain and patterned.

Elinor obeyed her in silence. She kept her order modest, though she could not resist a new pelisse with a fitted bodice, long sleeves and a full-length skirt which was buttoned to the waist. Two round

robes with fitted sleeves would serve her for day
wear, and her amber gown must suffice for evening
functions. Her ladyship would have none of it, insisting that Elinor chose another, to be made up in
either tiffany or sarsenet. To argue before *madame*
was out of the question, so Elinor did as she was
bidden.

Her ladyship's determination was evident also on
the following day, when confronted by the hairdresser. She made her wishes clear.

"No curls," she announced. "Miss Winton's hair
is fine and straight. With a short curled style, she
will spend her life in hair papers or with heated
tongs."

Monsieur René muttered to himself. A fashionable
crop was quite his favourite, especially as it could be
bound with either a fillet or a length of gauze for
evening, but he was forced to agree.

"And high off the neck, I believe," her ladyship
continued. "Such a style will enable Miss Winton to
wear neat earrings to the best advantage."

Hester sat patiently as the hairdresser continued
his ministrations, but when he had finished she could
not hide her pleasure. It was a transformation. Parted
in the middle, the gleaming wings of hair were
caught high at the back, lengthening her neck and
adding to her height.

"I look so different," she murmured in amaze-
ment. "Miss Temple, do you like it?"

"Hester, it is charming!" Elinor said truthfully.

She was not the only person to think so. On the
following day, John Charlbury's look of admiration

brought a flush to Hester's cheeks, though he was careful not to comment upon her changed appearance.

His visit was brief, and intended mainly to enquire if he could be of service to the ladies in their expeditions.

Hester was given first choice of the places she would like to visit, and settled upon a trip to see the menagerie in the Tower.

"Then, my dears, you will not mind if I do not accompany you," Lady Hartfield laughed. "The smell of those beasts is more than I can bear, even if I carry a nosegay."

"Ma'am, we may well choose somewhere else if you should wish it?" Hester's look was anxious.

"No, no, you shall leave me to my own devices. I have much to do."

The visit was planned for the following week and Charlbury took his leave of them.

The intervening days were filled with yet more shopping expeditions, until even her ladyship professed herself satisfied with the number of small hats trimmed with flowers or plumes, lace shawls, scarves and gloves which they had ordered.

"Best to get it done with now," she announced to Elinor. "As the weather improves, Hester will not wish to be concerned with such mundane considerations. I suspect that we shall all become well acquainted with the sights of London."

"Ma'am, you are very patient with her." Elinor gave the older woman a look of affection. She was beginning to grow fond of this forthright *grande dame* who brooked no nonsense.

"But this is such a pleasure for me, my dear Miss Temple. I had no children of my own, you know." For a moment her ladyship looked wistful. Then she straightened her shoulders. "Hester is improving, I believe. She is more at her ease with me now that we are better acquainted, and she will enjoy herself tomorrow."

She was not mistaken. Happy in the company of Elinor and John Charlbury, Hester made the most of their outing.

In her new pelisse of dark red wool, with a small fur hat and matching muff, she was warmly clad against the chill February wind, and her face glowed with pleasure as they wandered about the Tower. Even the rank smell of the beasts in the menagerie did not detract from her enjoyment, though Elinor wrinkled her nose.

The day was far advanced by the time they returned to Berkeley Square, and the street-lamps were already lit against the darkness of a winter evening. The wind was chill as they hurried indoors, with Hester still chattering about the wonders she had seen that day.

She hurried her companions through into the salon without stopping to put off her outdoor clothing. Then she stopped upon the threshold with a small gasp of surprise.

"My lord?"

"Yes, Hester...I am not a ghost." Rokeby was seated in a wing-chair with his injured leg stretched out upon a footstool. He reached out for the walking-cane beside him, and was about to struggle to his feet when Lady Hartfield stopped him.

"Marcus, kindly do not add to your folly. Hester and Miss Temple will excuse you."

Elinor could only stare at him. Her heart was pounding in a most unreasonable way as she looked at that familiar face. Now the firm mouth was curved in amusement as his eyes met hers.

"Lord Rokeby...what are you doing here? I had not imagined that you would be fit to travel so soon?"

"I was forced to escape my nurses," he said blandly.

"But, sir—"

"Now, Miss Temple, you shall not give me a roasting. My aunt has lectured me non-stop since my arrival. I confess it is hard to be taken to task when naught but the knowledge of my duties called me to your side." The blue eyes danced with laughter.

"Nonsense, Marcus!" her ladyship said briskly. "Doubtless you were bored at Merton Place."

"Quite true." Rokeby smiled up at John Charlbury. "John, this is no reflection upon your mamma, but I fear she intended to keep me bedridden for a twelve-month."

"And now you are in her black books?"

"I admit it, but I shall beg her to forgive me."

"So I should hope. What could you have been thinking of?" His aunt's forgiveness was not to be given so easily.

"Well, ma'am, it was the roads, you see. As it was, the horses almost foundered in the mire. Another week of rain and they would have been impassable. I might have been unable to join you for another month."

"We should have borne the prospect with forti-
tude," her ladyship announced.

"But sadly I could not." There was no mistaking
the glint in his eyes as he looked at Elinor.

Suddenly she felt breathless as her feelings threatened to overcome her. Rokeby was up to his old
tricks again. Now the peace of the last two weeks
was likely to be shattered into fragments. His behaviour was sheer folly, and she should have been
displeased, but her heart was filled with joy. It was
irrational to be delighted that she was wearing her
new walking-dress and was looking at her best.

Rokeby's eyelids drooped and he lay back in his
chair. "Most probably you are right," he murmured.
"I feel a little fatigued. Ma'am, if you will order my
carriage, I will go at once to Grosvenor Square…"

"To that great house, with no one to care for you?
You shall not think of it." Her ladyship rang the bell.
"Heaven knows what other folly you may commit.
You will stay here until you are quite well again."

"If you think it best," Rokeby agreed meekly. He
turned his head in Elinor's direction and the heavy
eyelids lifted. Behind them she saw a lurking smile.

She realised with exasperation that it was what he
had intended all along. She turned to John Charlbury
and gave him her hand as she thanked him for their
outing. He was about to leave them when her ladyship stopped him with an invitation to dine with them
that evening.

He demurred at first. "Marcus will wish to rest,"
he said quietly.

"Just give me an hour and I shall be myself again.
I look forward to sitting at a table and eating some-

thing other than gruel and broth." Rokeby gave him a cheerful grin.

"You may put that idea out of your mind at once, Marcus. You will go to bed and stay there, for this evening at least," Lady Hartfield said with resolution.

Elinor was tempted to laugh. It appeared that Rokeby had merely exchanged one strong-minded nurse for another and, as he had claimed to feel fatigued, he could not argue.

"I should be glad of a little company after you have dined," he murmured. His eyes were intent upon Elinor's face.

"I shall call in to bid you goodnight," Lady Hartfield promised.

Elinor's shoulders began to shake. From the look on Rokeby's face, that was *not* what he had in mind at all. Stifling her amusement she bore Hester away to change her gown.

The girl's high spirits had completely vanished, and her eyes were troubled.

"I wish Lord Rokeby had not come here," she announced when she and Elinor were alone. "It will not be the same..."

"You will see little of him," Elinor promised. "Her ladyship will insist that he takes care, and she will not expect us to change our plans."

"I did not expect him quite so soon. I was hoping that he might go to France again when he was well."

"My dear, you must not dread him quite so much. You have a staunch ally in Lady Hartfield."

"I know it, but Lord Rokeby is my guardian. He has come to make quite sure that I find a husband."

"He will find that a difficult task if he cannot get

about," Elinor said drily. "His lordship has, I fear, jumped from the frying pan into the fire."

Yet in one way Hester was right. With Rokeby's arrival, the atmosphere in the house had changed. Her ladyship did not succeed in keeping him in bed beyond the following day, as he advised her with conviction that the surgeon had advocated a little exercise.

"Very well, my dear boy, on the understanding that you will not overdo it. Perhaps you will make use of the library. We cannot spare much time for you, as Hester must go for fittings..."

"Pray do not change your plans for me. Shall you need Miss Temple with you? If she would but spare me an hour or two, it would help the days to pass..."

Thus appealed to, Elinor could do nothing but agree, though she did not trust Rokeby in the least. He appeared to have some machiavellian plan of his own, but what it was she could not imagine. He could hardly hope to seduce her in his aunt's home, with the servants always at his beck and call. The injured leg she dismissed as irrelevant. Such a trifling thing would be unlikely to stop him.

She was careful always to stay out of reach of those long arms, until at length he began to tease her.

"Your caution is commendable," he said one day. "I might almost imagine that you were afraid of me, Miss Temple."

"My lord?" Elinor's expression was as blank as she could make it.

His look was full of mischief. "I was referring to the fact that you keep the library table between us."

"Sir, we have our books upon it. That is its purpose, surely?"

"Fencing with me, my dear?"

"I am at a loss to understand you."

"I think not. You understand me very well, and have done so ever since we met."

"I do not care to be reminded of that evening," Elinor told him stiffly.

"Ah, yes...how shocked you were! You have not yet recovered? I wonder why the thought of human passions should disturb you so? It is a natural process after all."

"I do not think it in the least natural to have to pay for....for affection."

"You mistake the matter. We were not paying for affection."

"No, you were not," she cried bitterly. "You were paying to slake..." She could not go on.

"Our lusts? Well, that is natural, too."

"You are satisfied with very little, sir. There are other things to be considered in the connection between a man and a woman."

"And they are...?"

Elinor was silent.

"Go on!" he urged. "You interest me."

"I think you have not...well...what of respect and love?"

"Love, my dear? What is that? I have seen symptoms of infatuation in others. They led inevitably to disaster. I determined never to commit the folly of falling in love myself."

"That must be your choice, my lord. I will say only that infatuation is not love, in my own opinion."

"And you are something of an expert in these matters?"

The taunt brought a flush of colour to Elinor's cheeks, but she held his gaze steadily.

"I am not, sir, but should my affections ever be engaged, I should want something more than paltry coin."

"Your demands are high, my dear. You ask for a man's soul."

"No, I do not," she retorted hotly. "But I would wish to be treated as an equal in entrusting my life to that of another. Lord Rokeby, I cannot imagine how we came to discuss this subject. We shall never understand each other. You speak of one thing, and I of another."

"Bear with me," he suggested lightly. "Invalids have curious fancies—"

"And that is another thing," Elinor snapped. "Whenever you are routed, sir, you plead ill-health. I may tell you that it does not wear with me."

"Great heavens! I must be careful. Next thing you will kick my stick away and leave me prone upon the ground."

Elinor's lips twitched. "Sometimes you tempt me, sir."

"I only wish I did. Consider my position, ma'am. Here I am, an incapacitated rake, robbed of all opportunity to indulge my usual vices. Life is hard indeed. I had supposed you to be more understanding."

"Sir, you are quite impossible."

"I know it, and, ma'am, I am deeply sensible of your goodness in spending so much time with a reprobate." The firm, full-lipped mouth curved upwards at the corners. Under their heavy lids, the penetrating eyes were fixed upon her own.

"Lord Rokeby, I wish you will stop behaving in this odious way. You have no propriety of taste—"

"None whatever," he agreed promptly. "Propriety is dull you will agree?"

"And what is more, you are *utterly* without conduct…"

"You are right, of course." Rokeby hung his head in mock humility. "I am much in need of reform, as I believe I mentioned to you once before."

"The task is beyond me, sir." Elinor gathered up her reticule and left him. She was still smiling as she welcomed Hester and Lady Hartfield from their shopping expedition.

"You look more than commonly glad to see us, Miss Temple." Her ladyship drew off her gloves. "Marcus, I take it, has been at his most provoking…?"

"I believe Lord Rokeby is feeling more himself today, ma'am." Elinor's reply was carefully noncommittal.

"That, my dear, speaks volumes! Well, it will not do. You have spent far too much time indoors. A drive through the park will do you the world of good. We shall leave Marcus to reflect upon his misdemeanours."

Elinor hesitated. Rokeby was becoming restive with his enforced confinement. She thought of suggesting that he, too, was in need of a change of scene, but she could scarcely contradict her hostess. And she must not give her ladyship cause to think that she desired Rokeby's company.

It was not true, of course, except that she had

grown accustomed to the way his face lit up as she walked into the room. Even his chaffing she found entertaining, though she disagreed with his more outrageous statements. It was a challenge to be forced to defend her own ideas. Somehow, in his presence, there was always an underlying current of excitement.

She could not understand it. Was it his vitality, she wondered, or that impression of power barely under control? There was something unpredictable about him, and she found it impossible to guess what he would say or do next. He could always manage to surprise her.

It occurred to her that she was playing with fire, and she was unusually silent for the rest of the evening.

Chapter Eight

The weather on the following day was fine, with the promise of an early spring in the air. Somewhat to Elinor's relief, John Charlbury was an early caller, announcing himself happy to bear his lordship company as the ladies took their drive.

The air was chill, and Elinor had taken the precaution of wearing her warmest clothing, though they were amply provided with warm bricks for their feet, and fur rugs for their laps.

The green pelisse was becoming, as was her jaunty little hat with its curving feather, but she could not help thinking that she was wearing borrowed plumage. Not all her ladyship's assurances could convince her that it was right to accept more gowns from Madame Germaine's establishment.

"Ma'am, I have been thinking," she said shyly. "I am quite handy with my needle and the classical style of fashion is so simple. If I might buy some fabric, I might contrive something which would not disgrace you."

"Elinor, are you sure?" Her ladyship looked doubtful. "I do not mean to be unkind, but an aunt of mine was fond of remarking that many a girl had ruined her social position by attempting to make her own hats.''

She saw the humour of that startling statement as soon as she had made it, and joined in Elinor's peal of laughter.

"I promise that I shall not venture into the millinery trade," Elinor assured her. "But I have been accustomed to make my own gowns."

"Really? Well, my dear, I confess that I admire the way your garments seem to fit you to perfection." She reached up to tap the carriage roof, and directed her coachman to Bond Street.

It was as they were about to enter the portals of a well-known emporium that Elinor heard a voice behind her.

"Letitia, my dear?"

All three ladies turned to face the man who stood beside them. Of commanding presence, he was tall and burly, and his impeccable clothing proclaimed him a gentleman of fashion. He was smiling as he bent to kiss Lady Hartfield upon the cheek, but the grey eyes in the fleshy face were as cold as the winter sea.

"Dacre, I had not thought to see you here in town so early in the Season." Lady Hartfield was ramrod-stiff in his embrace.

"I needed some new guns, and Tobias wished to see his tailor. Ah, here he comes..." He bent a fond glance upon his son. "Will you not present us to your friends?"

Lady Hartfield's manner was so unlike herself that Elinor was startled. Normally pleasant and easy with her acquaintances, she made the introductions with

obvious reluctance. For the first time Elinor saw
something of the iron beneath the velvet glove.

"Miss Temple, this is my brother-in-law, Lord
Dacre, and his son, Tobias. Hester, my dear, I think
you have not met before. Dacre, this is Miss Winton.
Miss Temple is a friend of hers."

Dacre did not spare Elinor a second glance. His
eyes were upon the girl who was at that moment
making her curtsy to him.

"Miss Hester Winton? What a pleasure it is to
make your acquaintance, my dear. Such a tragedy
about your parents! You may not know it, but I have
always taken an interest in your welfare. I had hoped
to offer you a home, but Rokeby would not hear of
it."

Hester was too stunned to answer him. Her ladyship stepped into the breach.

"You will forgive us, Dacre. We are a little
pressed for time today." She gave him her hand and
turned away.

"Shopping for the Season? Quite right...quite
right! We shall hope to see much more of you in the
coming months." He bowed and bore his son away.

"That was unfortunate," Lady Hartfield muttered.
She was breathing hard. "In a busy street I could not
give him the cut direct, or the tale would have been
all over London, but how I longed to do so."

"Ma'am, I fear you are distressed. Should you
prefer to return at once to Berkeley Square?"

"No, not at all. Let us not disrupt our day." She
directed Elinor's attention to the bolts of fabric, but
it was clear that her mind was elsewhere.

Elinor made her purchases quickly, more disturbed
than she cared to admit. Dacre, she remembered, was

the man whom Rokeby held in such contempt. It was hardly surprising that Lady Hartfield should feel the same in view of his brutality towards her sister.

And this was the man who had hoped to become Hester's guardian? Elinor shuddered. She had taken him in dislike on sight, before she knew his name. There was something about his manner which spoke of violence barely hidden, and his eyes were stony.

As for the boy, Tobias, she had noted only that he was exceptionally handsome. Rokeby had described him as whey-faced, but that was an injustice. True, the boy was fair-skinned, but his classic features reminded her of a Greek sculpture. He had said nothing, other than to offer conventional greetings, and she guessed that he lived in his father's shadow.

It was not until they were alone that Hester questioned her.

"Lady Hartfield seemed so cross," she said in wonder. "She does not like Lord Dacre, does she?"

"It is an old story, Hester, and a family matter."

"I did not like him either, and…and he said that he might have been my guardian…" Her face grew pale.

"Well, now you will understand how lucky you have been. I'm sure you prefer Lord Rokeby."

"Lord Rokeby is alarming…but I do not think him a wicked man."

Elinor judged it time to change the subject, but once again she marvelled at Hester's quickness of perception.

"How did you like my purchases?" she asked. "I thought the worked muslin particularly elegant."

"They were very pretty. Miss Temple, do you think we shall meet that man again?"

"Not if Lady Hartfield can prevent it." Elinor smiled. "Hester, there is something I have meant to say to you before. Will you call me by my given name? If we are to be introduced as friends, rather than teacher and pupil, it will seem a little strange if you address me as Miss Temple."

"Oh, may I?" Hester flushed with pleasure. "We are most truly friends, are we not?"

"Of course we are." Elinor dropped a kiss upon her brow. "Now we should go down to join the others. They will wonder where we are."

"Do you go on ahead…I must re-tie my sandal."

The door to the salon was ajar, and as she walked towards it she heard Rokeby's deep tones. There was an urgency in his voice which was unfamiliar to her.

"Unfortunate is a masterpiece of understatement, my dear aunt. I had hoped to keep the knowledge of Hester's Season from him…"

"You must know that it would have been impossible." Lady Hartfield's voice was equally decisive. "Dacre is looking for an heiress for his boy. Where better to find one than the Season?"

"That is what worries me," Rokeby confessed. "He has always had an eye to Hester's wealth."

"But, Marcus, you are her guardian. You may accept or refuse any offers as you will. And pray do not imagine that I shall invite Dacre to this house. Nothing is further from my mind."

"I shall accompany you in future," Rokeby announced with resolution.

"My dear boy, is that wise? Your leg…?"

"Is much improved." His tone invited no argument, and, as Elinor entered the room, he rose to his feet.

"Miss Temple, I have been malingering," he told her with a smile. "I have just been explaining to my aunt that when one is cherished as I have been there is a great temptation to wish that it could last." He took a step towards her and appeared to stagger.

Elinor was beside him in a second to throw her arm about his waist. He chuckled as he looked down at her.

"You understand my meaning, aunt?" A smile of purest mischief lingered in his eyes.

"Only too well, Marcus. I am only surprised that Miss Temple has the patience to tolerate your nonsense."

"She doesn't find it easy, I assure you."

Elinor disengaged herself from his grasp. "I am glad to find you better in health, my lord. I imagine that you are now able to walk without your stick?"

Rokeby gave his aunt a look of mock despair. "You see how it is, ma'am. As far as this lady is concerned, I might be made of glass."

"I am delighted to hear that she is so well able to see through you." Lady Hartfield looked from one face to the other and gave an odd little nod of satisfaction. "Elinor...I may call you Elinor, may I not? I have been telling Marcus that I intend to start the Season by giving a ball."

"And I have promised to limp about, looking quite as distinguished as Lord Byron," Rokeby assured her.

"You will, of course, recite your poems, sir?" Elinor said demurely.

"No, I will spare you those. They are intended solely for the ears of my own true love..."

As always, he had had the last word, but the tense

atmosphere had lightened, and when Hester joined them she joined in the conversation with more vivacity than Elinor had imagined possible. Even the proposed ball appeared to hold no terrors for her, and Rokeby was constrained to compliment both Elinor and his aunt when Hester went upstairs to find a handkerchief.

"You have done wonders," he told them with a smile. "Hester will never be a beauty, but now she has a certain something."

"It is all down to perfect grooming, Marcus. Hester has a quiet charm, and not all men, you know, prefer a chatterbox."

"You are right. The thought of endless conversation at the breakfast table is enough to daunt the strongest heart." He grinned at Elinor, who ignored him.

"Well then, my dears, let us make our plans. I think possibly the beginning of April will be a suitable date. It is a little early, to be sure, but I'm sure we shall assemble sufficient company to make it a success."

"You are too modest, my dear aunt. Your invitations are prized like gold dust. I don't doubt but what we shall have a frightful crush."

His predictions were correct. In the intervening weeks Elinor had been too preoccupied with addressing cards and making herself useful wherever she could to note that most of the fashionable world intended to be present.

Her ladyship appeared untroubled by the need to oversee the preparations. Her servants were well trained, and her household continued to run with its customary efficiency as she made arrangements with caterers, florists and musicians.

"What will you wear, my dear? Have you a favourite gown?" Her question was meant kindly, but it succeeded in reducing Hester to a worried silence.

"Hester?"

"Yes, ma'am?"

"What is the matter, child?"

"I...I shall not know what to say to the guests, Lady Hartfield..."

"Then I will let you into a secret." Her ladyship twinkled. "Ask people about themselves. That fascinating topic is guaranteed to persuade them to talk so much that you need do nothing more than put in an odd word here and there. You may find this hard to believe, but it will gain you the reputation of being a brilliant conversationalist."

"Do you think so?" Hester looked doubtful, but she managed a faint smile.

"Nothing is more certain. Now, my dear, what do you say to these arrangements for the ballroom?" With a sheaf of drawings in her hand, she succeeded in diverting Hester's attention from the terrors to come.

"Aunt, will you tear yourself away from your labours for an hour or two?" Rokeby's limp was barely noticeable as he walked into the room. "I thought you might like to visit the Botanical Gardens today."

"What a splendid idea! The spring flowers will be at their best."

"Where is Miss Temple? She will like to join us, I expect."

"I believe she planned to busy herself with her sewing."

"Nonsense! The day is much too fine to be cooped up indoors. Hester, I shall rely upon you to persuade her."

"Oh, yes. I know she will wish to come." Hester gave him a shy smile as she hurried out of the room.

Elinor demurred at first. She was cutting out a plain white satin slip which would serve as an underdress beneath a number of open robes in different colours.

"But Lord Rokeby wishes you to make up the party," Hester pleaded. "He said so most particularly."

Elinor's heart gave a little jump. For the past few weeks, she had made an effort to keep his lordship at a distance. It had not been easy but she had countered all his pleas for companionship with murmured excuses. She was too busy...his lordship was almost recovered and well able to visit his friends...and should he wish to stay indoors, Mr Charlbury would bear him company.

"Losing your nerve, my dear Miss Temple?" There was dancing mockery in his eyes.

Elinor coloured. "Sir, I cannot imagine what you mean...I have explained..."

"So you have...and I don't believe a word of it. One might almost suppose that you felt yourself at risk from me."

Elinor's temper had risen. It was too close to the truth.

"You flatter yourself, Lord Rokeby," she had said coldly. "Why should I be at risk from you?"

"It was just a notion of mine. Perhaps the fancy

of a sick man? You must forgive me. For a libertine such as myself enforced withdrawal from the Polite World has been something of a strain, as I'm sure you'll understand.''

''From the Polite World, sir?'' The sarcasm in Elinor's voice had been evident. All her old distrust of him had returned in full measure. ''I would not describe your favoured company so.''

''I had not expected that you would. But then, your standards are so high, Miss Temple. Nothing but perfection will do for you. Could any man live up to that?''

''That is not true,'' Elinor had cried hotly. ''We all have our faults...myself as much as any-one...but...there are limits, sir.''

''Are there? Perhaps I have not found them.'' He had bowed and left her.

Since then she had avoided him, and he had appeared to have accepted her decision. For the most part he had not dined with them, and had been absent in an evening.

It had not taken long to revert to his old habits, Elinor reflected bitterly. For the past week they had merely exchanged civilities in passing. On occasion she had been aware of his return to the house in the early hours of the morning, and had remarked his absence at the breakfast table, but Lady Hartfield had not referred to it.

I wonder that she does not invite him to return to his own home now that he is well again, Elinor had thought to herself. For the time he spent in it, her ladyship's establishment might have been an hotel. Now, apparently, he intended to make amends.

Rokeby was all attention as he settled the ladies in the carriage.

"Aunt, do you care to drive through Hyde park first? You will see many of your acquaintances."

Lady Hartfield nodded. She was pleased to find that the town was filling up, as hopeful mammas came in from the country to present their daughters to the marriage market. Those with sons were more than civil to her, and the coach was pulled up again and again as she greeted old acquaintances.

Elinor was amused to find that she herself might have been invisible as far as the older women were concerned, though she attracted admiring glances from their sons. It was Hester who received an abundance of kind words and distinguishing condescension. The news that Miss Winton was an heiress must have spread through the town like wildfire for invitations rained upon her head, but though she smiled pleasantly enough she shot a pleading look at Lady Hartfield.

Her ladyship took pity on her. "Would you care to walk a little, Hester?" she enquired. "Elinor will accompany you, I'm sure. I must speak to the Princess Esterhazy for a moment. You may rejoin me at the far gate."

"A splendid idea!" Rokeby jumped down from the carriage. He offered an arm to each of the ladies and began to stroll through the busy throng.

"Why, here is Mr Charlbury!" Hester looked up with a happy smile as a horseman made his way towards them. Charlbury dismounted and began to lead his horse.

"This is Brutus." He gestured towards the splendid animal. "What do you think of him?"

He drew them a little apart to allow a party of fashionably dressed pedestrians to pass them.

Elinor had imagined that Rokeby was behind them, but he had been accosted by another horseman. Elinor recognised the man at once. She had last seen his flabby features at Rokeby's dining-table on the night of their arrival at Merton Place.

"Bad luck, Rokeby! I hear that your *chère amie* has found consolation elsewhere..." He must have imagined that his lordship was alone, for he made no attempt to lower his voice.

Elinor glanced at her companions, but they had moved a little way ahead of her, and were absorbed in conversation.

"Can't expect anything else, I suppose," the fat man continued. "That particular bird of paradise has expensive tastes, I'm told."

"Are you, indeed?" Rokeby's voice was icy. "I wonder that you should care to enquire."

"Oh, Lord, have I set you into a miff? A sore point, is it? Don't worry...plenty more fish in the sea...I hear there is a little opera dancer new in town. She might suit you..."

Rokeby bowed. "Kind of you to think of me, Talworth, but I'm not in need of a pander."

Elinor began to tremble. It was an insult which could only invite a challenge. She looked at the two men to find that Talworth had flushed an ugly red. Without another word he dug his spurs into his horse and rode away.

Rokeby's expression frightened her. He was breathing hard, and his lips were set in a tight line.

She turned quickly, hoping to convince him that

she had heard nothing of his conversation, but he caught her arm.

"Don't pretend!" he said roughly. "You could not fail to hear the whole."

"Sir, you are hurting me!" It was true. His fingers were digging deep into her wrist. "Let me go! How you wish to conduct your own affairs is no concern of mine."

"Ah, I had forgot! It would come as no surprise to you to hear that I kept a woman."

Elinor was scarlet with embarrassment. She did not reply.

"Merely confirms your opinion of me, does it?"

"Sir, please lower your voice. Do you wish Hester to hear you?" She almost ran towards John Charlbury.

All her pleasure in the day was ruined. As an eavesdropper she had got her just deserts, though it was through no fault of her own. Those few idle words had served to remind her of Rokeby's true nature, if she needed such a reminder. What had she expected...that Rokeby would spend his evenings in philosophical discussions? That he had been converted to a blameless life, indulging merely in card parties with his friends? Her lips curved in a bitter smile.

She had suspected...she had wondered how he spent his evenings, but it was appalling that the confirmation of her worst fears should hurt so much. She felt that someone had stabbed her through the heart.

She could not look at him, and turned away, thankful that the brim of her poke bonnet served to hide her face. To avoid any further conversation with him, she placed herself between Hester and John

Charlbury as they strolled towards the far gate of the park.

Her troubles were not yet over. As they reached the waiting carriage, she saw a figure she knew standing by the door.

"Good morning, ladies." Lord Dacre bowed and smiled. "Rokeby, I hope I see you well?"

"Do you?" Rokeby's answer was so abrupt as to be insulting.

"Why yes, of course! I have just been chatting to Talworth. He told me of your accident. Hard luck, my boy. I hear that it came at an inconvenient time." The smile on Dacre's face did not reach his eyes.

Elinor was startled by something in his tone. It was almost a warning. Certainly she felt a sense of menace.

"A broken leg is always inconvenient," Lady Hartfield murmured. "Dacre, we seem always to be rushing away from you, but we have promised ourselves a trip to the Botanical Gardens..."

"Then I must hope that, when we meet again we shall have more time for an interesting chat." He did not attempt to detain them further.

"A hateful creature," Lady Hartfield announced. "But, Marcus, really! Need you look like thunder? I thought you were about to strike him."

"He tries my temper, aunt."

"Well, kindly control it, sir. A fit of the sullens does not suit you. Neither does it please me."

Rokeby had the grace to apologise, but his light-hearted mood had vanished. Elinor too was silent until they reached the Gardens. There she roused herself to admire the blooms, until her ladyship was satisfied that whatever disagreement had occurred between

Elinor and her nephew was on the way to being resolved.

In that she was mistaken. In the course of the day Elinor had made a discovery which shocked her to the core of her being. She was in love with Rokeby. Libertine he might be, but she could no longer pretend, even to herself, that she did not care for him. He filled her mind to the exclusion of all else. When he smiled at her, her heart leapt in her breast, and when he touched her hand she felt herself begin to tremble.

The knowledge filled her with dismay. It was little short of disastrous, and panic filled her soul. She had known the danger and closed her eyes to it. Why had she been such a fool? Had she imagined that her disapproval of his way of life would protect her? It had not done so.

If only she could get away before she betrayed her feelings. Rokeby would despise them, believing, as he did, that love was an illusion. She could plead the need to visit her family, she thought wildly, but Lady Hartfield would find it strange to be presented with such a decision at this time. Then there was Hester to consider, and she had given her word that she would stay.

But where was it all to end? The answer was not far to seek. Hester would marry and she herself would be forced to find another position.

This was ridiculous. She was growing maudlin merely because she had been fool enough to allow herself to fall in love with a man so far beyond her reach that she could have no hope of happiness.

It must be a lesson to her. It would take all her strength of character to control her feelings until the

Season ended, but she must do so. The punishment for her folly would be to see him every day, knowing that her love was not reciprocated.

On the day of the ball she was standing in her undergarments when Lady Hartfield tapped upon her door.

"The hairdresser is here," she announced. "If you put on your dressing-robe, my dear, I will send him to you."

"Really, m'am, there is no need. It is kind of you, but—"

"Nonsense, Elinor! I wish you to look your best." Her eye fell upon the evening gown laid out upon the bed. "Shall you wear this? It is quite charming, but the spangled net becomes you even better." With an unerring eye she had decided upon the most expensive garment in Elinor's wardrobe.

"Silly child!" she said fondly. "I shall not allow you to stay in the background, which, I believe, was your intention. Weekes has already dressed Hester. She will come to you shortly."

Faced with such determination, Elinor could only submit to the ministrations of the hairdresser and her ladyship's personal maid.

The results surprised her. The silver thread of her gauzy overdress gleamed softly in the candlelight over a slip of jonquil yellow crepe. Cut low at the bosom it revealed her milky skin to perfection.

I look much too fine, she thought doubtfully as she studied her new hairstyle. Drawn high into a chignon at the back, she had been persuaded to allow a couple of ringlets to fall softly on each side of her face.

Still, at least she was not bedecked with jewellery. Fresh flowers were her only ornament. Satisfied that she would not disgrace her hostess, she drew on her long white gloves as Hester came to find her.

Clad in a delicate shade of apricot, Hester, too, had benefited from the hairdresser's attentions. The smooth fair hair shone like satin, and Hester could not resist a little preening in front of the dressing-glass.

She reached up a cautious hand to touch her new coiffure. "It does make a difference, doesn't it?" she asked anxiously.

"It does indeed. Did I not tell you that, 'Fine feathers make fine birds'? I can hear the music, Hester. We should go down to Lady Hartfield."

From Hester's expression, it was clear that she might have been condemned to enter the lions' den. Elinor tucked an arm through hers as they descended the great staircase.

Rokeby and his aunt were already stationed by the entrance to the ballroom. He was deep in conversation with Lady Hartfield, but as Elinor greeted them he turned to look at her. She heard a small intake of breath. Then he recovered and bent to kiss her hand.

"My dears, I must compliment you. You look quite lovely." Lady Hartfield smiled upon her protegées. "Marcus, as you see, is speechless."

"On the contrary, my dear aunt, I see that I must put in a bid for dances without delay. Hester, may I have your card?"

Hester blushed, but she did as she was bidden.

"And Miss Temple?" Rokeby's eyes were glowing as he looked at her. Scanning her card, he continued to mark dances until she took it from him.

"My lord, what are you about?" she murmured. "To dance with a partner more than twice must give rise to comment."

"Do you care? he whispered in her ear. "You look ravishing, my dear, though still, alas, unravished…"

"Kindly remember where you are," Elinor hissed at him. She had flushed to the roots of her hair.

"Marcus, pray give me your attention," her ladyship reproved. She looked towards the door. "Here is Mrs Templewood and her daughters."

"Both of them? Oh, Lord!" He raised a quizzical eyebrow as he took his place beside her in the receiving line.

"Hush! You wicked creature!" Lady Hartfield gave the first of her guests a gracious smile and directed them towards a room where they might leave their cloaks.

They were followed at once by Lord Bertram and his sharp-featured wife, who was engaged in shepherding a covey of young hopefuls.

"Lord preserve us!" Rokeby spoke with feeling as the guests moved on, but was silenced by a quick glance from his aunt.

Stationed at the end of the receiving line, Elinor was beginning to enjoy herself.

From the languishing glances cast at Rokeby by a number of young maidens and the arch remarks of their mammas, she gathered that his lordship was a prize much to be desired.

She could only admire his *savoir-faire* as he brushed aside both leading questions and innuendo with a bland expression and every profession of his deep regard. He must have used those skills to good effect to avoid being inveigled into matrimony, she decided.

Looking up, she caught his eye and he grinned at her. He had read her mind, and they were in accord. Oh dear, it would not do. She forced herself to attend to the woman who was at that moment addressing Hester.

"Charming, my dear girl! Charming! I have so longed to meet you. As to Henry! Well, he has spoken of nothing else these past three weeks..." She gestured towards a pale young man who looked as if he never spoke at all.

Hester smiled and nodded.

"Henry!" His mother nudged him in the ribs.

"Oh, yes!" Henry recalled the purpose for which he had been dragged here, much against his will. "Miss Winton, will you honour me with a dance?"

His speech was so clearly rehearsed that Elinor's lips began to twitch.

"He'll sweep her off her feet!" Rokeby had manoeuvred himself to stand beside her. "Such passion! What woman would be proof against it?"

Elinor's shoulders began to shake. "Sir, you are behaving very badly. Do, I beg of you, control yourself."

"You make it very difficult, Miss Temple." There was no mistaking the glint in his eyes.

Chapter Nine

Marcus had no opportunity to speak to Elinor again for some time as the press of guests converged upon them. It was a full hour before her ladyship felt able to leave her post. Few members of the *ton* had refused her invitations, which were not given lightly, and the crush was a clear indication that the evening would be a success.

The room was growing warm, and body odours mingled with the scent of French perfumes, some of them stale, which drifted towards her as she shook hands endlessly at the end of the receiving line.

As the crowd began to thin, Lady Hartfield gave the signal for the dancing to begin.

"Now, Hester, shall we start the proceedings?" Rokeby drew his ward's hand through his arm and led her on to the floor. "The quadrille is quite your favourite, I believe?"

"I hope I shall remember the steps," Hester murmured nervously.

"Of course you will...and if not, I shall prompt you...very quietly, of course."

As he smiled down at the girl, Elinor's heart

turned over. Her eyes were fixed with great intentness upon his face. The firm, well-defined mouth curved up at the corners, and against the swarthy skin his teeth showed very white. Tonight he was in full evening dress and in deference to his aunt's wishes, he wore knee-breeches and silk stockings. A starched neck-cloth, meticulously arranged, rose in splendour above a waistcoat of watered silk.

He was quite the most distinguished-looking man in the room, Elinor decided. The black swallow-tailed coat fitted his athletic figure to perfection, and he moved with a grace surprising in such a large man.

An urgent voice beside her broke into her musings.

"Miss Temple, they are making up the numbers, and you promised me this dance, if you recall…?"

Elinor turned to face a young sprig of fashion, who had dared to brave the dagger-looks of his mamma in order to claim her hand.

Shaking off her preoccupation, she accompanied him towards a group of dancers, only to find, to her dismay, that she was in Rokeby's set. Knowing him as she did, she felt quite sure that he would attempt to enliven the evening by an effort to shake her composure.

Well, he would not succeed. She turned to her partner and exerted all her charm to put him at his ease. He was very young, and clearly dazzled by her beauty to a degree which made him tongue-tied.

Elinor persevered, and soon she had him laughing gaily as he told her of his visit to Astley's Amphitheatre.

"I am not quite in the way of things just yet," he admitted. "Mamma was not best pleased that I should go there, but I had a famous time. She thought, you see, that I should take more dancing lessons.'' At that moment he missed a step, and gave her a rueful look. ''It seems that she was right.''

''You dance very well,'' Elinor encouraged. ''It may be that I am a little clumsy myself. This is my first large ball...''

''Is it?'' His face cleared. ''I should not have thought it, ma'am. You look...well, you look so perfectly at your ease.'' The effort of making the compliment, artless though it was, caused him to blush to the roots of his ginger hair.

At that moment, Rokeby took his partner past her in the figure of the dance. His brows went up at the sight of her companion's face, and his eyes were filled with laughter.

This time it was Elinor who missed a step.

''There, you see, sir. Now you must believe that I am a novice in this art...''

''Is it over?'' The boy gave an almost audible sigh of relief as the musicians struck the final chords, and Elinor was tempted to chuckle. Instead, she nodded gravely.

He realised at once that he had shown a remarkable lack of tact. ''Oh, pray do not think that I did not enjoy it,'' he said quickly. ''I meant only...well, I hope I did not disgrace myself...''

''It was kind of you to partner me,'' Elinor said gently. ''Now, I believe that you should find your partner for the next dance. It is a waltz...''

He looked alarmed. ''Ma'am, I have not yet learned to waltz. My mother disapproves...but if I might bring you a glass of lemonade, or fruit cup if you should prefer it? It is very warm, is it not?''

"It is indeed!" Rokeby was beside them, and his deep voice made Elinor jump. "How thoughtful of you to offer refreshment, sir. Your mother will be glad of your attention...she is looking fatigued."

"But I have just offered to fetch something for Miss Temple..." Uncertain, the boy looked at the faces of his companions.

"Miss Temple will excuse you. She is promised to me for the waltz, you see." Rokeby's face was bland, but his expression brooked of no argument.

"That was not well done of you, my lord." Elinor looked at the boy's retreating back and frowned. "To send him back to his mamma as if he were a child...?"

"He is little more." Rokeby was unrepentant. "I imagined I was coming to the rescue."

"Of whom?"

"Of your young admirer, naturally. The boy appears to be besotted. Was it wise, I wonder, to exert upon him the full weight of your charm? From his mamma's expression she does not seem to have missed a word or a look. At present, I imagine, she is wishing you elsewhere."

"How dare you criticise my conduct, sir? Your own leaves much to be desired. Are you telling me that I have stepped beyond the bounds of propriety?" In her anger, Elinor had forgotten that she was addressing her employer.

"Alas, no, Miss Temple. I live in hopes, but it would appear that I am always to be disappointed." He grinned at her in such a provoking manner that Elinor was robbed of speech for an instant. "Even should such a moment arrive, I should not dare to mention it."

"One day, sir, you will go too far," she forecast darkly.

"I am waiting for that happy moment to arrive. Will you not tell me how I may go about it?"

"I was not referring to your light manner towards myself, which serves, apparently, to amuse you. Take care, my lord. The duennas in this room may take your banter for serious intent. Then where will you be?"

"I shall be fleeing for my very life." His laughing face was very close to hers. "The waltz, Miss Temple?" He took her hand preparatory to leading her out.

Elinor pulled away from him. "I do not care to waltz with you," she said stiffly.

"You promised." He took her hand again. "To refuse me now really would be a breach of propriety." He led her on to the floor and slid an arm about her waist.

Elinor tried to hold herself away from him.

"No, no!" he urged. "You must enter into the spirit of the dance...just trust yourself in my arms..."

Elinor gave him a withering look and he chuckled.

"An unfortunate remark on my part," he admitted. "You will never do that."

He was holding her closer than propriety dictated and she felt unaccountably breathless. In an effort to change the subject, she glanced about her.

"I do not see Mr Charlbury here tonight. Is he otherwise engaged?"

His mouth seemed to harden. "He is. Shall you miss him?"

"Hester will most certainly do so. She looks to him for support on these occasions…"

"I did not ask you about Hester." Beneath their heavy lids, the blue eyes were studying her face.

Suddenly Elinor was exasperated beyond belief. "You cannot imagine, sir, that I have the least interest in Mr Charlbury, or he in me. He is a friend, and has shown us much kindness but that is all."

"I am glad to hear it," he said smoothly.

"And you believe me?" It seemed important that he should do so.

"Yes, I do. I have never known you lie." He was silent for a few moments. "Miss Temple, I think you should prepare Hester for the fact that she may not see John Charlbury for some time. I believe he intends to return to Kent."

"But why? The Season is only just beginning…?"

"That is part of the reason. He has been aware for some time that, by acting as her constant escort, he may be considered as Hester's accredited suitor."

"And would that be so very dreadful?" Elinor cried without thinking. "She is already more than half in love with him, though she does not know it."

"He is aware of his position," Rokeby told her shortly. "He will not dangle after an heiress."

"And you agree with him?" Elinor did not wait for his reply. "I might have known it. What did you tell him? That Hester is destined for someone far above his touch?" She looked at him straightly and was surprised by his look of anger.

"What an opinion you have of me," he gritted out. "Must I remind you that Charlbury is a friend of mine?"

"Yet you do not encourage his suit?"

"Miss Temple, I cannot force him to offer for Hester. He believes, as you do, that she is too young for marriage."

"But you do not, my lord?"

"You know my opinion on the subject. It least you will agree that she should be given these next few months to look about her before she makes her choice."

"I thought you intended to make it for her," Elinor retorted. "Lord Rokeby, you do not know her as I do. Once having given her affection, she will not change."

"You taught her that?" There was a curious expression in his eyes.

Elinor shook her head impatiently. "That is not something one can teach…it is a question of character."

"I see."

A silence fell between them as they pursued their own thoughts. Elinor had been considerably surprised to hear that Rokeby had discussed Hester's future with John Charlbury. And how like the latter it was to refuse to stand in the way of a splendid match for her. His sudden decision to return to Kent was understandable in the circumstances, but Rokeby's announcement that his friend would not dangle after an heiress spoke of something more.

"My lord…" She faltered. "Am I to understand that Mr Charlbury is growing attached to Hester?"

"I cannot speak for him." There was an underlying note of anger in Rokeby's voice. "I advise you to put the matter out of your mind, Miss Temple."

But Elinor could not. Preoccupied with her musings, she was unaware that Rokeby had signalled to the musicians to continue with the waltz. It was indiscreet of him to depart from custom in such a way and it resulted in a number of indignant looks from the elderly ladies who were seated by the side of the ballroom.

Rokeby ignored the buzz of gossip. He was an excellent dancer, moving with grace and dignity as he held her lightly in his arms, and Elinor matched her steps to his. As he whirled her about the floor, she gave herself up to the music almost insensibly, revelling in the pleasure of the dance.

"That's better!" He looked down at her with a smile. "I knew that we should partner each other to perfection. Now, Miss Temple, I cannot ask for yet another reprise or I shall be in serious trouble with my aunt. May I offer you the refreshment which you missed?"

Recalled to the present, Elinor looked about her as the music stopped. She and her partner were the cynosure of all eyes, and many of the glances thrown in their direction were hostile.

"Sir, we are giving rise to comment," she murmured in a low voice. "Please take me back to Lady Hartfield. You must seek your partner for the next dance."

"Not just yet. My leg is paining me, you see." It was said with a chuckle, and Elinor gave him a suspicious look.

"It is the unaccustomed exercise, I assure you," he continued blandly. His limp was pronounced as he led her from the floor.

"I am not surprised, my lord," she hissed, aware for the first time that he had prolonged the dance deliberately. "That was thoughtless of you..."

"On the contrary, I gave it some considerable thought. The opportunity to hold you in my arms is all too rare. I felt that I should make the most of it."

"You deserve to be in pain," she ground out. "You are impossible!"

"Pray do not glare at me, Miss Temple. That will give rise to further gossip. You will be glad to hear that I am in severe pain, and have been for some time, from a wounded heart, as much as from an injured leg…"

Elinor gave him a fulminating glance and walked to where Lady Hartfield stood in a group of friends.

"How well you and Marcus dance together, my dear! It is a pleasure to watch you, but the waltz is so exhausting, even for young people. Marcus, where are your manners? Miss Temple will be glad to rest for a time, perhaps with a little refreshment…?"

"Ma'am, I have just suggested it." Rokeby smiled down at her.

"Will you not join us, Lady Hartfield?" Elinor said in despair.

"No, no, my dear…off you go." Her ladyship dismissed them with an airy wave of her fan. "I will join you later."

"Foiled again, my dear?" Rokeby took Elinor's arm and led her away. "Everything conspires against you, and in my favour."

Elinor had reached a decision. It was time to put an end to Rokeby's folly. If she did not do so without delay, she would acquire an unenviable reputation as his lordship's latest flirt, if not worse.

Unresisting, she allowed him to lead her to a secluded embrasure, and sat quietly as he went away to procure her a glass of lemonade. As she waited, she cast about in her mind for some way to discourage his casual attentions. She was still lost in thought when he returned.

"So grave, Miss Temple?" He handed her the glass. "Let me assure you that I have not added some mysterious potion to this liquid which will rob you of your senses."

She gave him a long look and set the glass aside.

"I am here because I wish to talk to you, my lord."

"At last! I am delighted to hear it. Can it be that my patience has been rewarded?" He grinned as he took a seat beside her.

"Mine has been sorely tried, Lord Rokeby. It is not kind in you to attempt to destroy my reputation."

"I shall never do that." His smile vanished. "I would not seek to harm you, as you know."

"But I do not know it. I cannot think you a fool, sir, and you must realise that I am in a difficult position in this household?"

"Beloved by all? Come, ma'am, is that such a very dreadful fate?"

Exasperated, she raised her face to his. "That is exactly what I mean. Must you say such things? They are quite meaningless, and serve only to distress me."

He took her hand in his and began to stroke her fingers in an absent way. She could feel the warmth of his flesh even through the fabric of her gloves and it disturbed her. She tried to draw her hand away, but his fingers closed about hers.

"And if it were not meaningless? Would it distress you still?"

Elinor froze for a moment. Then the colour rose to her face.

"I shall not pretend to misunderstand you, sir. I am astonished that you should offer me such insult under your aunt's roof." She stood up swiftly and removed her hand from Rokeby's grasp.

He was too startled to do more than stare at her. Then, in a single lithe movement, he was beside her, reaching out to take her in his arms.

"Elinor..." His words died on his lips as Talworth moved towards them, smirking.

The fat man did no more than bow as he walked by, but his face wore a look of secret satisfaction.

Elinor wished that the ground might open at her feet. Talworth, she guessed from his expression, had heard the whole of her conversation with his lordship, and would judge the pair of them accordingly.

"Damnation!" Rokeby swore beneath his breath. "What is he doing here? Does my aunt not know that he is the worst rattle in London?"

The tears sprang unbidden to Elinor's eyes. She could have wept with mortification. Now she longed only to run up to her room.

"I hope you are satisfied," she choked out. "I shall be a laughing-stock..."

"Stay here! I'll go after him and explain."

"Explain what? That you offered me a *carte blanche?* He knows it already..." Without waiting for his reply she ran from the room.

Her hopes of escaping before the end of the ball were dashed as she was claimed by first one partner and then another. Later she could recall nothing of the rest of the evening other than Hester's wistful face as they bade their guests farewell.

"Mr Charlbury did not come. I wonder why?" she appealed to Lady Hartfield.

"Oh, Hester, I forgot to tell you in the bustle. He sent a message to explain why he must fail us for this evening." Her ladyship patted Hester's cheek. "You did not want for partners, my dear. In fact, you were a great success and we were proud of you... Is that not so, Elinor?"

Elinor nodded, but her heart was moved to pity by Hester's disconsolate expression.

"He...he is not ill?" the girl asked, and there was no hiding the anxiety in her voice.

"Nothing like that, my love. Some little difficulty, I understand, which may force him to return to Kent."

Hester looked stricken. "You mean that we shall not see him for some time?"

"It may not be for long." Her ladyship dismissed John Charlbury from her mind. "Now tell me, Hester, which of your partners did you find the most agreeable?"

Hester murmured something in reply, but her mind was not upon the conversation and suddenly she looked weary.

"My dear ma'am, Hester is ready for her bed." Elinor pleaded. "Will you excuse us now that the last of the guests have gone?"

"Yes, yes, my dears...I hope you enjoyed it...it was a success, I believe."

Her two companions murmured all that was proper, adding their thanks to all their compliments, and her ladyship was pleased.

"Now, where is Marcus?" she said suddenly. "I have not seen him this age. Ah, there he is, by the door. I might have guessed that he would not fail in his observance of civilities.'' She moved across to stand beside her nephew.

Elinor seized the opportunity to take Hester by the arm and hurry her away. Another confrontation with Lord Rokeby at that hour of night would be beyond bearing. After the events of that evening she doubted if she could face him again with any degree of equanimity.

Talworth would talk, she was convinced of it. He would not miss such an opportunity to be revenged on Rokeby for the insult offered to him in the park. The news that his lordship desired to take Elinor in his keeping would be discussed in every drawing-room in London before the following day was out. She felt that she must die of shame.

The cynical eyes of the Polite World would be upon her from now on, and she felt that she could not bear the sly remarks and the innuendos which were sure to be her lot.

How could Rokeby have behaved so ill? Apart from all else, he might have considered his aunt. The ensuing scandal could not fail to affect both Lady Hartfield and Hester.

Misery gave way to anger in Elinor's mind. She would not, could not, love a man who thought only of self-gratification, destroying those about him as he pursued his lusts. She would speak to her ladyship and explain that she must leave Berkeley Square at once. It was the only course open to her.

She knew, of course, that for a wealthy man to keep a mistress gave no cause for comment among the *ton.* The lack of such an arrangement might be more surprising, but the gorgeous birds of paradise who gave their favours in return for charming little houses, dashing curricles, and a profusion of jewellery and clothing were not of her world. Some of the fair Cyprians made it their profession, whilst others, such as actresses and opera dancers, used such arrangements to augment their slender incomes.

And she was thought willing to be added to their number? Her face grew hot. When had she given Rokeby any indication that he might suggest it to her? She was tempted to ask him, but she dared not. She could not be sure that she had not betrayed her love with an unguarded look or a word, and it could not be denied that she had responded to his kisses with a passion which had shaken her beyond belief.

She had always thought that she knew herself so well, she thought sadly. Now it was clear that there were hidden depths within her soul which were unknown to her.

Was she truly a wanton at heart? With his experience of women, Rokeby must have sensed it and thought himself justified in appealing to her sensual desires. Perhaps it was she herself who was to blame?

Consumed by a miserable feeling of guilt, she found it hard to sleep. It was not much consolation to think that, if it were she who was at fault, she would most certainly be punished for it, either by leaving those she loved, or being forced to face the censure of the world.

In the event, neither of those dreaded fates awaited her. She came down next day to find that Rokeby had decided to accompany John Charlbury to Kent. That was some respite, she thought with relief.

She had viewed her first appearance at Almack's with trepidation, fearing that she could not avoid the open disapproval of the powerful patronesses, but it came as a surprise to find that she was greeted with the same civility proffered to Hester and Lady Hartfield. Perhaps Talworth had gone out of London? She hoped so with all her heart. It was becoming clear that he had not yet spread his evil gossip. She had no way of knowing what Rokeby might have said to him, but whether his lordship had resorted to threats or persuasion, his efforts appeared to have been successful.

It was as she was chatting quietly with Hester that Lord Dacre approached them, accompanied by his son. He greeted them effusively, but Elinor noticed once again that his grey eyes were as cold as the winter sea.

"Not dancing, my dear Miss Winton?" he said in a jovial tone. "That will not do. Tobias would enjoy nothing more than to partner you."

Hester had no alternative but to take the young man's arm and allow him to lead her away.

"I do not see Rokeby here tonight." Lord Dacre scanned the room. "A pity! I wished to speak to him on a matter of some importance."

Elinor felt a small twinge of anxiety. She was well aware of the antipathy between the two men, and she sensed at once that, whatever her present companion had in mind, it could bode no good.

"His lordship is gone into Kent," she told him quickly. "We do not know when he will return."

"Very wise of him...under the circumstances." His look was almost a leer and Elinor grew cold. It said more clearly than words that he had learned of her conversation with Rokeby on the night of the ball. She did not answer him.

"Lady Hartfield's ball was a great success, so I understand," he continued. "Doubtless my own invitation must have gone astray..."

Elinor could not look at him. She would not lie, but he knew as well as she did that no invitation had been sent to him. She cast about wildly for something to say, but she could think of nothing. If only someone would rescue her. She looked around, but Lady Hartfield was speaking to a friend at the far end of the room, and did not seem to have noticed that Hester was dancing with Tobias.

"I heard reports of your own success," Lord Dacre went on smoothly. "Your beauty won more than one heart..."

"I am not aware of it," Elinor said stiffly.

"No?" His smile was one of disbelief. "Come now, you will not expect me think that you did not receive at least one offer?"

Elinor stared at him. She felt like some helpless animal mesmerised by a snake. She longed to escape, but her limbs refused to obey her.

"Elinor, my dear, why is Hester dancing—? Oh, I beg your pardon, Dacre...I did not know that you would be here tonight." Lady Hartfield did not trouble to hide her annoyance.

"Else you would not have come, Letitia?" The big man's expression did not change from its customary benevolence. He wagged his head and turned to Elinor. "These family feuds, Miss Temple! With your own background, I'm sure that you cannot approve of them."

"I was not aware that you knew anything of my

background, sir.'' The words were out before Elinor had time to think of their possible consequences.

"Surely you have no secrets, my dear, especially from Lady Hartfield?'' There was a note of warning in his voice.

It was at this point that her ladyship's patience snapped. "Dacre, I do not know what game you may be playing, but if you are thinking of Hester for Tobias you may forget the idea. Rokeby, I assure you, will have none of it.''

Lord Dacre bowed. "I hope to persuade him to change his mind, my dear Letitia. Will you let me know when he returns to London?''

"You will be wasting your time…'' The older woman took Elinor's arm and turned away.

"That man! He puts me out of all patience, Elinor. I am tempted to scream at him like a common fish-wife!''

"I know the feeling, ma'am.'' Elinor made an attempt to recover her composure, but she found that she was trembling. Her conversation with Lord Dacre had been short, but in those few moments he had convinced her that not only did he know of Rokeby's offer to her, but that he would not hesitate to tell Lady Hartfield of it. And he had mentioned her own background. Was he referring to her parents? She would not put it past him to have made enquiries in Derbyshire. She realised that it was yet another threat.

But why should he threaten her? She was not a danger to him. Perhaps it was her imagination, but she could not shake off an underlying sense of menace.

"Elinor, do not look so troubled,'' Lady Hartfield

urged. "The man is unpleasant beyond belief, but he is a fool if he imagines that Marcus would consent to a match between Hester and his son."

Elinor shuddered. "I should hope so, ma'am. I could not bear to think of Hester in his power."

"Now you are letting your imagination run away with you. One dance with Tobias can do no harm. Even so, I could wish that it had not happened, and I find myself wishing even more that Marcus had not taken it into his head to go back to Kent at this particular time."

Silently, Elinor agreed with her. Rokeby, however trying his attitude to herself, was more than a match for his formidable enemy. It came to her suddenly that beyond the excitement which she found always in his company there was a feeling of security.

The knowledge puzzled her. How could she feel secure with a man who had but recently made her a dishonourable proposal and wished for nothing more than to persuade her to become his mistress?

Her feelings were irrational, but at that moment she longed to see him walk into the room with that teasing smile and nonsensical banter upon his lips. He would know how to counter Lord Dacre's threats, she was sure of it.

It was two days later that her prayers were answered. She was standing in the hall with Lady Hartfield and Hester, when Rokeby ran lightly up the steps.

"You are lucky to have caught us in, my dear Marcus." Her ladyship allowed him to kiss her on the cheek. "We were about to drive out to the park."

"I will go with you. Have you missed me?" His

question was directed to his aunt, but his eyes were upon Elinor. Something in her expression caught his attention. Under their heavy lids the penetrating eyes asked another question, but it was not until later that day that she found herself alone with him.

"Something is worrying you...what is it?" he asked without preamble.

In a very few words she told him of their meeting with Lord Dacre at Almack's. "My lord, I am sorry that Hester was persuaded to dance with Lord Dacre's son," she said.

Rokeby looked at her. "That is not it. Why are you so frightened?"

It was all too much for Elinor. The tears welled up and she found herself in his arms.

Chapter Ten

"My little love! I should not have left you." Rokeby rained kisses upon her brow, her cheeks, and the tip of her nose.

"Sir, you must not." Elinor struggled to free herself. "I am sorry to be so foolish...but...but please listen... I must warn you—"

"Warn me of what?" His eyes were tender as he looked down at her.

"Lord Dacre is aware...I mean...he knows of our conversation at the ball."

"I see. Then Talworth must have told him. I could not find him on that night, else he would not have spoken." There was a grimness about his mouth which startled Elinor. "You fear the gossip, is that it?"

"No...that is not all. I cannot think how it came about, but I felt that he was warning me. He spoke of having secrets from Lady Hartfield...and...and he mentioned my background..."

"What the devil has that to do with him?"

"I do not know, my lord," Elinor told him truthfully. "He may intend to write to my parents..."

"Warning them of your life of dissipation?" Rokeby leaned against the mantelpiece. His tone was light, but his eyes were wary. "Have you told me everything?"

"No, sir. When Lady Hartfield told him that you would not countenance a marriage between Hester and Tobias, he seemed to believe that he could persuade you to change your mind."

"A forlorn hope, you will admit, my dear one?"

Elinor did not return his loving look. "Lord Rokeby, I beg that you will be serious. I cannot trust Lord Dacre. If you had but heard him...I cannot say exactly...but I would swear that he has some scheme in his mind."

"You have told my aunt of this?"

"No, I did not wish to worry her with my fancies."

"I am flattered that you have no such scruples about worrying me." His lordship walked towards her and slipped an arm about her waist. "That is as it should be, my little love."

Elinor summoned her few remaining shreds of dignity. "I wish you will not address me so, my lord. It does not please me, and in any case, I am not little. For a woman, I am tall."

Rokeby gave a shout of laughter. "Of all the inconsequential remarks! You are adorable!"

"Sir, you go too far!"

"No, I do not. I do not go nearly far enough, but my time will come. Now, my dear, what do you suggest? Shall I beard Dacre in his den? Will that set your mind at rest?"

There was doubt in Elinor's eyes as she raised her

face to his. "It might be as well to find out what he has in mind. That is, if you think it best...?"

"Deferring to my judgment, my dear Miss Temple? Wonders will never cease! I must be grateful to Lord Dacre if he has brought about this change of heart." A lean finger slipped beneath her chin and he bent towards her.

"No, you must not!" Elinor turned her face away.

"Why not? You will admit that we have both enjoyed our kisses up to now. Must I suppose that your heart is given to another? Alas, it was a mistake to leave you unattended and at the mercy of the marriage market."

"Marriage has not been mentioned to me," Elinor said in glacial tones. "And a market in flesh can only be disgusting."

He did not release her. A strong hand cupped her chin and he forced her to look at him. "How you despise us!" he said softly. "I do not care to see that look upon your face."

"You are mistaken. I have met with much kindness from your aunt, and from the Charlburys. I am no ascetic, sir, and I appreciate the elegance of all I see about me..." Elinor had no idea why she was protesting, but it did not change the bleak look upon his lordship's face.

"So all we lack is heart?" he murmured. "I wish I could persuade you otherwise."

"Sir, I do not mean to sound censorious. I am not fool enough to despise the advantages of wealth and position which are so important to your world. It is just that..."

"Yes?" he prompted.

"I have not been brought up to believe that an

advantageous match should be the main aim of a woman's life…or a man's either." Her voice was so low that he could barely catch her words.

"That has been clear to me from the moment that we met!" There was a harshness in his tone which surprised her.

"I do not expect you to understand," she added quietly.

"I should do, ma'am. Our mutual friend, John Charlbury, has been expressing similar sentiments to me for these past few days. You and he should deal famously together…"

"No, sir, we should not," Elinor cried indignantly. The words came out with more vehemence than she had intended, and she knew at once that she was on dangerous ground. In protesting a lack of interest in John Charlbury, she must not give Lord Rokeby cause to believe that his own advances might be welcome to her, even though she had repudiated them up to the present time.

"We have both missed his companionship, especially Hester," she murmured. "Does he plan to return to London?"

Rokeby gave her a sharp look. "I am not privy to his plans, Miss Temple. And for the present I believe that we have much else to occupy our minds. I will see Dacre in the morning."

His lordship was unable to carry out this plan, as Lord Dacre, so he was informed, had left the city for an unspecified length of time.

Rokeby had not much time to speculate on his enemy's reasons for such a sudden departure. Within the next few days, he received three offers for Hester's hand.

When he summoned her to his study, he had expected that Elinor would accompany her, but in that he was disappointed. Elinor had decided to accompany Lady Hartfield to the Florida Gardens, believing that no words of hers should influence the girl.

"Do you know why I have sent for you, Hester?" He motioned his ward to a chair.

"No, sir." Hester sat bolt upright, tension apparent in every line of her body.

"There is no need to be nervous," he told her gently. "I must tell you that three gentlemen have offered for your hand. I wish to know your opinions..."

Hester's eyes grew huge with fright, but she did not speak.

"I think we need not consider Mr Thorne, unless you have a particular *tendre* for him? He is very young, and not yet in control of his fortune..."

Hester swallowed convulsively, and shook her head.

"I am glad that you agree with me," Rokeby continued smoothly. "Barrington is a much more suitable match, although he is a widower..."

Hester could contain herself no longer. "No, no, I cannot marry him. Oh, sir, you will not make me do so? He is old, and when he looks at me I feel..." She stopped as a deep flush of colour rose from beneath the neckline of her gown and suffused her face.

"You were saying?"

Hester was driven beyond endurance. "I feel that I am not wearing any clothes... I cannot bear it..."

"There will be no need for you to do so. I had

already decided against him," Rokeby continued in an imperturbable tone.

"Then why did you mention him?" Hester choked back a sob.

"My dear, it is only right that I should tell you of all offers. Now, as to the third…"

"Yes?" Hester lifted her head, and her eyes were filled with hope.

"Pangbourne, my dear. His suit, I hope, will meet with your approval. He is a young man, and his father's heir."

"Sir, he is a fribble." Hester's disappointment had made her bold. "I cannot spend the rest of my life with a man whose main concern is the height of his shirt-points." She looked at Rokeby, expecting an explosion of wrath but, to her surprise, he smiled at her.

"Very wise, my dear Hester. We shall do better than that for you." It was an effort to restore her spirits, but Hester did not respond. She had hoped against hope that the third offer might have come from John Charlbury, and her disappointment was obvious.

Rokeby strolled over to her, and cupped her face in his hand.

"Chin up!" he advised. "All is not lost. You may yet gain your heart's desire, as I hope to do myself."

"You, sir?" Hester stared at him.

"Why yes, my dear. I am not made of stone, you know."

"Sir? I…I do not understand you?"

"Sometimes, Hester, I fail to understand myself." He gave her a rueful look. "There, do not trouble yourself with my problems…you have many more

interesting matters with which to occupy yourself.''
His voice was more gentle than she had heard it.

"I may go, my lord?"

Rokeby nodded his assent, and was surprised when
she sought to thank him.

"For what, my dear?"

"For not forcing me to accept one of the...the
offers, sir.''

"You must make your own choice, my dear
Hester.''

"But I thought that you were to decide?"

Under their heavy lids, his blue eyes were filled
with amusement. "My function is, I believe, to check
the gentlemens' credentials. After all, we cannot
have you carried off by some fortune-hunting villain
who would lock you in a dungeon until you agreed
to his demands. Miss Temple would never forgive
me..."

"You are making game of me, my lord." Hester
had caught a little of his gaiety. "I promise that you
would hear my screams.''

She left him then to sit by the window in the salon.
Bursting with news, she was impatient for the return
of Elinor and Lady Hartfield. And, as she waited, she
thought of her interview with his lordship.

His attitude had come as a surprise to her. Perhaps,
after all, he was not so lost to all human feeling as
she had believed. In the end, she had felt more at
ease with him than she had done since their first
meeting. She was still wondering at her discovery
when Elinor walked into the room.

"Well, my dear?" From the expression on
Elinor's face she guessed that both her friend and
Lady Hartfield knew of the offers. It was only to be

expected that Rokeby would have mentioned them before he spoke to her, but she found that she was blushing.

In halting words she told Elinor of her conversation with her guardian.

"But it will be all right," she murmured. "Lord Rokeby is not angry with me."

"Of course not, my love! How could he be? He could scarce expect you to take any of the three..."

Privately, Elinor had been appalled at the idea that Hester's hand might be given to any of them, but Rokeby had warned her not to attempt to influence the girl.

"You think highly of Hester's intelligence, do you not?" he had demanded. "Pray allow her to use it, madam."

"Then you will not insist?"

"No, I will not." It was clear that he was annoyed, but he made a quick recovery. "It is early in the Season," he told her lightly. "Doubtless there will be other offers."

With that she had to be satisfied, though his easy acceptance of the fact that Hester would refuse all three of her prospective suitors had surprised her.

From the beginning, Rokeby had claimed that he wished to see Hester married as soon as possible. Now, it appeared, he intended to give her at least some choice in the matter. But how long would his patience last?

Hester had given no sign of being attracted to any of the men who were quick to claim her hand to partner them at the many balls and routs which they attended. Her confidence had grown, and her modest, pleasant manner had won her several friends among the younger ladies.

Effusive compliments still caused her to withdraw into her shell, whether they came from her partners, or from their predatory mammas.

Elinor sighed. She had long suspected that Hester's heart was already given to John Charlbury. The girl might not yet have recognised her affection for what it was, but Elinor knew without being told that Hester compared her present companions with the man she missed so much, and found them wanting.

She was alone in the salon, still lost in thought, when Rokeby came to find her.

"Frowning, my dear? I had thought to find you overcome with joy?" The penetrating eyes were intent upon her face, though his tone was teasing.

"I must thank you, sir." Elinor looked up at him.

"For allowing Hester to show us that she is no fool? That should not surprise you." His lordship sat down beside her and took her hand. Before she realised his intention he had raised it to his lips, and Elinor began to tremble as his warm mouth caressed her palm.

"What are you doing?" she cried quickly. "Please, I beg that you will not..."

"I am claiming my reward, my love. Confess it, Hester is in charity with me. Surely that must please you?"

Elinor removed her hand from his grasp and rose to her feet.

"No, do not run away from me!" he begged, and she heard the laughter in his voice. "I wished merely to know if you would care for an expedition to the Vauxhall Gardens? There is to be a concert there this evening, and we might order supper. I will take a box...''

"That is thoughtful of you, sir." Elinor took a seat as far away from him as possible. "Hester will enjoy it. She has longed to see the fireworks."

"And you? Perhaps you feel that there are enough fireworks here in Berkeley Square?"

Elinor refused to rise to the bait. "I too, should enjoy it, sir...that is, if Lady Hartfield agrees."

Rokeby chuckled. "Don't worry! I had not intended to lure you there alone, delightful though the prospect seems. You will be well protected from my importunate advances."

"I am glad to hear it," she said stiffly. "I wonder that you should not grow tired of all this nonsense, my lord."

"I am an optimist," he told her with a wicked grin. "I have not abandoned hope of capturing your heart."

"You will not do so by continuing in your present manner." Elinor had not reflected before she spoke and paid the penalty at once.

Rokeby walked towards her and raised her to her feet. With his hands resting gently on her shoulders, he looked down at her.

"But if I should change? What then?" There was no mistaking the glitter in his eyes.

She had no answer for him. Her feelings threatened to overcome her as he gazed into her eyes. She tore away from him before she betrayed herself and fled from the room.

She was in sombre mood as she took her seat in the carriage that evening. It was becoming increasingly difficult to keep his lordship at arm's length.

This very morning her resolution had been sorely tried. When he had held her close and had looked at her in just that tender way, she had longed to throw caution to the winds and respond to his embrace. She stifled a little moan of anguish. Such heartache was difficult to bear.

The evening was unseasonably warm, and all three ladies felt that lace shawls would be sufficient for their comfort in the open air. Elinor's was of a deeper tone than her straw-coloured gown of Berlin silk, high-waisted and cut low at the neck as fashion dictated. She could not doubt that her toilette met with Rokeby's full approval. He did not take his eyes off her on their journey across the river.

There her attention was diverted by Hester's pleasure in the Gardens. They entered the brightly lit enclosure by the water-gate and made their way through the tastefully planted groves of trees to the main arena which was lined with private boxes.

"It is like a fairyland." Hester pointed to the coloured lamps which were strung between the trees. "How wonderful! I had not thought that anything could be so fine..."

"You will see more wonders later," Rokeby promised as he led them to his box. "Supper first, I think...then the Rotunda...We must not miss the start of the concert."

Even Lady Hartfield could not fault the supper, though she had expressed doubts that it could match the efforts of her own chef. Elinor was unmoved by the excellence of the various dishes. She could not have said what she was eating.

All her attention was focused upon the tall, athletic figure beside her. Tonight he was clad in a well-fitting coat of corbeau-coloured cloth and tight-fitting pantaloons with gleaming Hessian boots drawn over them.

As he pressed her to take a little of the trifle, the creams or the jellies which ended the meal she could not look at him. The urge to take his hand and press it to her lips was overwhelming.

"We should go to the Rotunda." Rokeby consulted his time-piece. "In the interval between the two halves of the concert, I shall show you the Cascade…"

He was as good as his word, as Hester exclaimed with delight at the spectacle before her. The scene drew visitors from far and near to marvel at the life-like replica of the country vista, with its water-mill, its bridge, and its rushing waters. She could not be drawn away.

Lady Hartfield smiled at her enthusiasm. "Marcus, do you accompany Miss Temple back to your box. We shall be more comfortable if we watch the fireworks from there. I will bring Hester to you."

"Aunt, they do not begin until after the concert is ended."

"Oh yes, I had forgot! Come, Hester, we must take our seats again." She took Hester's arm and smiled at Elinor. "Shall you wish to hear the rest of the concert, my dear?"

"I would not miss it for the world," Elinor told her truthfully. A passionate lover of music, she had found long ago that the soaring cadences of sound transported her to another world where she could forget her present cares.

She had another reason for not wishing to leave her companions to stroll back to the private box with

Rokeby. All evening she had been aware of the sly looks and malicious smiles on the faces of those who greeted them. She wondered that Lady Hartfield had not noticed it.

She was too much in Rokeby's company, and to walk back alone with him could only give rise to further comment among the *ton.*

It was unlike Lady Hartfield to be oblivious of such gossip. Her ladyship was ever quick to detect the least breath of scandal, especially when it concerned her family, or anyone close to her.

Elinor resolved to speak to her when the opportunity arose. She had wondered for some time at Lady Hartfield's attitude towards herself and Rokeby. On occasion it had seemed to her that her hostess had been eager to leave them together. She could not disguise that fact, even from herself, but she could not understand it.

She trusts us, Elinor thought sadly. It had not occurred to her that her beloved nephew might be ailing at seduction, or that Elinor herself might be in any danger from him. It would not be easy to mention her own worries so tactfully that she did not give offence.

As the concert began again, she tried to give her full attention to the music, but she found that she could not. There was something wrong...something in the atmosphere of the Rotunda that night which she found disturbing.

She looked about her at the circle of rapt faces. All eyes were upon the musicians, or so she thought. Then a movement caught her eye. There was someone standing in the shadow of one of the colonnades to the side of them.

A slight breeze had sprung up, and the coloured lights strung between the trees began to sway, throwing beams where there had been none before. As Elinor looked towards the darkened colonnade, the shadows lifted and she recognised Talworth. He moved back at once, but not before she had seen the expression on his face.

His eyes were fixed upon Lord Rokeby and in them was a look of hatred.

Elinor gasped and turned to her companion, but a strong hand grasped her arm and held her still.

"I have seen him," Rokeby murmured. "You must pretend that you have not done so."

"But, my lord, he looks as if he might plunge a dagger in your back." Drowned by the music, her words did not reach the others. "You will take care?"

"I will take care," he promised. "Don't worry! Talworth has not the courage for such a violent course of action. His revenge is likely to be of a more subtle kind."

"I could wish that you had not quarrelled with him in the park that day…"

For an instant his mouth seemed to harden. "You would have had me ignore his remarks? That was not possible, my dear."

Elinor was silent. It had been an ugly scene, and Talworth, however much he deserved it, would not forgive his lordship's words. To be called a "pander' was the worst of insults, and must result in a challenge.

Yet Talworth had not issued that challenge, and must, therefore, be regarded as a coward. Elinor realised that this, as much as the insult, was the cause of Talworth's hatred.

She began to tremble.

"Steady!" Rokeby murmured. "You will not wish to worry my aunt. I assure you, there is no need for concern."

Elinor longed to believe him, but she could not rid herself of the impression that some threat hung over him.

Common sense told her that behind the laughing, teasing manner was a man well able to take care of himself, but was he proof against treachery?

Later, as they strolled back through the crowds towards their box, she found herself starting at every shadow which moved beside the long avenues of trees. Her eyes searched faces in the press of people, but she saw nothing to alarm her.

Rokeby appeared to be untroubled. With his customary courtesy he settled the ladies at the front of the box and took a seat behind Elinor.

Hester was on her feet as the first rockets soared into the sky, and she found it impossible to sit down as the various set-pieces were set alight.

Lady Hartfield had seen the spectacle several times before and soon found more diversion in chatting to an acquaintance in the neighbouring box.

"Tonight you look lovelier than ever." Rokeby leaned forward until his lips were close to Elinor's ear. "In those tawny shades, with the candlelight upon your hair, there is a certain glow about you."

Elinor tried to hush him.

"No! Listen to me!" he insisted. "Won't you allow me to tell you—?"

"Lord Rokeby, I know that you are trying to divert

me from all thought of Talworth. It is kind of you, but there is no need. I am quite myself again.''

''I think not, but you must believe that I shall take care of my own—''

Elinor seized upon a gap in Lady Hartfield's conversation to comment upon the fireworks. She took care to give Rokeby no further opportunity to speak to her alone that night.

In recent weeks she sensed that his attitude towards her had changed. Sometimes she fancied that his words were almost a declaration of love, but that could not be. It was more likely that as one method of seduction had failed he would try another.

On the following day she sought out her hostess as her ladyship was writing letters.

''Ma'am, may I have a private word with you?'' she said.

''Of course, my dear. What can I do for you?''

Elinor found herself at a loss for words although she had rehearsed what she wished to say. Somehow the expression in those keen black eyes made her worries seem trivial.

In desperation, she plunged ahead. ''Ma'am, I have been thinking. It is so long since I visited my family. Would you think it wrong of me to leave you now? Hester, I know, will be quite safe in your care…and…and…''

''And there are other reasons?'' Lady Hartfield turned from her writing desk to give Elinor her full attention.

Elinor felt the colour rising to her cheeks. ''Yes, ma'am, but, if you please, I would rather not discuss them.''

"I see. Well, Elinor, I shall not press you to give me your confidence, but to leave now…in the middle of the Season? Hester has suffered one disappointment, as you know. You are her dearest friend. Is it right, do you suppose, to ask her to suffer another?"

Elinor felt her resolution waning, but she made a last attempt to press her case. "Hester has had offers, ma'am. It cannot be so long before she is safely settled. Then, as you know, I must seek employment elsewhere."

"That is in the future, my dear. Knowing Hester as we do, I cannot think that she will make her choice in London."

Startled, Elinor grazed at her. "Then…then you know?"

"Of course I know. Did you think me blind, my dear? In her quiet way, Hester has set her mind upon John Charlbury."

"But, ma'am, he will not offer for her, or so Lord Rokeby gave me to understand…"

Her ladyship made a gesture of impatience. "Men are such fools, my dear Elinor, but we shall not give up hope. A clever woman will often find a way to circumvent their preposterous notions."

Elinor felt oddly comforted. It seemed that Lady Hartfield did, in fact, favour Hester's choice.

"I could wish that Hester were not an heiress," she admitted. "That will seem strange to you, perhaps, but it does seem to be a stumbling-block."

"It will be overcome." Her ladyship, who was not demonstrative, leaned forward to drop a kiss upon Elinor's brow. "Now, my dear, let me beg you to forget your present worries. Why not write to your family? You might promise to visit them in the autumn. Meantime, none of us can spare you...indeed, we are not willing to do so.''

Elinor did not argue further. Her good intentions had been defeated but, rather than being saddened by her failure, she felt a sudden surge of joy. The thought of leaving Rokeby had struck like a dagger to her heart. She could only wonder at her own folly. Heartache beckoned, there could be no doubt of it, but she felt powerless to resist. Fiercely she castigated herself for her want of character. She should stand firm against him, but she could not.

She descended the great staircase, still absorbed in her thoughts, as the outer door opened to admit Lord Dacre.

Rooted to the spot, she stood in silence as Rokeby came towards him. Then the two men disappeared into Lady Hartfield's library.

Elinor could not imagine that Lady Hartfield knew of the sudden appearance of her brother-in-law. Her ladyship had not mentioned it, and Dacre was not a welcome visitor. She waited in the salon until he left, and Rokeby came to find her.

Chapter Eleven

Elinor looked at him with a question in her eyes.

"Tobias," he said briefly. "He has offered for Hester...at least, his father has."

"But you refused?"

"Of course. Could you doubt it?" He began to pace the room, looking so unlike himself that Elinor was troubled.

"My lord, is there something more?"

Rokeby hesitated. "There is," he said at last. "He threatens to apply to the courts to remove Hester from my care."

Elinor's blood ran cold. "But...you are her guardian," she faltered. "How can that be possible?"

"Anyone may challenge my suitability," he told her. "In this case there are witnesses to confirm that my way of life is so depraved as to put my ward in danger."

"Talworth?" Suddenly Elinor felt breathless.

Rokeby nodded. "As you say."

"But that is nonsense!" Elinor rushed to his defence. "Suppose you do consort with...er...with lightskirts. Does not every man in London do the same?''

''Every man in London does not admit his ward and her companion to his home when he is entertaining ladies of the town.''

''But that was not your fault,'' Elinor cried hotly. ''I shall swear to it. We came to Merton Place without your knowledge...''

When he looked at her his face was grave. ''There is yet more,'' he said. ''I am thought to be in the act of seducing my ward's companion...a respectable woman who should, in the normal way of things, be assured of my protection.''

He looked so disturbed that Elinor lost her temper.

''That worm, Talworth!'' she cried in fury. ''He shall be made to eat his words! How dare he malign you so?''

Rokeby leaned forward and touched her hand. ''Elinor, you are generous,'' he said quietly. ''I have given you no reason to think well of me.''

Elinor was too angry to think before she spoke. ''I will see Lord Dacre. When I assure him that you had no such thought in mind, he must believe me!''

''He has a witness. Don't forget Talworth.''

''Talworth was mistaken. He misunderstood your words, as I did myself.''

''Did you, Elinor?'' His eyes held hers for a long moment. ''You did not allow me to explain, but sadly it is too late. My way of life has not been such that anyone would believe me.''

''You cannot mean it?'' She looked at him in horror. ''Do not say that you will allow Lord Dacre to take Hester from us?''

"I shall fight the case, naturally, but I cannot offer much hope that Dacre will not succeed."

"He must not and he shall not. Oh, there must be a way to stop him... If Lady Hartfield were to speak on your behalf?"

"It would not serve. As a woman, my aunt has no rights in this matter..."

At his words Elinor's anger increased, and a faint smile touched his lips as he saw her wrathful expression.

"I know your views, my dear, and I must agree. When it comes to good sense, both you and my aunt are the equal of any man. In fact, you have more than most of my acquaintance, but the law does not recognise it."

"Then the law is wrong," she told him with a kindling eye. "Is Hester to be handed over to a brute merely because he is a member of the male sex?"

"I cannot say." Rokeby began to pace the room, lost in thought.

"There must be something we can do," Elinor pleaded. "If we returned to Kent...? Or perhaps we might take her to some other part of England?"

"It may be too late for that. I do not know what steps Dacre may have taken before he came here. He must have known that I would not consent to the match."

"What steps could he take? He cannot force his way into this house to take her by force."

Rokeby looked at her and she grew cold with apprehension. "Oh, no!" she cried. "That *must* be against the law."

"It has been done before. I do not say that he would take her from this house, but I suspect that he has set men to watch the place. At the first suggestion that we planned to leave, he would make his move.''

''Abduction?'' she cried in horror. ''No magistrate would allow it!''

He came to her then and took her hands in his.

''Don't look like that!'' he begged. ''I cannot bear that you should suffer so. It is all my fault. Had I not been such a fool, this could not have happened.''

Slow tears rolled down Elinor's cheeks. ''Do not say so, my lord. I believe that you intended from the first to do your best by Hester.''

''You will give me credit for good intentions, my dearest?'' He lifted her tear-stained face to his. ''Ah, if only I could tell you...'' His mouth came down on hers and the world was lost to both of them.

Elinor clung to him as if her very life depended on it. She could fight him no longer, whatever his reputation. With her arms about his neck, she held him to her. Then the full implications of that embrace came home to her.

''Sir, this is wrong,'' she whispered. ''How can we hope to keep Hester with us if I allow...?''

''There is one way, my love.

Elinor pulled away from him to gaze into his eyes.

''You have thought of a solution?''

''I have.'' His arms were still about her and the firm, full-lipped mouth curved into a smile. ''Elinor, will you marry me?''

For a moment she could not believe her ears. She looked at him in stupefaction. ''My lord?''

''I asked you to marry me. Is it such a dreadful suggestion?''

Elinor's head was spinning. It was the last thing she had expected.

Her legs seemed unwilling to support her, and she reached out an arm to grasp the back of a chair.

"But why?"

Rokeby helped her to a sofa and sat beside her with an arm about her waist. Then he began to stroke her hands.

"Elinor, please consider," he said softly. "I know that you do not care for me in the way that I should wish. I am no plaster saint, God knows, but with me you would have security. And I give you my word that you would have no further cause to think ill of me. I should not humiliate you by...by...seeking other company."

"You have not answered my question," she whispered.

Rokeby looked ill at ease. He rose and began to pace the room.

"I can think of no other solution," he said at last. "If we wed it will put an end to all the gossip."

Elinor was beginning to understand, and her heart felt like a stone within her breast.

"I see! As a married man your suitability as a guardian would be beyond question? How clever of you, my lord! I had not supposed you capable of such a sacrifice."

Rokeby paled as if she had struck him a mortal blow.

"You misunderstand. Elinor, have I not shown you how much I want you?"

"You have, sir. Your intentions were all too plain, though I did not imagine that they included marriage." In her anger she longed to hurt him. "Your offer is an insult, my lord."

"I regret that you should find it so." He was as

white as Elinor, and his anger matched her own. "I offer you my name and my protection, only to have it thrown back in my face...? Well, madam, I shall not insult you further. You must prepare yourself for Hester's imminent departure from this house." He made as if to leave the room, but Elinor stopped him.

"Wait, I beg of you!" Her thoughts were in chaos, but one fact alone stood out in her mind. Hester must not be handed over to Lord Dacre.

"Lord Rokeby, I spoke in haste," she told him frankly. "Will you give me time to consider your...er...proposal? That is, if you are still of the same mind?"

He bowed. "The offer holds, Miss Temple, though I should warn you that there *is* no time."

"One hour is all I ask?" Her eyes were pleading, and he gave her a brief nod. His set expression told her that she had pushed him beond the limits of endurance. She was on the verge of tears as she hurried to her room.

There she sobbed as if her heart would break. Rokeby's offer had been little short of blackmail. He wanted her, and if he could have her no other way then it must be marriage. And there had been no word of love. His object was to gratify his lust, and to achieve it he had used Hester as a pawn.

Wildly, she cursed her own beauty. Had she been plain everything might have been so different. Rokeby would not have given her a second glance.

Such thoughts were useless, she reflected as she grew a little calmer. At least she, too, had a bargaining tool; she would use it.

To save Hester she would marry Rokeby, but upon her own conditions. His lordship should not learn of them until after they were wed. Then he would discover that a match arranged simply to foil his enemies could have no place in it for love and passion.

She would be cheating him, she knew, but he had cheated her of the love for which she longed. She stifled the small voice which told her that she was also cheating herself.

It would not do to examine her own motives too closely. A guilty conscience was an uncomfortable thing with which to live, and so was self-delusion. Had she not admitted that she loved Rokeby to distraction? She brushed the disturbing thought aside. In time the pain would lessen.

She bathed her face in cold water, washing away all traces of her tears. Then she returned to the salon.

Rokeby stood by the window, still and silent. He turned as she came into the room.

"Well, Miss Temple? What is your decision?"

Elinor hesitated for only a moment. "Sir, you feel that this is the only course of action open to us?"

"I do." His eyes betrayed no emotion, and he did not move towards her.

"Very well then. I...I will accept your offer, sir."

"You have made me the happiest man alive." He gave her an ironic look. "Shall we ask my aunt to share our joy?"

The swarthy face was so austere that Elinor was seized with panic as she nodded her agreement.

"Come, then, I believe we shall find her in the study."

Elinor swept past him as he opened the door for her. His sneering manner was hateful. She had been playing with fire, and now, it seemed, she was about to get her fingers burned. And she had promised to marry him?

Outside the study door she checked. There was still time to change her mind.

"Afraid of me?" he jeered.

"Certainly not!" With her head held high she walked into the room.

To Elinor's astonishment, Lady Hartfield showed no surprise at their announcement.

"I have been longing this age to wish you both happy." She enveloped Elinor in a hug.

"Ma'am?" Elinor's face was warm with colour, and her ladyship laughed.

"You have been slow about your wooing, Marcus." She tapped his face affectionately. "I had begun to think that I must make the offer for you."

Rokeby kissed her. "There was no need, my dear. I knew it was your dearest wish."

Her ladyship looked at him in mock reproach. "You will not tell me that *my* wishes weighed with you, wretch! Do you believe me to be blind?"

"I do not think it for a moment." He took Elinor's hand and raised it to his lips. "Aunt, shall you be disappointed if we have a quiet wedding? We wish to be married without delay."

"You must do as you think best, my dears, but Elinor will wish for her parents' permission."

"A letter shall be sent today. I will see to it." He sat down at the writing desk, and applied himself to the task. At length, he turned to Elinor. "Do you wish to add to it," he asked, "or perhaps you will desire to write at length?"

In silence, Elinor took the pen from him and scribbled a few sentences. Her parents would think it strange, but she could not think it wise to undertake a long explanation of her sudden decision to marry Lord Rokeby. Her father knew his daughter well, and he would not sanction any match which had resulted from coercion. Unwittingly, she might betray her reasons for agreeing to the marriage.

Rokeby took the letter and left the room as Lady Hartfield turned to Elinor.

"Marcus was right, my dear child. I consider him the luckiest man in the world. How I prayed that he would win you in the end, though in recent weeks I have had no doubt of it. You love him dearly, do you not?"

To her ladyship's consternation Elinor burst into tears.

"There, there," the older woman comforted. "It is the strangest thing, but tears of happiness are just as real as those of grief."

Elinor dabbed at her eyes, and blew her nose upon the scrap of lace proffered by her companion. How could she explain that there was no cause for celebration in her forthcoming marriage? She had accepted Rokeby for all the wrong reasons, and misery awaited her. He would never forgive her. She had seen it in his eyes.

She turned away as Hester came to join them.

"Elinor has a surprise for you," her ladyship cried gaily. "I will leave her to tell you of it. I must find Marcus. I have a thousand things to say to him." Beaming, she bustled away.

"Elinor, what is it?" Hester's eyes were intent upon her friend's face. "Why, you have been crying! Is something wrong?"

"Nothing at all, my love!" Elinor managed a wa-

tery smile. "It is just that...well...I am to marry
Lord Rokeby—"

"No! You can't! I won't believe it!"

"It is true." Elinor took Hester's hand in hers.

"No, no! You don't even like him." Hester
snatched her hand away. "What has he said to you?
How has he forced you to agree? There must be some
reason."

"I love him," Elinor said with perfect truth. "Is
it so strange that we should wish to make each other
happy?"

"You don't look happy to me." Hester ran from
the room.

Elinor followed, but it was only with the greatest
difficulty that his ward could be persuaded to offer
Rokeby her congratulations later that day.

He accepted them with grave courtesy, affecting
not to notice that her eyes were red with weeping.
His aunt threw Elinor a significant glance and kept
the conversation going at the dinner table with various items of inconsequential gossip. Even so, the air
of tension in the room could not be denied.

To Elinor, the meal seemed interminable. She
looked about her sadly. This should have been an
occasion for celebrations but it was not.

At length, Lady Hartfield rose from the table, leaving Rokeby to his wine. She had hoped to offer
Hester a few words of consolation for the loss of her
friend, but Hester would not wait for the arrival of
the tea-tray. Pleading a headache, she begged to be
excused.

"Pray do not worry about her, Elinor." Lady
Hartfield comforted. "Your news has come as a

shock. In a day or so she will grow accustomed to the idea that you are to wed.''

''Ma'am, I am sorry that she has taken it so badly. It is disrespectful to both Lord Rokeby and yourself.''

''We shall both make allowances, my dear. She is very young, and then, you know, for the past few years you have been her only friend.''

As Elinor sipped her tea, she prayed that her ladyship was right. Rokeby had sat through the meal in a silence unusual for him. Hopefully Lady Hartfield would put this down to his disapproval of Hester's conduct.

''Now here is Marcus come to claim you.'' The older woman twinkled at her nephew. ''I do not propose to sit here like a gooseberry, sir. You may have your bride to yourself, though I hope that you will not keep her from her bed for long. She looks a little tired this evening.''

''It is the excitement, ma'am.'' As Rokeby opened the door for her he bowed, but his smile did not reach his eyes.

Alone with him at last, Elinor was lost for words. Then he broke the silence.

''I believe it may be best that I go into Derbyshire myself to see your father,'' he announced.

''Oh, pray do not!'' Elinor's involuntary exclamation brought an expression of quelling severity to Rokeby's face.

''You have changed your mind?''

''No, it is not that...but perhaps...''

''You think he may take against me?'' The sensitive mouth curved in a sneer.

Privately, Elinor believed that in his present mood

it would be impossible for his lordship to convince her parents of his regard for her. Her father would sense at once that there was something strange about this sudden betrothal, and Rokeby's insistence upon an early marriage.

"Of course not!" she disclaimed. "I thought merely that it might be better if I went myself.

"You cannot go alone, and it would be unwise of us to leave Hester without protection at this time. That is, unless we take my aunt into our confidence?"

"Oh, no! It would hurt her so to learn the true reason for our marriage. Let us leave matters as they are. You have sent the letter?"

"I have not. It is impossible to offer your father such discourtesy. I don't flatter myself with the notion that you will miss me, but I shall travel fast. The journey should take no more than a few days."

He would not be dissuaded, and Elinor realised that further argument was useless.

"You have messages for your family?" he asked briefly.

"Will you give them my love?" Elinor struggled for composure as she swallowed the lump in her throat. "When do you plan to leave, my lord?"

"At first light. Elinor?" He stretched out a hand towards her, but she had turned away and did not see it. Rokeby's arm fell to his side. "If you wish to write to them you may leave the letter in the hall. I shall not forget it."

"Thank you." Her voice was colourless and her eyes were fixed upon the carpet. Absently, she smoothed at the skirt of her gown with trembling fingers. If only he would lose his temper and rail at

her, instead of treating her with his present distant
courtesy. He might have been speaking to a stranger.

"You wish to continue with this farce?" she asked
quietly.

"I told you. I have no choice."

"There is always a choice," she said. "You might
walk away from your responsibilities—"

"As you intend to do? Your opinion of me is so
low that you would deny me a sense of honour? No,
ma'am, we shall go on. You shall not find me wanting in that respect."

"Then, if you will excuse me, I shall write my
letter." As she walked towards the door he spoke
again.

"You know the danger? You will keep Hester
close?" Elinor nodded her assent and left him.

As she had expected, the letter to her parents
caused her much soul-searching. She tore up her efforts again and again, and it was well into the early
hours of the morning before she had completed it to
her own satisfaction.

She sealed the envelope and, taking a candle, stole
down into the darkened hall. A gleam of light shone
beneath the door of the study, and she guessed that
Rokeby had not yet retired.

She had no wish to see him. She was too exhausted to indulge in any conversation, but as she
laid the letter upon a small brass tray a drop of burning candle wax fell upon her hand. The pain made
her jump and her fingers caught the tray, sending it
crashing to the marble floor.

The door of the study opened, and Rokeby looked
at her. Then he held out his hand for the letter. She
gave it to him without a word.

"I have written to Charlbury to ask if he will support me at our marriage. You agree?"

"Of course...whatever you wish..."

For a second a faint smile of mockery played about his lips. "I fear it will take all your powers of persuasion to induce Hester to attend you."

"I am quite sure that she will do so." Elinor told him stiffly.

"Perhaps! But only if she were convinced that I should make you happy. A vain hope, I imagine..."

"Goodnight, my lord." Elinor did not trust herself to say more. She picked up her candle and turned towards the stairs.

"Not so fast, my promised bride!" He moved so quickly that she had no opportunity to evade him. "Shall we not seal our bargain with a kiss?"

His arm was about her waist, and Elinor was acutely aware that she was clad only in a diaphanous night-robe beneath her filmy dressing-gown. Her maid had taken down her hair from its fashionable chignon and brushed it until it shone. Now the tawny mane hung in a cloud about her shoulders.

"Charming!" His lordship observed in a silky tone. "What pleasures I have in store..." There was no tenderness in his voice, and the note of cynicism roused her to fury. Bitterness and despair made her throw caution to the winds.

"You will not be the loser by our bargain," she cried angrily. "Doubtless you will make sure of that."

"Indeed I shall." He was stroking her shoulders. "Kiss me, Elinor!"

"Let me go!" She struggled furiously. He did not love her. Nothing but expediency had forced him to offer for her, and had it not been for Dacre's threats he would never have done so. "You will wake the servants."

"They will not think it strange that I should wish to salute my betrothed."

"In the early hours of the morning, and when I am clad only in...in...?"

"In gauze, my dear? It is vastly becoming, and leaves little to the imagination."

Elinor threw back her head and looked at him. There was a dangerous glitter in his eyes, and in that moment he looked capable of anything.

There was an air of reckless abandon in his manner, and it frightened her. She sensed that it was born off frustration, but surely he would not attempt to seduce her here, in his aunt's home?

"Pray allow me to return to my room, my lord," she said more quietly. "If you wish to talk, we may do so in the morning. At present you are not yourself."

"You are mistaken. I am very much myself, and I have no wish to talk. That is not my object at this moment."

His mouth came down on hers, and it was only with a supreme effort of will that she managed to offer no response. With every muscle tensed she stood statue-like in his embrace.

After a moment he released her, looking at her strangely.

"You wish to talk?" he muttered. "Well then, let me offer you a glass of wine." Seizing her hand, he thrust her ahead of him into the study.

Elinor began to tremble.

"You are cold, my dear? Allow me to make you

more comfortable." He slipped out of his coat and placed it about her shoulders. "Here, drink this! It might help to thaw the ice."

Elinor did not answer him.

"I hope you do not intend to cheat me, Elinor." He was standing with his shoulders propped against the mantelpiece. "If you have any thought of banishing me from your room when we are wed, you may forget it now."

Elinor felt the hot colour rising to her cheeks. Some such idea had occurred to her, it was true. It would serve him right for his callous approach to their marriage, but she had dismissed it as unworthy of her. He might not love her, but she would keep her part of the bargain.

"I shall not cheat you," she whispered. In her own heart, if she were honest, she knew that she could not bear to do so. When he kissed her, it had taken all her self-control not to throw her arms about his neck and melt against his lips.

"I am glad to hear it. Who knows, in time you may grow to think of me more kindly."

There was an odd note in his voice, almost of pleading, but she knew that she must be mistaken. She turned away and did not answer him.

"No? I see that you do not agree with me. Ah well, it is not a condition of marriage after all. We must make the best of it. Others do so every day."

Elinor was close to tears. Her heart felt like lead within her breast. He had succeeded in crushing all her dreams of happiness, and the future looked bleak indeed. She choked back a sob.

"No tears, I beg of you! I would not have you distress yourself unnecessarily. You will not find me a demanding husband. You may go your own way if you should wish it, though, of course, I shall expect the same understanding.''

Elinor rose to her feet, feeling that her heart must break, and he did not attempt to detain her.

As she stumbled blindly to her room, she came to a decision. She could not go on like this. Tonight had been the final insult.

Rokeby had left her in no doubt of his meaning. He had offered her an arrangement which was not unknown among the *ton*. Once she had given him an heir, she would be free to take a lover more to her taste.

How could he? she thought wildly. It was an offence to every finer feeling.

From the hall below she heard the front door open, and then close. She guessed that he was gone to seek more congenial company. The thought of him in another woman's arms struck like a dagger to her breast.

Was this what she must suffer in the years to come? She would not do it, not even to save Hester. Tomorrow she would put an end to her betrothal.

Chapter Twelve

Elinor did not close her eyes that night, and she rose at first light. Rokeby had planned to leave for Derbyshire at dawn, but now his journey was unnecessary. He must return her letter.

She was unsurprised to find that his lordship had not spent the night at home. He too must have had second thoughts. It was only to be expected after the away she had repulsed him. His change of heart was for the best—it would save much argument.

She would speak to him before she broke the news to Lady Hartfield. After all, a broken engagement was not uncommon when the parties found that they had been mistaken in their feelings for each other.

She should have felt happier now that the decision was made to free herself from an intolerable situation. Instead, she was convinced that she had never been so miserable in her life.

Only Hester would be pleased, and she, poor child, had no idea of the probable fate in store for her.

She stared at her face in the mirror. It did not seem possible that such pain would not have left its mark but, apart from a certain heaviness about the eyes, she looked just the same. She buried her head in her hands. If others could but look into her mind, it would be a different story.

What a coil it was! And how could she, the cool and sensible Miss Temple, have become embroiled in such a situation?

As she grew calmer she began to reflect upon a possible course of action. There was no time to lose. After one last unpleasant interview with Rokeby, she would take her leave of Hester and Lady Hartfield and return to Derbyshire. She had no intention of spending another night beneath the same roof as his lordship.

Lady Hartfield would be upset and Hester would be distraught at the thought of losing her. Her heart misgave her as she wondered what on earth she was to say to them. Only that she had been mistaken in her affections, perhaps? But would that be considered sufficient reason for her sudden departure?

She could not explain to either of them that Rokeby had tried to molest her.

And what of Hester? If Lady Hartfield knew the truth about Lord Dacre and his threats, she might find some solution to the problem. Rokeby had assured her that it was impossible for her ladyship to intervene, but was there not a chance?

In her distress, Elinor knew that she was clutching at straws, but she felt trapped. Whatever happened, she must get away from Rokeby. She felt that she was fighting for her very life, and her decision to leave must be irrevocable.

It was noon before she joined the others at the nuncheon table. Rokeby had not returned, but Lady Hartfield saw nothing strange in this.

"Dear Marcus!" she said fondly. "Is it not like him to rush away to Derbyshire so soon? He cannot wait to claim you, my dear Elinor."

Elinor's response was non-committal, and Hester gave her a sharp glance. Her ladyship did not appear to notice it.

"He had no sleep, you must know, which was foolish of him, but we cannot blame a young man in love." Lady Hartfield helped herself to a wing of cold chicken and some salad, and then exclaimed at the lack of appetite shown by the others.

"This will not do, Elinor. You will be worn to a shade before your wedding day. Marcus will not be away for long, and he will not care that you should pine for him."

Obediently Elinor filled her plate, but she took no more than a mouthful of the food. Preoccupied with the thought that this might be the last meal which she would eat with her companions, she took no part in the conversation.

"Elinor, you are dreaming!" Lady Hartfield challenged. "It is natural, though I hope you have not forgot. Tonight we are promised to the Morcotts for their evening party."

"I have not forgotten, ma'am." Elinor gave her hostess a mechanical smile. For all she knew, Rokeby might have decided upon some days of debauchery. She could only wait for his return.

As the long hours dragged, by it took all her self-control to behave as if nothing was amiss. She had no choice but to dress for the party, and to join the others in the carriage.

In the crush of the Morcotts' overheated rooms she

bowed and nodded to her acquaintance, but later she could not recall a word of their conversation.

Thankfully there was to be a musical recital after supper, though Lady Hartfield had announced her intention of making up a table at cards. Hester had been borne away by some hopeful scion of a noble house with a promise of a glass of cooling lemonade.

Elinor sank into a chair beside a window, half-hidden by the heavy draperies, as she waited for the recital to begin. The music, at least, would relieve her of the need to exchange inanities with those about her. She closed her eyes as the first chords sounded, and was lost to all sense of time until the piece had ended.

When she opened them it was to see an unwelcome sight. Lord Dacre was standing in the doorway, with Hester by his side.

Elinor rose to her feet with the intention of joining them, but the rows of small gilt chairs, each occupied, barred her path. The music had begun again and angry looks were thrown at her as she tried to pass.

Panic seized her. In desperation she turned towards the long window behind her chair. It was unlocked, and led on to a terrace. She slipped out, praying that she might gain access to the house again by another window further along. This too was unlocked and led into another, smaller salon. She pushed through the crowd of chattering guests, but she could see no sign of Hester.

Dear God! Would Dacre abduct the girl in full view of the Polite World? She could not think it, but her terror grew as she moved among the diners, and those who were playing cards. Hester was nowhere to be found.

She appealed to her hostess, striving to keep her voice as calm as possible. "I am looking for Miss Winton, ma'am. Have you seen her?"

"She is gone into the garden, I believe. She found it warm indoors…" Mrs Morcott was only half attending. She turned back to her guests.

Elinor was terrified. In the darkness anything might happen. She brushed past the people in her way, ignoring their startled looks, and ran on to the terrace.

At first she could see no one. The Morcotts' garden was not large, but it was long and narrow. As she picked her way along the path, the shrubs on either side threw dark shadows in the moonlight.

She had reached the far wall which separated the house from the road which ran behind it when she saw Hester. The girl was sitting on a low bench in the gazebo. Thankfully, she was alone.

"My dearest, what are you doing here? You will take a chill without your shawl." Elinor's voice was shaking with relief.

"It does not matter. Nothing matters…" Hester did not raise her head.

"Is something wrong? What has happened? I saw you speaking to Lord Dacre…" A nameless dread filled Elinor's heart.

"You lied to me," Hester said dully.

"Hester! How can you say such things? I have never lied to you."

"But you did not tell me the truth, did you? It is much the same…"

"I cannot imagine what Lord Dacre has been saying to you, but will you not tell me? I cannot bear to see you so distressed. Dacre is not to be trusted, you must know that?"

"I do." Hester gave a convulsive swallow. "I did not believe him at first. He asked if I knew of Lord Rokeby's evil reputation and then…"

"Yes?"

"Then he said that Lord Rokeby planned to ruin you." She would not meet Elinor's eyes.

"But you knew that was not so," Elinor cried warmly. "Have I not just accepted his lordship's offer of marriage?"

Hester raised her head and gave Elinor a level look.

"Why did you do so, Elinor?"

"Because I loved him. Did I not tell you so?"

"I didn't believe you then, and I don't believe you now. Was it not to give my guardian some semblance of respectability? Lord Dacre told me that he had planned to apply to the courts for permission to take me into his own care."

"Hester, you are overwrought…"

"I am not blind. You are not happy, are you, whatever Lady Hartfield may say?"

"My dear—"

Hester rose from her seat and bent to kiss Elinor's cheek. "You shall not sacrifice yourself for me," she said quietly. "Shall we go indoors? The wind, I find, is cold."

It was true that she was shivering, but Elinor suspected that it was as much from shock as from the chill night air. She took Hester's arm and hurried her towards the house.

"Let us speak of these matters later," she urged. "I'll explain... I must make you understand."

Hester stopped at the entrance to the salon.

"I do understand. I have been both foolish and selfish. I should not have refused all the offers made to me."

"Oh, do not say so," Elinor pleaded. "That is not true. Hester...?" She sighed as the girl brushed past her and entered the crowded room.

This was a very different Hester from the girl who had always taken her advice. There was something about the set expression upon that small face which gave her cause for deep anxiety.

She would make it right, she vowed to herself. If she could but talk to Hester for an hour...but what was she to say? How could she convince his ward that she was in love with Rokeby when she had decided on that very day to break off her engagement?

The problem seemed insuperable, but she would think of something... She could not leave matters as they were. In Hester's present mood the child might do something irrational.

Later that evening she was unable to carry out her plan to speak to Hester. On their return to Berkeley Square the girl was quick to plead exhaustion and beg to be excused.

And Rokeby had not yet returned from the illicit pleasures which were doubtless still detaining him.

Despair filled Elinor's heart. She hated him, but if only he would come back. She *must* tell him what had happened at the Morcotts'. Without him, she had the odd sensation of being on shifting sands, not knowing when she might be sucked down into unimaginable horror.

* * *

On the following morning she was surprised to find Hester at the breakfast table before her. The girl was polite and pleasant, and totally unapproachable. The presence of the servants made it impossible for Elinor to do more than make casual conversation.

Elinor cast a covert glance at her as they made their morning visits later in the morning. Lady Hartfield was punctilious in her observance of the social niceties and she nodded her approval of Hester's calm civilities.

"We shall make something of her yet," she whispered happily to Elinor. "She is growing more mature."

Elinor fought the urge to tell her ladyship all. Her anxiety was increasing. This cool, composed creature was a Hester she did not know. Pray heaven the child had not decided upon some wild plan of her own. If so, she must discover it before any harm was done.

She was given no opportunity to do so. For the rest of that day Hester took care not to be left alone with her, and retired at once after their evening visit to the opera.

Elinor followed as soon as it was practicable to make her own excuses, and hurried along to Hester's room.

"Miss does not wish to be disturbed." The maid who opened the door to her announced.

"I shan't keep her a moment." Elinor brushed past her and walked over to the bed. To all appearances Hester was already asleep, but Elinor was undeceived. It was clear that Hester did not wish to speak to her. With a shrug of resignation, she turned away. She would try again in the morning.

* * *

But on the following morning, Hester sent a message to her hostess. She had the headache, and believed that she should stay in bed.

"Do you believe her, Elinor?" Lady Hartfield's face was stern. "I had imagined yesterday that she was becoming resigned to your marriage. I do not care to think that she has given way to another fit of the sullens."

"Ma'am, I am sure that it is not so. I will go to see her." Elinor half rose from her chair.

"No, you will not! Sit down, my dear! You are much too careful of Hester's whims and fancies. I will see her myself. Sometimes, I confess, she puts me out of all patience with her."

"But, ma'am, she may indeed have the headache." Elinor thought it more than likely, after the events of the past few days.

"Then she shall stay in bed, but we shall not change our own plans, my dear Elinor." She summoned a footman and ordered her carriage.

When she came downstairs her expression of severity had softened.

"Hester does look pale," she admitted. "She tells me that it is a certain time of the month. I have advised her to rest. The pain will ease in a few hours time if she takes the dose I recommended."

Elinor did a few calculations, well knowing that there was something wrong. It was not time...though the shock might have upset Hester's normal functions.

A little niggling doubt stayed with her throughout their drive through the park. She was impatient to get back to Berkeley Square, but their carriage was stopped again and again as Lady Hartfield's friends approached them. To her the hours seemed endless, as greetings were exchanged and invitations offered.

She could not repress a sigh of relief when the coachman was free at last to whip up his horses. Her hand was on the carriage door almost before he had drawn to a halt.

Then, as she followed Lady Hartfield up the steps, the door flew open and an agitated butler hurried towards them.

"Ma'am, it's Miss Winton," he gasped. "We can't find her anywhere."

"Nonsense, man! She is in her room."

"No, your ladyship, she isn't. What's more, her outdoor things are gone, and so is her bandbox!"

Elinor ran through the hall and up to Hester's room. It was all quite true. Very little of Hester's clothing had disappeared, but enough had gone to fit into a bandbox, and of the girl herself there was no trace.

"Elinor, the maid found this. It is addressed to you…" Lady Hartfield sat down suddenly, looking much older than her years. "What can have possessed the child? Has she eloped? She gave no sign of a preference for any particular man…"

With shaking fingers, Elinor ripped at the envelope. The note was brief, and it begged her forgiveness. Hester had decided to marry Dacre's son.

Elinor went scarlet and then white. Her world seemed to reel about her and she put out a hand to steady herself. Lady Hartfield gripped it tightly and took the note from her nerveless fingers.

"What does this mean?" the older woman asked. "Hester gives no explanation. Were you aware of her affection for Tobias?"

Elinor shook her head. She could not trust herself to speak.

"Then I cannot understand it. She has not met Tobias above three times, and she always confides in you. This is Dacre's doing, I make no doubt, but how did he persuade her? I thought she held him in dislike."

"She does," Elinor replied briefly. "Ma'am, I should have told you, but I did not wish to worry you. Lord Dacre spoke to Hester at the Morcotts' ball. He...he told her something which distressed her very much."

"And what was that?"

"He...he tried to blacken Lord Rokeby's character..."

"I see." The sharp black eyes were intent upon Elinor's face. "There is something more, I think. Won't you be honest with me?"

Elinor flushed painfully, and turned her head away.

"Come, my dear, out with it! Hester may despise my nephew, but it would take more than a recital of his shortcomings to cause her to leave her friends. What is behind her decision?"

"Lord Dacre convinced her that his lordship offered for me merely to lend himself respectability. Otherwise Hester would be removed from his care." Elinor's eyes filled. "Worst of all, she now believes that I accepted him in order to save her."

Her ladyship gave a snort of disbelief. "Is the child blind? Does she not see what is beneath her nose? Elinor, you must have told her of your love for Marcus..."

"I did." The slow tears were rolling down

Elinor's cheeks and she made no effort to wipe them away. "She did not believe me. I disliked him so, you see, and I made no effort to hide it. She said that she could not allow me to...to sacrifice myself for her."

Lady Hartfield shook her head. "Sometimes you young people make me wonder. Hester does not understand you very well, I fear. If your affections were not engaged, you would never have agreed to marry Marcus, whatever pressure might be brought to bear upon you. I am sure of it."

Elinor dried her eyes. Now was not the time to explain that she had decided to end her betrothal.

"I will go to Lord Dacre," she announced. "If I can but see Hester, I know I can persuade her to return with me."

"Is that wise? Do but consider, my dear. We have not heard from Dacre. Hester may not yet have reached him. If he learns that she is missing from her home, that is yet another reason for him to claim a lack of care for her well-being. And then, you know, we may have misjudged her reasons..."

Elinor stared at her companion and was disturbed by her ladyship's expression.

"Ma'am?"

"You will not like what I have to say, but Hester may not have been perfectly open with you, Elinor. I confess that I thought she had an affection for John Charlbury, but Tobias is a handsome boy. Young girls are not always true to their first love, my dear."

"Your ladyship, I think you are mistaken." Elinor told her steadily.

"Perhaps so, but it is not impossible, and you will admit that Hester has a secretive side to her nature."

"She is reserved and shy, but I have never known her to lie, and she is incapable of deception."

"Very well, I shall not quarrel with you, but if I am right and she had but told us of her feelings, Marcus might have reconsidered—"

"What might I have reconsidered?" Tall and straight, Marcus stood in the doorway, looking from one face to the other.

Elinor's heart began to pound. She longed for nothing so much as to run to him and throw herself into his arms, but the memory of their quarrel stopped her. His behaviour and his cruel words could not be forgiven. She stared at him, her lips almost as pale as her face.

"Thank heavens you have come back to us." Lady Hartfield reached out a hand to him. "Oh, Marcus, what is to be done?"

Rokeby dropped a kiss upon her brow and then he turned to Elinor. "What has happened?" he asked quietly. "The servants are running about like headless chickens. At the very least, I imagined a death in the family."

"Hester is missing," Elinor told him stiffly. "We were out this morning, Lady Hartfield and myself. When we returned, Hester had gone—"

"And she is gone to Dacre," her ladyship broke in. "She wishes to marry Tobias."

"Rubbish." Rokeby's reply was pithy, to say the least. "Did she give you a reason for this sudden decision?" There was silence, but a glance at Elinor's face told him all he wished to know. A smile of utter contempt curved his lips. "I'll go to Dacre at once," he said.

There was something in his face which frightened

Elinor. His jaw was set, and the mobile mouth had hardened into a thin line. The expression in his eyes was murderous.

"Take care!" she cried involuntarily. "He is a dangerous man."

"And so am I, as he will soon discover. I will bring Hester back with me," he promised. "You have not long to wait."

Elinor's heart turned to lead within her breast, as terror consumed her. "You will take no chances?" she pleaded.

Rokeby bowed. His face was enigmatic. "I thought I had taken those already." Without more ado he strode from the room.

Elinor sat in silence, picking aimlessly at the lace trimming on her gown, and unaware of her companion's bemused expression.

"You disappoint me, Elinor," her ladyship said at last. "I thought that we were friends. There is so much about this situation which I do not understand. Won't you trust me?"

Elinor cast about wildly in her mind for some words which might express what she wished to say, but she could find none.

"Very well," her ladyship said at last. "I won't press you, but, my dear, you will remember, will you not, that I shall always stand your friend?" She rose to her feet as if to leave the room, but Elinor caught her hand.

"Lady Hartfield, forgive me! I have no wish to deceive you, but I can say naught at present. It is only fair that I speak to Marcus…to Lord Rokeby, before…before I can take you into my confidence."

"You have quarrelled, have you not?"

Elinor nodded. Her lips were trembling and her heart was too full for speech.

"I thought so." Her ladyship patted Elinor's hand. "My dear, we can't always be in agreement with those we love, and lovers' quarrels are soon mended. Take heart! Both you and Marcus are under a strain at present, and this business with Hester cannot help."

"It is more than that," Elinor told her sadly. "We may have been mistaken in our feelings for each other."

Lady Hartfield shook her head. "My dear Elinor, for two intelligent women, both you and Hester have been singularly blind. How can you doubt my nephew's love for you? Do you not see the way he looks at you, and the way his voice changes when he speaks your name?"

Elinor looked at her with brimming eyes. "That may have been so before...before... But, ma'am, he had no word for me just now. You must have been aware of it."

"He will come back to you, my love, no matter what your present differences."

"I don't know." Elinor felt unutterably weary. "I am confused... I don't know what to think."

It was true. She had been determined to end her betrothal, but at the sight of Marcus a wild surge of love had shaken her to the core. She could not deny her passion for him, try as she might.

And now she was filled with dread. Lord Dacre hated him, and she shuddered to think of the outcome of their meeting. A duel in which Dacre was the victor would resolve Hester's future without recourse to the courts.

Dacre would see it as an answer to his problems, especially if, as she suspected, it would not be a fair fight.

She pictured Rokeby's lifeless body stretched upon some lonely field of turf. The thought was unbearable and she swayed in horror.

Please God, anything but that. Let Rokeby leave her for his lights-o'-love. She could bear it, if only he were safe. She put a hand up to her eyes as if to shut out the spectres which tormented her. Then she found herself in Lady Hartfield's arms.

"Don't, my love. Please don't look like that. You shall not be so frightened. Marcus will come back to us and then you will be happy again."

"I wish I could believe it," Elinor cried in bitter despair. "Did you not see his face? There was murder in it."

Lady Hartfield shook her gently. "You know his temper, Elinor, but it will not lead him into folly. He has you to think of now, as well as Hester."

"He no longer loves me. I know it."

"Then you are more foolish than I had imagined possible. He was yours from the first moment of your meeting. I never doubted it from the day he asked me to choose a gown for you. It is not quite usual, you know, for a gentleman to be so exact as to the colour of a lady's eyes, her height, her build, and the way the candlelight reflected the tawny beauty of her hair." There was a chuckle in her voice. "You were always with him, Elinor, in his mind's eye. A love like that is not easily destroyed."

Elinor dried her eyes. "Ma'am, you are very good to me," she murmured. "I am ashamed to have worried you at a time like this."

"Then you shall not continue to do so," her ladyship said briskly. "As for Hester, when Marcus brings her back, that young lady will learn what I think of her behaviour."

Her promise was not destined to be soon fulfilled. Marcus returned within the hour, but he was alone. As both women looked at him, he shook his head.

"She is not there. Dacre has not seen her."

"He is lying," Elinor cried wildly. "Surely you don't believe him?"

"Perhaps not his words, but certainly his actions. His men are scouring London for her."

"No, it is a trick! He would tell you anything to get his way. He *must* be hiding her."

"I think not." Rokeby's face was grim. "You did not see his face. It is a picture of baffled rage. Hester was to arrive at his house by noon. That he did not deny. When she did not, he thought she'd changed her mind. Now he is as anxious as we are ourselves."

"Though not from any care for Hester's safety, you may be sure." The lines on Lady Hartfield's face had deepened. To Elinor she seemed to be ageing by the minute.

"Quite so! He sees his prize eluding him, my dear aunt."

"I don't believe him, whatever you may think." Elinor sprang to her feet and began to pace the room. "He is deceiving you."

"Will you not sit down?" Rokeby was alarmed by her pallor. "Whatever else, I think we may believe Tobias. The boy is distraught. Hester has been kind to him and he holds her in affection."

"Then it is true? Hester has agreed to marry him?" Lady Hartfield looked more hopeful.

"She has agreed...and without my permission. That I shall never give." Rokeby's face might have been carved in stone, his jaw was set, and his mouth a tight line.

"My dear boy! Are you not being unreasonable? Hester must marry, you said as much yourself. This match may not be what we would wish, but if the two young people hold each other in such high esteem, why then should you stand in their way?"

"And leave them at the mercy of Dacre? No, ma'am, I cannot do it. You know something of him, but I know more. Once married, Hester might not live out the year." He looked at their horrified faces and turned away.

"Oh, Marcus, you cannot mean...murder?" Lady Hartfield's voice was little more than a whisper.

"Why not? He is capable of it, and he is deep in debt. An accident might be arranged...it would not look like murder."

"Then he would be in control of Hester's fortune? Oh, my dear, I cannot believe it..."

"But I believe it, ma'am." Elinor rose and faced them. Her face was as set as Rokeby's own. "What I will not believe is that Hester loves Tobias. Now we are wasting time. Hester must be found without delay."

"Agreed, but where are we to look? Do you recall if she had any money by her?"

"She had not used up her allowance—"

"Then I'll send men to the coaching depots. Someone may remember her." Rokeby pulled at the bell-rope.

"But where would she go?" Elinor cried in anguish. "She can't return to Bath...the school is closed…and she would not go back to Kent…to Merton Place.''

"To Kent?" Rokeby stood lost in thought for a few moments. "What of the Charlburys? She is fond of them, and they of her."

"I don't know…they are friends of yours… She might not think it wise…"

"Where then? Can you think of anyone else?" He stood at the far end of the room, cool and unapproachable.

"No, I can't." Elinor's look was pitiful. "She has never ventured out alone before, and she knows no one in the city."

"She has one or two friends among the younger girls," Lady Hartfield pointed out. "Though, of course, their mammas would not encourage her to leave the protection of her guardian."

"That's true, aunt. She would have been returned to us at once." Rokeby was quick to issue his instructions to the men who came in answer to his ring. Then he turned back to his companions. "Try to think," he urged. "Has she ever mentioned anything which might tell us of her present whereabouts?"

"I have racked my brains these last few hours," Elinor said in a low voice. "I believe she intended to go to Dacre as he told you. Something must have happened on the way."

Thoughts of the nearby river rose unbidden to her mind and she sat down suddenly as her legs gave way beneath her. Then Rokeby was on his knees beside her.

"What is it?" he said gently.

She choked out her reply so quietly that he had to bring his lips close to her ear to catch her words.

"Do you think she might have decided to...to do away with herself?" she whispered. "Rather than go to Dacre?"

"No I do not. One does not pack a bandbox with suicide in mind." He slipped a lean finger beneath her chin and forced her to look at him. "Let us not fear the worst, Elinor. Hester, as you know, is unaccustomed to travel alone. She may simply have given a wrong direction to whichever hack took her up."

"I wish I could believe it." She would not be comforted, and she could not hide her agony of mind. "Even now she may be in danger of abduction, or, at best, being accosted in the street by some unscrupulous creature. We must look for her...I will fetch my cloak."

"You will stay here," Rokeby told her firmly. "Hester may yet return, having thought better of her foolish plans. Besides, my aunt has need of you."

"Oh, ma'am, I am so sorry!" Elinor turned to Lady Hartfield in quick contrition. "How selfish of me to be thinking only of myself! Will you not let me help you to your room?" She was as alarmed as Rokeby by the ashen pallor of the older woman's face. "If you were to rest for an hour? I will come to you at once if there is any news..."

"Thank you, my dear." Her ladyship struggled to her feet, but the spring had gone from her step as she allowed herself to be supported from the room.

Beyond the door, she paused to allow a stalwart footman to take each arm. "My dresser and the maid will look to my needs," she told Elinor in a thread-like voice. "Do you go back to Marcus. You may yet think of a way to bring Hester back to us."

"No, I shall not leave you," Elinor protested. "Ma'am, you don't look at all the thing..."

"Neither do you, my love, but I know that you will not rest. You may leave me now. I know that you will both do all you can."

Elinor knew that further argument would be useless. With a sinking heart she returned to the salon. Marcus raised his head as she approached him, and she shrank back at the expression in his eyes. His face was dark with anger, and she was reminded of their first meeting when she had believed that she would hate him for the rest of her life.

"Well, madam, it seems that the fates conspire against me. Now I am to be repaid in full for my transgressions."

"You are tired, and worried about your aunt as well as Hester," she said quietly. "Pray do not blame yourself...the fault is mine."

"How can that be?" His lips curved in a cynical smile. "Hester believes that I am the devil incarnate...she would go to any lengths to prevent our marriage!"

"She did not understand. She thought it was a sacrifice on my part."

He came towards her then and took her hands.

"I thought so myself, Elinor. I would not believe that you could care for me, and it almost drove me into madness. It was only when your father told me that you would never marry without love that I—"

"My father? You have seen him?"

"Of course!" As he looked at her his face changed. "You knew that I was going into Derbyshire...?"

Elinor could not meet his eyes, but she flushed to the roots of her hair.

"I had supposed that after...after that night...you would not care to go..."

"I see." His voice was that of a stranger. "I wondered why you had not asked about your family. Do you care to tell me how you imagine I have spent my time these last few days?"

She did not answer him. In the silence which followed, the ticking of the clock on the mantelshelf was clearly audible, and when it struck the quarter-hour she jumped. She moistened her lips and tried to speak.

"No!" he said sharply. "There is no need to explain. Your expression tells me all I wish to know, and it has convinced me of one thing. There will never be trust between us, will there, Elinor? You couldn't believe that I should keep my word to you."

She put out a hand as if to ward off his accusations. The bitterness in his voice had wounded her to the heart. She had misjudged him yet again, and now she knew that she had lost him. He would not forgive her lack of trust. She told herself that it was for the best.

"Please..." she murmured faintly. He would never know what she had been about to say, for at that moment there came the sound of a commotion in the hall.

Rokeby strode over to the door and flung it open as Elinor raised her head.

There, in the doorway, stood Hester. Behind her was the tall figure of John Charlbury.

Elinor heard a rushing in her ears and the world seemed to spin about her before she slipped into darkness.

Chapter Thirteen

Elinor returned to consciousness to find herself supported by Rokeby's arm. He was holding a glass to her lips but her first sip of the strong spirit made her cough. She struggled to sit up unaided.

"Don't move!" his lordship ordered. "In a few moments you will feel better…then you shall go to your room."

"No…no, I won't. I must know… Oh, Hester, where have you been?" She looked down at the girl who knelt beside her, chafing her hand as the tears rained down upon her fingers. "Are you unhurt?"

"Hester has not been harmed, though why you should care I can't imagine." Rokeby's face was dark with anger. "She has forfeited any claim to consideration."

Hester's sobs increased.

"Don't be angry with her," Elinor pleaded. "I'm sure she believed that her actions were for the best."

"Then she is even more of a fool than I had supposed. Get up, you stupid child! It is too late for tears."

"Marcus, you will not address Hester in that

tone." John Charlbury spoke for the first time. His normally gentle manner had vanished, and there was anger in his eyes.

"I shall address her in any tone I please. Must I remind you that I am her guardian?"

"You have not exactly shone in that capacity, have you?"

Within the circle of his arm, Elinor felt Marcus stiffen. Gently, he laid her back against a pile of cushions and rose to his feet. Oblivious of her pleading looks, he walked over to his friend.

"Would you care to explain what you mean by that remark?" he said very quietly.

Elinor could not bear the tension in the room. She began to speak, but Rokeby hushed her with a look.

"I am waiting," he continued.

"Then you need wait no longer, Marcus." Charlbury's look was long and deliberate. "I had thought better of you. Imagine my feelings when I found Hester wandering alone in Berkeley Square. She was attempting to hire a hackney carriage...and at the mercy of any passer-by who cared to accost her."

"*Your* feelings? What of the rest of us? My aunt is overcome with worry, and Elinor has been near-demented..."

"I am sorry for it, but the fault is yours."

"You think so?" Rokeby's eyes narrowed. "You came upon Hester quite by chance, I suppose? Or had you planned to help her leave this house?"

Charlbury took a step towards him. His fists were clenched. "Do not try our friendship further," he warned. Then he checked and his voice grew calmer. "I make allowances for your natural anxiety,

Marcus. You will not believe that of me if you consider. Why should I bring her back to you?"

"Why indeed?" his lordship jeered. "Would you have me think that you met her by coincidence?"

"Is it so strange?" Charlbury had regained his self-command. Now he turned to help Hester to her feet, and handed her his handkerchief. "Sit down, my dear, and wipe your eyes," he said gently. "There is no need to be afraid."

"No?" His tenderness towards the girl had served only to incense his lordship further. "Take care, my friend, you presume too much..."

To Elinor's astonishment Charlbury began to smile.

"In your high ropes, Marcus? Come down, I beg of you, and listen to what I have to say. I was coming to you anyway. Did you not invite me to attend your marriage?"

Rokeby would not be mollified. "How fortunate that you were just in time to succour a maiden in distress." The sarcasm brought a tinge of colour to Charlbury's cheeks.

"Yes, she *was* in distress," he replied. "To save Miss Temple from an unfortunate marriage, she had planned to agree to Lord Dacre's suggestion that she betroth herself to his son, Tobias."

"Remarkable." Rokeby sneered. "I had no idea that she was besotted with the boy. Must I give you my permission to wed him, Hester?"

"Oh, please don't!" Hester cried in falling tones. "I don't wish to marry Tobias in the least—"

"It is out of the question," Charlbury intervened.

Rokeby stared at him, and when he spoke some of the anger had left his voice.

"I suppose we must be thankful that you have

talked her out of that piece of nonsense,'' he said grudgingly. ''But did it take all day? You might have brought her back before. Is that the action of a friend?''

''Hester is also my friend. She had no wish to return.''

''And her wishes are paramount?''

''They are with me.''

''Then I wonder why you brought her back.''

''I came for a purpose,'' Charlbury said deliberately. ''I wish to marry Hester.''

''To save her from the cruelty of her wicked guardian?''

''Marcus, don't be such a noddle-cock. I want to marry Hester because I love her.''

''Indeed!'' Rokeby turned away, but not before Elinor had seen the sparkle in his eyes...it was the old familiar glint of mischief. ''You surprise me! Here is Hester, on the verge of betrothal to Tobias? She will find it hard to make her choice. The boy is devoted to her. He told me so himself.''

Charlbury chose to ignore such baiting. ''You may not like the idea,'' he said steadily, ''but Hester has promised to be my wife.''

''I have not said that you may pay your addresses to her.'' Rokeby took a leisurely pinch of snuff. ''Upon consideration, I do not think I can allow it.''

''You must! We are betrothed.''

''Dear me! I fear I shall be forced to call you out for your importunate behaviour. Shall we say at dawn tomorrow? You may name your friends.''

Hester gasped. Her face was as white as her gown. It was Elinor who broke the silence.

''Marcus, the joke has gone far enough,'' she reproved. ''Hester thinks you mean it.''

"But I do!" When he turned, Rokeby was laughing. "I should like nothing better than to challenge this idiot." He gave Charlbury a friendly blow upon the shoulder. "A noddle-cock, did you call me? What of yourself? If you hadn't been so damned stiff-necked, none of this need have happened. You have known from the first that this is what I wished for you."

He shook Charlbury warmly by the hand, and then he turned to Hester.

"You deserve a beating, miss, but I shall leave that to your husband. You had best go to my aunt, and take John with you. It may take some time to persuade her to forgive you."

"Pray do not be too hard on her," Elinor faltered when they were alone. "She meant it for the best."

"Your forgiveness comes readily," he replied. "I could wish that it applied to me." Once again he might have been a stranger. "Your father believes that you must have some regard for me. Can it be true?"

"I think you did not tell him all, my lord."

"No, I did not." His face was sombre. "I am not proud of my behaviour on the night I left."

Elinor was silent, and he turned away.

"It is over between us, then?" he asked. "Well, it is no more than I deserve."

"There is no trust between us," Elinor cried brokenly. "You told me so yourself."

"That's true!" There was a quality of stillness about him which filled her with despair. "You were quick to believe that I had left your arms to return to the women of the town. I suppose I cannot blame you. My life has not been such that you could doubt it."

Elinor was silent. His words were true, and she could not deny them.

Rokeby straightened his shoulders. "Do you wish to tell my aunt at once that we no longer plan to marry?"

"I don't know." Elinor plucked at the trimming on her gown. "Lady Hartfield has had a shock. Another may be too much for her."

"As you wish. We shall keep up the charade for another day or two." He bowed and made as if to leave her.

"My family?" she pleaded. "Will you not give me news of them?"

He paused, looking down at her, and then his expression softened.

"I beg your pardon. That was remiss of me." He took a seat beside her. "They are well, and I have a letter for you." He reached inside his coat.

Elinor sat in silence, turning the envelope in her hands.

"I should tell you that your parents received me with great kindness. They were sorry only that you could not accompany me." His air of formality was forbidding. "They hope to see you soon."

"Yes…yes, of course. I will go to them," she said mechanically. She thought that she had never been so miserable in her life. She could not bear to open the letter. It must contain such loving wishes for her future happiness that each word would turn the knife in her wounded heart.

"You will stay for Hester's wedding?" Rokeby enquired in a cool tone. "I imagine it will not be long delayed."

Elinor nodded, but it was only with an effort that she managed to speak calmly of the coming nuptials.

"I am glad that you are pleased with Hester's choice," she murmured. "She and Charlbury are ideally suited to each other."

"Indeed. Their betrothal is all that reconciles me to Hester's folly. Had Charlbury not convinced himself of my neglect, he might never have offered for her. Her fortune was the stumbling-block."

"Hester will be happy with him. He is a man of honour."

"Unlike myself?" His smile was bitter as he looked at her. "Well, what's done is done, and we cannot change it. There is no point in going over it again."

"None whatever," Elinor agreed. She was close to breaking-point. "If you will excuse me, my lord."

She had reached the door before he spoke again.

"Elinor!" There was anguish in his voice, but she did not turn her head. She must be strong in her resolve to leave him, but the urge to run to his arms was overwhelming. She thrust it aside. There could be no future for them.

She walked slowly through the hall in a daze of misery, only half aware of a knock at the outer door. Her hand was on the newelpost of the staircase when she heard the sound of an altercation with the footman who had opened it. The voice was familiar, and she paused.

All visitors were to be denied, but beyond the servant's brawny figure she caught a glimpse of Tobias.

"But I must see Lord Rokeby," he was saying. "At least send in my card..."

Elinor walked towards him, dismissing the footman as she did so. "I'm sure his lordship will see you, sir. I'll take you to him."

"Oh, ma'am, have you any news of Hester...Miss

Winton, I mean?'' His anxiety was piteous and Elinor took his hand.

''She has returned and is quite safe,'' she reassured. ''Lord Rokeby will tell you what has happened.'' She led him into the salon.

Rokeby favoured him with the briefest of nods, but Elinor's pleading glance persuaded him to mend his manners.

''You had best sit down,'' he muttered. ''This may take some time...''

''Is something wrong?'' Tobias looked from one face to the other. ''Miss Temple said that no harm has been done.''

''None to Hester,'' Rokeby told him briefly. ''But you will not care for what I have to tell you.''

''I...I don't understand...''

''Hester is betrothed.''

The news came as a brutal shock to Tobias. He flushed scarlet and then his face grew pale.

''She...she eloped?'' He sounded as if he could not believe his ears.

Elinor felt a pang of pity. ''No...no...she is not married, but she has accepted the offer of an old friend. She has loved him for some time.''

''I can't believe it.'' Tobias was bewildered. ''Father was so sure that she would marry me. I did not care for the idea at first, but then I found that she was not so...so frightening as the other girls. She has been very kind to me.''

''She is a gentle soul,'' Elinor agreed quietly. ''And she is lucky to have you as her friend, but if you are fond of her you must wish only for her happiness.''

''I do.'' Tobias was the picture of dejection.

"But...well...Father said she wished above anything to be my wife ."

"Your father was mistaken," Rokeby told him grimly. "Pray give Lord Dacre my compliments when you tell him that his hopes are dashed."

"Thank you, my lord." Tobias was unconscious of the irony in Rokeby's words. "He is sure to be disappointed."

"I don't doubt it," came the brief reply.

"Do you think...well...may I see Miss Winton? I should like to wish her well."

"At present she is resting, but I will give her your good wishes." Elinor knew what he was feeling and her heart went out to him as he took his leave. She could only imagine that Tobias had inherited his gentle nature from his mother. There was nothing of his father in him.

She said as much to Rokeby when they were alone.

"The lad is well enough," he replied with a gesture of impatience. "Doubtless he fancies himself ill used, but he won't be allowed to pine for long. Dacre will wed him to the next heiress to appear in the marriage market. That is, if he can find some reason for such a girl to take him."

"Tobias was not thinking of the money," Elinor said quietly. "I believe he has a genuine regard for Hester."

"And your heart bleeds for him?"

Elinor flushed at the sarcasm in his voice.

"Bear up, my dear," he continued in the same tone. "Tobias will not die of unrequited love. It is a condition which is soon mended."

Elinor's temper rose. "Naturally you would think so," she accused. "What is your remedy, my lord?"

"Why, Elinor, I thought you knew it." His eyes held hers and his meaning was unmistakable. "Have I not given you evidence enough?"

"Indeed you have! To you, one woman is as good as another." She flounced out of the room.

She was breathing hard as she climbed the stairs to Lady Hartfield's boudoir. Rokeby was impossible. He had no finer feelings. Who could look upon the young man's misery and remain unmoved? Only someone with a heart of stone. Let him go to his birds of paradise. She was well rid of him.

She was still clutching her father's letter in her hand, but she would not read it yet. She needed all her composure to face Lady Hartfield.

Pushing the letter into the pocket of her skirt, she stood quietly for a moment before she tapped at her ladyship's door. Then she took a deep breath before she entered the room.

Her fears were not unfounded. It was an uncomfortable trio which faced her. There was a reserve in Lady Hartfield's manner which Elinor had not seen before, and John Charlbury's calm appeared to have deserted him. It was clear that he was very angry.

Elinor went at once to Hester, saddened to see her swollen face and reddened eyes.

"This is no time to be weeping, my love." She slipped an arm about the girl's shoulders. "I had thought you must be very happy."

"Hester deserves no happiness," her ladyship snapped at once. "When I think of the trouble she has caused... She is a selfish, stupid girl."

John Charlbury stepped forward, but Elinor intervened before he could reply.

"I believe Lord Rokeby would like to see both you and Hester," she said quickly. "Will you go down to him? There are arrangements to be made…''

Charlbury read the message in her eyes. She wished to be alone with Lady Hartfield. His sigh of relief was almost audible. He reached out a hand to Hester and drew her to her feet.

''Do bathe your face, my dear,'' Elinor suggested. ''John will wait for you.''

Hester was quick to hurry from the room, with John behind her. She neither spoke nor raised her head.

''The girl is a fool,'' her ladyship announced with snapping eyes. ''She deserves a beating, and were she not betrothed I should see to it.''

Elinor sat down beside the chaise-longue and took Lady Hartfield's hand. For all the tension apparent in the older woman, Elinor could not repress a smile.

''I see nothing in the least amusing, Elinor. Perhaps you had best leave me.''

''Forgive me, ma'am, I do not mean to be uncivil. It is just that…well…sometimes you are very like his lordship. You echoed his words to Hester.''

The black eyes stared at her. ''And you persuaded him to forgive her for her folly? You will not get round me so easily. I cannot abide a fool!''

''Ma'am, will you not consider? Hester was wrong to run away, and to cause you so much worry. I know how you must feel. I could have shaken her myself, but it is a natural reaction, rather like the urge to whip a child who has just escaped some dreadful danger.''

Lady Hartfield tossed her head and looked away.

''Please don't destroy her present happiness,'' Elinor pleaded. ''Hester has had so little in her life…''

"She had one piece of good fortune."

"Ma'am?"

"She has you to stand her friend. She doesn't deserve you, Elinor, nor that charming man who has been weak enough to offer for her. I fear she is one of those wishy-washy creatures who will always lean on others."

"You are wrong." Elinor stood up. "It took courage to do what she has done today. She fears Lord Dacre, yet she went to him for my sake."

"Now, Elinor, don't go into alt! Sit down...sit down. We shall not quarrel, you and I. Hester will wed, and there's an end to it. I can't say that I shall be sorry to see her settled, as much for your sake as for her own."

"Then I may tell her..."

"You may tell her and her bridegroom that I wish them well. It is the truth." A faint smile curved the corners of her lips. "Marcus is delighted, I suppose. It is what he has wished from the beginning."

"He has given them his blessing," Elinor told her in a neutral tone.

Lady Hartfield cast a sharp glance at her face. Then she lay back and closed her eyes. "I suppose we must be thankful that some good has come from Hester's folly, however well intentioned it may have been. Elinor, you may leave me now. I think that I shall rest before I dress for dinner."

"Must you come down this evening, Lady Hartfield? If you wish it, I should be happy to bear you company in your room," Elinor coaxed in the hope that her ladyship would consent. Beneath the fashionable paint, her skin was the colour of ancient parchment, but she shook her head.

"I am just a little tired. It has been a trying day, but I shall join you later."

She would not be dissuaded, so Elinor left her to the ministrations of her maid. As she walked back to her own room the rustle of paper in her pocket reminded her that she had not yet read her father's letter. The sight of his familiar writing brought a lump to her throat, and her vision blurred as tears rose to her eyes.

She dashed them away with an impatient hand and began to read, though she was forced to lay the letter aside on more than one occasion as her feelings threatened to overcome her.

As she had expected, her family's love reached out to her across the miles which separated them. Their affection flowed towards her from those few sheets of paper. How they rejoiced in her good fortune! Lord Rokeby had convinced them, even on short acquaintance, that he was worthy of her, and who, they asked, could be more deserving of his love?

Elinor smiled through her tears. No one would ever convince them that they were not biased in her favour. A tide of homesickness swept over her. Suddenly she longed to lay her present cares aside. In Derbyshire there were no luxuries, except for kindness, good-will and the warmth of tenderness. If she were asked to choose, it would be no hardship to give up all the gaieties of the London season in return for a home such as her own.

Yet it was but a dream. She might return to her family for a short time, but poverty would drive her away again to make her own way in the world. She would not be a charge on them. In their present circumstances, one more mouth to feed would mean disaster.

She lifted a hand to her eyes as if to shut out a dreadful vision. Her future must be bleak indeed. Her lips trembled as she thought of the letter she must write. It would end all their hopes for her. As yet she could not bring herself to set pen to paper. Perhaps it was deceitful, but she would give them another day or two of happiness.

What a coward she was, she thought wretchedly. A sterner character would have grasped the nettle at once, and set about the painful task. But how was she to explain her change of heart? She was still wrestling with the problem when she heard a tapping at her door. Dear God! Was she never to be left in peace?

Hester came towards her with a contrite look. She sensed at once that her company was unwelcome.

"I...I expect that you do not care to see me, Elinor," she faltered. "But won't you say that you forgive me? I cannot bear to think that we are no longer to be friends."

Elinor held out her arms. "There is nothing to forgive, my love. You must excuse me. It is just that I had a letter from my father...and...well...perhaps I feel a little homesick."

"It must be hard to be away from them." Hester sat by her feet. "How stupid I have been. I never think of you as being lonely. You always seem so...so..."

"Self-sufficient? Perhaps I have been too much so." Elinor shook her head as if to free it from unpleasant thoughts. "Enough of me. Now tell me, are you truly, truly happy?"

"I can't believe it!" Hester told her simply. "Am I really to be John's wife? It all seems like a dream. If I pinch myself, I shall wake up."

"Then you must take care not to pinch yourself," Elinor teased. "You will believe it when you are ordering your household and looking to your children."

Hester's eyes were filled with rapture. "I've loved him for so long, you know, but I never thought he'd look at me."

"Oh, I don't know about that... Some men have a curious longing to wed a monster of depravity." Elinor began to twinkle.

"Have I been depraved? Oh dear, I had not thought to be so..."

"Of course not, goose! John loves you because you are kind and gentle, and your interests are his own. My dear, I wish you all the happiness in the world. No two people could be better suited to each other."

"I wish that Lady Hartfield thought so," Hester told her wistfully. "She was very cross with me."

"Her ladyship was worried about you, Hester. Her anger stemmed partly from relief to find that you were safe. She sent her good wishes to both you and John, and she meant them sincerely."

"I will go to thank her—"

"No! At present she is resting. It may be best to speak to her this evening. Have you made your arrangements with Lord Rokeby?"

Hester brightened. "There is such a lot to do...before a marriage, I mean. Did you know that banns must be called...that is...if John does not get a special licence?"

"I had heard of both banns and a licence," Elinor said drily. "My dear, there is much to consider when you are deciding where to marry. John will wish, perhaps, to have his family to support him?"

"Oh, yes! Lord Rokeby has left it to us to decide whether we shall marry from here or from Merton Place. Either way, his parents must be there... Elinor, now I have a family like yours."

"So you have, my dearest, and they will love you as mine loves me." Her smile was tinged with sadness. Had things been different between herself and Rokeby, she too might have worn that inner glow which gave the girl beside her a radiance of her own.

Hester reached out to slide a confiding hand into hers.

"It is strange," she whispered softly. "Already the world looks different. I can't explain it, but even ordinary objects look beautiful. I feel as though I've just been born, and am seeing everything about me for the first time."

Elinor bent and kissed her. "Hold on to that special feeling, Hester. Not everyone is lucky enough to know it, even in a lifetime."

"You sound sad. Oh, Elinor, I didn't mean to hurt you. It will happen to you, you'll see." She hesitated.

"What is it, Hester?"

The girl buried her face in Elinor's skirt, and muttered a few words, but they were inaudible.

"What is troubling you?"

"I was just thinking...now that I am to be John's wife there will be no need for you—"

"To stay with you? Of course not!"

"I did not mean that," Hester muttered. Then her words came out in a rush. "You need not marry Lord Rokeby, need you?" She lifted a pleading face, and was startled by Elinor's sharp intake of breath.

When it came, the reply was uttered in a toneless voice.

"No, I need not," said Elinor.

"I'm so glad," Hester told her earnestly. "I know you said you loved him, but I knew that you could not. He's such a harsh, unfeeling man, and he would not be kind to you."

"Your beloved John thinks well of him." Irrationally, Elinor was spurred into a protest.

"John thinks well of everyone. He is the best of men—"

"Spare me a list of his perfections," Elinor cried sharply. "My dear, I am sorry, but I have the headache. Will you excuse me if I rest before we dine? I crave your pardon. I did not mean to snap at you."

As a subdued Hester stole away, Elinor threw herself upon her bed. Her nerves were at breaking-point. What was happening to her? She had been on the verge of snarling like a madwoman. Surely she could not be jealous of Hester's happiness? That would be unthinkable.

If it were true, it showed a want of character, a lack of generosity. It revealed an aspect of her nature which she did not care to examine too closely.

She lay on her bed dry-eyed, staring at the ceiling. She *did* wish happiness for Hester, but she prayed heaven that John Charlbury would be impatient to claim his bride. Then, her promise to Hester fulfilled, she would go away and put all thoughts of Rokeby from her mind.

Chapter Fourteen

Later that evening Elinor joined the others to find them deep in a discussion of the forthcoming nuptials. They broke off at her entrance, and John Charlbury came towards her.

"I have much to thank you for, Miss Temple." He raised her hand to his lips. "How beautiful you look tonight! You remind me of some sea-nymph, newly risen from the foam."

"A poetic thought, my dear John! Love has made you lyrical..." Rokeby's voice was soft, but Elinor detected an undertone of sarcasm. He, too, kissed her hand, and it took all her self-command not to drag it from his grasp. Even through the fabric of her glove she felt that his lips must burn her skin.

"But it is true." Hester gave her a fond look. "Lady Hartfield, don't you agree?"

"I do!" Her ladyship patted the seat beside her. "Elinor, come and sit by me." She subjected Elinor's gown to a critical look. "That misty gauze is exactly right for you, but I cannot decide if it is blue or green..."

"It is a turquoise shade, I believe. Ma'am, are you feeling better?"

"I am quite recovered. Did I not say that I was just a little tired? Enough of that, we have need of your counsel, my dear. Here is Marcus, insisting on a London wedding…"

"It will not do, old friend." Charlbury took the hand of his bride-to-be. "A quiet country service will suit us better. We have few friends in London, and my family must be there."

Hester glanced at him with gratitude. The thought of a crowded ceremony, in a fashionable London church, filled her with dread.

"Well, that is better than to wed by special licence," said her ladyship with a flash of her old spirit. "That would be a havey-cavey thing to do. I am surprised to hear that you considered it."

"Ma'am, it was to be a last resort." Charlbury gave her his enchanting smile. "I feared that in the end I must abduct my bride. Marcus offered to call me out, you know."

"Marcus has an unfortunate tendency to levity," her ladyship said severely. "It is high time that he controlled it."

Elinor stole a glance at Rokeby. He was smiling, but there was no amusement in his eyes. As if aware of her regard he looked at her, but she turned away.

"Well then, that is settled. Mr Charlbury, you may take me in to dinner." Lady Hartfield laid her hand upon his arm.

Escorted by Lord Rokeby, Elinor and Hester followed them in silence. As they took their places at the table Elinor resolved to exert herself. It was ridiculous to allow what should have been a celebration into a funeral wake.

She turned to John Charlbury. "When do you return to Kent?" she asked. "I expect you will have much to do."

"I don't quite know, Miss Temple. That must rest with you and Marcus, as you will wed before us, and I have promised to stand up with him."

Elinor thought she must be turned to stone. She heard a gasp of surprise from Hester.

"But, Elinor," the girl began. "Did you not tell me...?" She subsided at a warning look.

"We have changed our plans since we received your news," Rokeby announced smoothly. "I believe we shall now wait until the end of the Season. We cannot cope with two such ceremonies in the course of the next few weeks."

"We could make it a double wedding," Charlbury suggested happily. He was puzzled by the ensuing silence. "Oh, I see! I beg your pardon, Marcus. I was not thinking. A quiet wedding will not do for you. The world and his wife will come to wish you joy."

Lady Hartfield jumped into the breach. "You young men have no idea—" she sounded a little breathless "—announcements must be made, and bride clothes chosen..."

"I quite understand," Charlbury's brow cleared. "I hope that we have not put you about."

"Not at all." Elinor forced out the words through stiff lips. She could not go on.

"We are disposed to wait," Lord Rokeby assured him. "Elinor wishes to see her parents."

That much at least was true, but it was an ambiguous remark which failed to satisfy John Charlbury.

"I thought you had but just come from them," he said.

"I went alone to ask for Elinor's hand. Her family longs to see her." His words did not invite further comment, and Charlbury did not pursue the subject. He had begun to wonder if Marcus had not received the welcome for which he'd hoped.

"My place in Yorkshire is yours for the asking," Rokeby continued in a softer tone. "You will wish to take Hester away after you are married. It is kept fully staffed. You will be comfortable."

Charlbury looked at Hester's sparkling eyes. Then he turned to Rokeby in gratitude. "Thank you," he said simply. "It is a generous offer, and we'll be happy to accept. From there we might go on to Northumberland. I have an old aunt. She is too frail to make the journey into Kent, but she will want to wish us happy."

Elinor's eyes were fixed upon her plate. She felt as if she were upon the rack. The talk of her own marriage had been torture to her, now that all her hopes of happiness had vanished. Later, she could not have described the rest of the conversation at the dinner-table, and it was with a sigh of relief that she followed Lady Hartfield and Hester into the salon, leaving the men to their wine.

Her ladyship rang for the tea-tray.

"Elinor, will you pour?" she said.

Elinor was only too thankful to busy herself with the task. The evening had been a trial, but such trying situations promised to be her lot for the next few weeks. She glanced at her companions, but they were engaged in planning Hester's wardrobe. At least her ladyship appeared to be more in charity with the girl, and for that she must be grateful.

Hester's mind was only half on the discussion. Her eyes strayed constantly towards the door, and when

Charlbury appeared, accompanied by his lordship, she gave them a radiant smile.

"Hester, the night is fine. Mr Charlbury will wish to see the gardens." Lady Hartfield dismissed the lovers to a welcome tryst.

Rokeby sat down, but he was restless. At length he began to pace the room.

"Marcus, for heaven's sake! Pray take yourself off if you cannot be still. It makes me tired just to look at you."

"I beg your pardon, aunt. Pray excuse me if you will. I should send off the announcements to the papers." He bowed to both of them and left the room.

"Now then, my dear, this will not do, you know." Her ladyship's sharp eyes were intent upon Elinor's face. "Am I to understand that all is at an end between you?"

"We had hoped to keep it from you, ma'am."

"Then you must think me a fool. When Charlbury spoke of your coming marriage, I feared that you would faint."

Elinor did not reply.

"And you must not forget that I know my nephew very well," the older woman continued. "He is not the same man. Has your father refused his permission for Marcus to address you?"

"No, it is not that." Elinor's expression was bleak. "My family thought him charming."

"Clearly his charm has been wasted upon yourself. Oh, my dear, whatever he has done or said to you, will you not find it in your heart to forgive him? He loves you so."

"You are mistaken, ma'am. Things have been said which cannot be forgotten. Forgiveness is not enough. There is no trust between us."

"I see. My love, I am so sorry. I had such hopes for both of you." She was silent for some time, seeming almost to shrink within herself. "Elinor, what will you do?" she asked.

"I have promised to stay with Hester until she weds. Then I must find another post."

"Will you not make your home with me? I have felt for some time that I shall not wish to live alone again. You would be my friend, as well as my companion."

"How kind you are!" The tears sprang unbidden to Elinor's eyes. "But, Lady Hartfield, it would not do. I could not bear—"

"To see him constantly? Before you came, his visits were infrequent. We might arrange it so that you were not in his company."

Elinor shook her head.

"Well, promise me at least that you will think about it? You are overwrought, my dear. Perhaps if you paid a visit to your family?"

"They will be so sad for me." Elinor was weeping openly. "This news will hurt them so."

"Need you tell them yet? Why not go to bed and sleep on it? You are so tired, but you will feel better in the morning. Now give me a kiss before you go."

Elinor hurried away before the others could return. John and Hester would wonder at her reddened eyes, and above all, Rokeby must not see her weeping.

She would not sleep...she was convinced of it, but nature was too strong for her.

It was morning before she opened her eyes. A glance at the clock on the mantelshelf showed her that it was early, but the sun was already peeping through a gap in her drawn curtains.

Her sleep had not refreshed her, and the leaden feeling in her limbs persisted. She longed for a breath of air, and rising, she dressed quickly in her thinnest muslin gown. She met no one as she made her way down to the garden door.

How cool it was out of doors! She pressed her hands to her burning face. Within an hour or two the sticky heat of a summer's day would return, but meantime she was free to wander along the flagged path towards the fountain at the far end of the garden.

There she sat down upon the raised stone wall that surrounded the pool and dabbled her fingers in the water. A green frog stared at her from a lily pad, and in the depths she could see the flash of golden carp.

Then a shadow fell across the pool and she turned quickly to find Rokeby by her side. She was on her feet at once.

"No, don't run away!" He said curtly. "I wish to speak to you."

"We...we can have nothing to say to each other," she faltered. She would not look at him.

"On the contrary...I have much to say. My aunt tells me that you have refused the offer of a home with her."

"I am sorry that she found out...I mean..."

"She could scarce miss it, could she, Elinor? We have no gift for dissembling, you and I. John's remarks last night were less than fortunate, though he could not know it at the time."

Elinor said nothing.

"That is not the point I wished to make." Abstractedly his lordship tossed a pebble into the pool, watching the widening ripples as it broke the surface and sank into the depths. "What is your objection to this plan? You are fond of my aunt, as she is of you... It would seem to be a solution."

"Would it?" She turned to him then, her eyes ablaze. "My lord, you may not order my life for me. My future can be no concern of yours. I am sensible of her ladyship's generosity, but nothing would persuade me—"

"To risk yourself in my company? You need have no fear of that. When Hester is wed I intend to go abroad again to Europe. That is...if this peace with Napoleon should hold."

"And if not?"

"Why, then I shall offer my services to a grateful country."

"You would fight if the war should break out again?" Elinor's face grew pale.

"Other men will do so. Would you have me hide behind their valour?"

"But...but you might be killed!"

"Very possibly. That is not unknown in time of war, my dear Elinor." A cynical smile curved his lips. "It would be no great matter, I assure you, and then you would be rid of me for good."

"That is foolish talk," she cried sharply. "I have no wish...I mean...a broken engagement is no reason for you to throw your life away."

"How true!" His eyes flickered reflectively across her face. "Let us forget these morbid thoughts. The Treaty may hold and possibly it will not come to war, though I must doubt it. Napoleon, so I understand, is using these months of peace to good effect."

"He is preparing?"

"I believe so." He tossed another pebble into the pool. "Elinor, what will you do when you leave us?"

"I shall go home to Derbyshire for a while. It will give me time to look about me…"

"And then…another teaching post?" His voice sounded oddly harsh.

"If such is to be had," she told him lightly. "I enjoyed my work at Bath…" He could have no notion of the despair which filled her heart.

"I don't doubt it. You have qualities of courage and endurance which are rare. I could wish…" He stopped and rose to his feet. "The sun grows warm and your head is unprotected. Will you not come indoors?"

Elinor looked up at him, willing him to go on with what he had been about to say. What did he wish? His eyes were sad, and his expression tore at her heart. If only the events of that dreadful night had not occurred, or if the cruel words which had passed between them might be unsaid…

She bit her lip. Wishing would not change matters now. It was better that she knew him for what he was…a man capable of brutality. He could have no idea of how badly he had frightened her, else he would not have gone into Derbyshire to ask her father for her hand.

She walked ahead of him in silence and went up to her room. She had no wish to eat, but she made a dutiful appearance at the breakfast-table, to find herself alone with Hester.

"Lord Rokeby is gone out," Hester told her cheerfully. "Elinor, I think I like him better now. He has been very good…I mean about my marriage."

Elinor looked at her. Does she not know that she is treading on my heart? she thought in anguish. Nothing of that must show upon her face.

"Lord Rokeby is happy for both of you." Even to

herself her voice sounded unnaturally calm, but Hester did not notice.

The shy little creature who had been so sensitive to the feelings of others was now oblivious to everything but her love. She chattered on until John Charlbury was announced. Then her face lit up, and she flew into his arms.

Charlbury kissed her gently. Then he disengaged himself, though he kept her hand in his.

"I am come to take my leave of you, Miss Temple. Today I go to Kent."

"We shall miss you quite dreadfully, shan't we, Elinor?" Hester gave him an adoring look and raised his hand to her cheek. "I shall be miserable."

"No, puss, you will not. You will have much to do, and the time will fly. It is but four short weeks, and then we shall not part again."

"Must you go so soon?" Hester pleaded. "Lady Hartfield will wish to see you... Shall I tell her you are here?"

He smiled his assent and Hester hurried away.

Charlbury was silent for a moment. Then he sat by Elinor's side.

"I am sorry if I caused you pain last night," he said. "I did not know, you see, but Marcus has explained. This is distressing news and must have been the cause of much unhappiness."

"We did not intend to deceive you," Elinor murmured. "We kept up the pretence for Lady Hartfield's sake. She was not well..."

"And I gave the game away? She did not take it amiss, you know. I spoke to her last evening, when you had retired. The old can be surprisingly resilient. They see much in the course of a lifetime, and they learn to endure...and also to hope."

"She must not hope," Elinor told him quietly.

"As you do not?" A large hand covered her own. "Miss Temple, love is not so easily crushed. Who should know better than I? I might have sacrificed both Hester's happiness and my own for the sake of pride. I could not bear that the world should see me as a fortune-hunter."

"Who could think that of you?" Elinor managed a faint smile.

"Myself for one. She is so very young, and all the advantage is on my side."

"What nonsense! You are all that I could wish for her. Hester needs protection...and, above all, love. You will transform her life, and I wish you joy with all my heart."

Charlbury raised her hand to his lips. "What a friend you are!" he said unsteadily. "I see why Hester is devoted to you, but so is Marcus, believe me."

"Please...I wish you would not speak of him." Her voice was not quite under her control.

"I must, my dear. He too is my friend. Won't you reconsider? Marcus is not perfect. He would be the first to admit it. He has a hasty temper, and sometimes it leads him beyond what is acceptable, but then it is over like a summer storm."

"Leaving wreckage in its wake? Oh, I know that you mean well, but..."

She was spared the need for further argument, and fell silent as Hester came to join them.

"Her ladyship is still abed. She sends her compliments, John. You are to give her love to your mother, and—"

"I will leave you to your farewells." Elinor gave

him her hand. "May I too send my regards to your family?"

"Thank you. There is one more thing, Miss Temple. Should you think of visiting your family...after the wedding, I mean, we should be happy to have your company on our way into Yorkshire. Is that not so, Hester?"

"I should like it above anything," Hester agreed earnestly. "Do say that you'll come with us."

"Would you have me play gooseberry?" Elinor smiled in spite of herself. "I should be *de trop*. To quote the old saw there are occasions when 'Two is company but three is none'."

She shook her head at their protestations, but they would not let her go until she had promised to consider travelling with them.

Hester returned to the subject later that day.

"I shall miss you after I am wed," she said wistfully. "And Derbyshire, you know, is on our way to Yorkshire...at least, it would be only a little out of the way, and I should like to meet your family. You've told me so much about them."

"You might call on your way home. And John, you know, will wish for your undivided attention."

"He shall have it...for the rest of our lives...but I do wish..."

"Well, there is time enough to decide," Elinor told her briskly. "At present we are neglecting Lady Hartfield, and I know she wishes to speak to you."

They found her ladyship at her desk, absorbed in making lists. She looked up as they entered.

"There you are, my dears. Hester, we must consider your bride-clothes without delay."

"Ma'am, shall I need more? We seem to have bought so much..."

"Foolish child! Your present wardrobe can form but a small part of your trousseau. And what of the ceremony itself? The choice of a bridal-gown is not to be lightly undertaken."

Hester was quick to agree. "Though, ma'am, other than that...well...we are to live in the country, you know. John says that we are to have the Dower House on his father's estate."

"You will not lead a hermit-like existence, Hester." There was a note of exasperation in her ladyship's voice. "A bride is asked everywhere, and there is your honeymoon to be considered. Your gowns are well enough for the summer season, but autumn will soon be upon us."

Hester subsided, though she threw a despairing glance at Elinor, knowing well enough that the next few weeks were likely to be hectic.

She was not mistaken. The announcement of her coming nuptials brought a flood of invitations from milliners, mantua-makers and purveyors of boots and shoes, begging her to inspect their stock.

Two days later Elinor found her gazing at an enormous pile of cards and letters.

"I'd like to throw them all away," she told Elinor ruefully. "But some are letters from her ladyship's acquaintance, inviting us to various functions." She picked up a gilt-edged card, and placed it on the mantelshelf. "This one is from Lord Dacre."

Elinor felt a spurt of anger. "That, at least, is unlikely to be accepted. Have you shown it to your guardian?"

"I have not seen Lord Rokeby. I expect that he is busy. He has returned to his own house, you know."

Elinor nodded. Rokeby had kept his word, but whether or not it was to persuade her to make her home with Lady Hartfield she could not guess. It was strange, but without him life had lost all its savour. She no longer looked for his tall figure whenever she entered a room, but how she missed the way his eyes lit up at her appearance. That swarthy face had a curious way of softening when he looked at her, even as his eyes devoured her.

In his company life had an edge to it…a sense of excitement. Without him it was bleak indeed.

"Elinor, look at this!" Hester held up another card. "It is from a tradesman, but it is so interesting."

"I wonder why it has been sent to you? These goods are bespoke for gentlemen…"

"I know, but I must have a wedding gift for John, and I don't know any other shops." She looked at the address. "Could we find it, do you think?"

Elinor examined the card. "It is somewhere between St James's street and Piccadilly, I believe. The finest shops for men are in that area, but, Hester, no lady may walk along St James's street. It isn't done. You will not persuade her ladyship to agree to such an expedition."

"Must we tell her? We need not walk, you know. If the carriage were to drop us at the door and wait for us, the purchase would not take long…"

Elinor frowned. "I think not. I don't like it, Hester. We had best forget it. Lady Hartfield will know of somewhere else."

Hester's face fell, but she accepted the decision with good grace, though it was not possible to ask her ladyship's advice that morning. Their hostess was much preoccupied with answering letters and adding to her list of things which must be done before the wedding. She sent word that they were to drive in the park without her.

Time and again their carriage was stopped as members of the *ton* came up to offer their good wishes. Elinor was aware of a few dark looks from fond mammas whose hopes of a wealthy heiress for their sons had just been dashed, but these were balanced by the obvious relief of those whose daughters had not yet received an offer. Hester was to marry an unknown, which left more glittering prizes still within their grasp.

As they left the park and drove down Piccadilly, Hester clutched at Elinor's arm.

"There is the street," she cried excitedly. "I recognise the name. May we not stop just for a moment?" She called to the coachman.

"Hester, please!" Elinor made a vain attempt to catch at her sleeve, but she was too late. Hester was out of the carriage, and was already disappearing down the narrow street.

"Stay here! We shall not be above a moment." Elinor ignored the startled look upon the coachman's face, and hurried in pursuit.

Hester was well ahead of her, gazing intently at the names above the shops. Then she vanished round a corner.

Elinor began to run. The street was dark and noisome, and in the summer heat the foul smell from the gutters was overpowering.

As she turned the corner she saw Hester standing irresolute on the pavement.

"We must go back," she cried. "We have come far from Piccadilly. Hester, this is folly. Let us return at once."

"I can't find it," Hester said. "It must be here...we are almost at the end of this lane."

"Can I help you, miss?"

Both girls turned to face a rough-looking man in a muffler. He seemed to have materialised from nowhere. His smile did nothing to reassure them as it revealed a mouthful of broken teeth. From his flattened nose and mighty thews Elinor guessed him to be an ex-pugilist.

"No, thank you!" she said sharply.

"He might know," Hester protested. "We are looking for Cleggs."

"Bless you, miss, you're almost on the doorstep. There it is...across the street."

Hester darted away, leaving Elinor with no choice but to follow her. She gave no further thought to the man who had accosted them, and then was startled to find that he was behind her as she entered the shop.

A warning bell rang in her head. There was something wrong. She turned to find the pugilist leaning against the door. He was no longer smiling.

Hester looked perplexed. "This can't be the place," she murmured. "There is nothing here..."

The interior was very dark, but as Elinor looked about her she realised that the room was empty. It was also thick with dust, and showed no signs of occupation.

"Let us go at once." She turned towards the door, but found her way barred. Arms folded across his breast the man stared down at her.

"Get out of my way," she cried. "Hester, this is a trap."

Then a cloth was thrown about her head, muffling her screams. She fought and kicked, but all to no avail. She was picked up without ceremony and carried into an inner room. Almost immediately she heard a bolt drawn back.

"All clear?" her captor asked.

"Aye! Let's get these hellcats into the coach."

She heard the sound of nailed boots on cobbles, and then she was flung on to a leather seat. Elinor fought to free her head from the folds of cloth, but her captor held her close.

"You won't see nothing, miss. Nor will folks see you. The blinds is drawn. Be still now, or you'll do yourself an injury."

Elinor stopped struggling. The man was right. Her puny efforts were no match for his strength, and she would need all her own to face what lay ahead.

She was still dazed by the speed of the attack. To be abducted in broad daylight? It did not seem possible. She could not have imagined it in her wildest dreams.

Her mind was racing. What had these men in mind? She was certain that they were not the principals. She had seen only one of them, and briefly, but it was enough to tell her that he could not have been the instigator of such a careful plan.

And careful it had been. She and Hester had been lured into that narrow side-street in the cleverest way. Someone had taken pains with that apparently innocent advertisement, couching it in terms which could not fail to appeal to an inexperienced girl.

Suddenly Elinor was aware that the coach had stopped. Their journey had not taken more than a few moments. It was clear that they were still in central London. She lay inert as she was lifted from the coach and carried across a cobbled courtyard. Her captor then mounted a staircase, opened a door, and laid her upon a couch. Then the enveloping cloth was whisked from about her head.

"Welcome, Miss Temple!" The voice was only too familiar. She raised her head to find Lord Dacre standing by the door.

Chapter Fifteen

"What is the meaning of this outrage?" Elinor asked in icy tones. "How dare you treat us so?"

"Spare me your display of temper. You had best see to the girl…" His face was impassive as he gestured towards Hester, who lay huddled in a chair. Her eyes were closed, and Elinor guessed that she had fainted.

"Get me some water," she snapped out. "Have you no pity for her?"

"Not much. She is a fool, Miss Temple, but then, I was able to rely upon that. You, I believe, are made of sterner stuff, but we shall see."

Elinor ignored him as she sprinkled a few drops of water on Hester's face. After a few moments the blue eyes opened, and Hester struggled to sit upright.

"What has happened?" she whispered. "Those awful men…are they gone?" Her glance rested upon Lord Dacre. "Did you save us, sir? I can't think how you found us…"

"Save your thanks, my dear Hester. We were brought here on Lord Dacre's orders. Is that not so, my lord?"

Dacre bowed. "My apologies, Hester. You were roughly handled, but there was no help for it. I doubted that you would accept a formal invitation to my home."

"I don't understand." Bewildered, Hester looked from one face to the other. "Why are we here?"

"There is a simple explanation, my dear. I fear you have been misled into an unfortunate betrothal. Did you not assure me that you wished to marry Tobias?"

"My lord, I was mistaken... I agreed only when you threatened to harm Elinor and Lord Rokeby. I am sorry. I have no wish to hurt Tobias, but my heart is given elsewhere."

"May I be allowed to hope that you may change your mind?" Dacre's eyes had almost disappeared in the folds of flesh surrounding them.

"Never!" Hester cried stoutly. "I love John Charlbury and I intend to marry him."

"Really? You are fond of your friend, I think." With a speed surprising in so large a man, his hand flashed out to grasp Elinor's hair. He twisted her curls around his fingers and pulled hard. The pain brought tears to Elinor's eyes, but she did not speak.

"Please don't!" Hester cried in anguish. "If it is the money I will give you all I have."

"I doubt if your guardian will agree to that." Dacre dragged Elinor to her feet. "I'm afraid that it must be marriage to Tobias." He stroked Elinor's hair, then his hand caressed her neck, and swept down to her bosom. The red face was very close to hers, and Elinor could smell the wine upon his breath. He bent his head to find her lips, and she began to struggle.

"I am not surprised that Rokeby finds you irresistible," he murmured thickly. "Will he want damaged goods, I wonder?"

"Let her go!" Suddenly Hester was on her feet, beating vainly at his shoulders. He swept her aside as if she were a fly.

The force of his blow sent Hester spinning. She landed heavily in one corner of the room, twisting her ankle as she did so.

Dacre forced Elinor back against the cushions on the couch. The powerful hands reached out to unfasten the ribbons of her gown. Then he slid it from her shoulders, feasting his eyes upon her milky skin.

"No! Please stop!" Hester took a painful step towards him.

"It is up to you, my dear. A word of consent, and your friend will remain unravished. Otherwise, you may watch as I deflower her. You are a virgin, are you not, Miss Temple?"

Elinor spat full in his face. It was a mistake. He tore the last shreds of her gown away and threw himself upon her. She was suffocating, helpless beneath his bulk. Then she heard a thread-like voice.

"I will marry Tobias," Hester said.

Dacre was not listening. His face was suffused with passion and he was breathing hard. A large vein beat hard in his temple, and for a heart-stopping moment Elinor believed that nothing could deter him from his purpose.

Hester plucked wildly at his shoulder. "Stop!" she cried again. "Do you not hear me? I've agreed to marry Tobias."

His eyes blinded with lust, the great bull-like head turned at last in her direction.

"Let Elinor go," she shouted. "That is my condition."

With a grunt Dacre heaved himself to his feet, and began to rearrange his clothing.

"You shall tell Tobias," he ground out. "And no tricks, mind. The boy must believe you. I want no trouble with his delicate ideas of honour."

Elinor lay as he had left her. Her eyes were closed, but she was thinking fast. They must play for time. By now the coachman must have given the alarm, unless he imagined that they had been so distracted by their shopping that they had forgot their promise to return at once.

Dacre pulled at the bell-rope, but he did not admit his servant to the room.

"Send my son to me," he ordered through the half-opened door. Then he walked over to where Elinor lay dishevelled on the couch. "Cover yourself," he snapped. "If you are wise, you'll keep a still tongue in your head. Remember that I can hold you here as long as I care to do so."

"But you promised to let her go." Hester raised a tear-stained face to his.

"That must depend on your behaviour, my dear Hester. Now I think I hear Tobias...it is up to you."

As the door opened he moved to stand in front of Elinor, blocking her from his son's view.

"Good news, my boy!" he announced in a jovial tone. "Here is Hester come back to us. She has been over-persuaded by her so-called friends, I fear, but now she has something to say to you."

Tobias hesitated, looking at Hester's wan face. "You look strangely, Miss Winton. Is something wrong?"

"I...I have been stupid enough to turn my ankle..." Hester whispered. "It is very painful."

"I will get help. It should be bound up."

"Stay where you are, Tobias, and listen to what Hester has to say to you. She is now quite sure that she wishes to become your wife."

"Can it be true?" The boy's face lit up. "Oh, Hester, tell me that it is what you wish—"

"Of course she does not wish it." Elinor struggled painfully to her feet. "Hester has agreed because your father threatened to harm me. Look at my gown!"

"I warned you!" With cat-like ferocity, Lord Dacre turned and struck her a fearful blow across the face. Elinor fell unconscious at his feet.

She returned to consciousness to find herself in semi-darkness. Her head was pounding, and she could taste the saltiness of blood upon her lips. Gingerly she lifted a hand to discover the source of the wound, and found that she had a deep cut on her brow. She must have struck something when she fell.

Beside her Hester was sobbing quietly, and Elinor reached out towards her.

"Where are we?" she murmured.

"He has locked us in a cellar. Oh, Elinor, I thought that he had killed you."

"Where is Lord Dacre now?"

"I don't know. Tobias ran from the house and his father followed him."

"Then we are saved. Tobias will go to Rokeby…"

"He may not. He is terrified of his father."

"You misjudge him, Hester. Tobias is a man of honour." Elinor spoke with a confidence she was far from feeling.

Tobias had good reason to fear Lord Dacre yet, even had he resolved upon defiance, would he have the courage to seek out Rokeby and tell him the full story? If so, he would most certainly sign his father's death warrant.

"We shall not have long to wait," she comforted. "Marcus will find us..."

"It is all my fault," Hester said dully. "I should have listened to you."

"Don't blame yourself. Lord Dacre is a ruthless man. If one plan had failed, he would have found another."

"We shall never be safe from him," Hester wailed.

"Of course we shall. You will marry your John and go to live in Kent. Then you will forget all this."

"I wish that John were here in London..." It was a pitiful whisper. "Perhaps I shall not see him again."

"You will. I promise you." Elinor squeezed her hand. "Have you looked about you, Hester? There may be some way of escape...?"

Hester shook her head.

"Then let us do so now." Still dizzy from the blow to her head Elinor struggled to her feet. "There may be a chute for coal, or even a window. These cellars must extend below the house."

They found the window in the adjoining passageway. It was high on the wall and very small.

"Could you squeeze through there?" Elinor asked.

"Perhaps, but how are we to reach it?"

"There may be some bricks, or boxes...even old furniture...anything which will bear our weight."

In the third of the cellars they found a wooden packing-case.

"Help me to drag it under the window," Elinor

urged. "Quickly...we do not know when Dacre will return."

The box was large and heavy, but they tugged it into place at last. Elinor helped Hester up, but she could not reach the window.

"Let me try." Elinor took her place and found herself on a level with the glass. She pushed at the dusty frame with all her strength, but she could not move it.

"It's stuck," she cried in despair. "I doubt if it's been opened since the house was built. Find something heavy, Hester...some tool...a piece of wood...I'll try to force it open."

"Get down," Hester cried in terror. "Someone is coming!"

The creak of the cellar door was loud as the bolts were drawn back. Both girls saw the flicker of a lantern.

"Pretend to be unconscious," Hester whispered urgently. "If it is Lord Dacre he may not hurt you further."

It must be Dacre, Elinor thought in despair. It was too soon for Rokeby to have found them. She closed her eyes as she heard the sound of feet upon the steps. Then a large hand closed about her chin, moving her head from side to side.

"I must have hit her harder than I thought. A pity I did not break her neck." Dacre brought his ear to Elinor's mouth. "She's still breathing... Make haste there...we must get them away. That son of mine is fool enough to fetch the Bow Street Runners."

Once again Elinor found herself enveloped in a blanket. Through the muffling folds she heard Hester's voice rising to a shriek.

"Let her go," she screamed. "I gave you my word. Is that not enough?"

"Not now, my dear. Tobias does not believe you. His finer feelings are offended."

"Whose fault is that?" Had you not struck Elinor in that brutal way, I might have persuaded him."

"I doubt it. What could you have said? That your friend had torn her own gown to give me the lie? What an innocent you are! Enough of this. Will you walk to the coach or must we carry you?"

"You shall not touch me," Hester said with dignity. "What do you intend to do with us?"

"Well now, I haven't quite decided. Tobias, alas, is lost to you, but there are other possibilities. Rokeby may be persuaded to pay a handsome price for your return...that is, if you are still in your virgin state."

"And Elinor?"

"That is another matter. I have an old score to settle with your guardian. He may keep his paramour...when I have done with her. Will soiled goods hold the same appeal, I wonder?"

The blood in Elinor's veins turned to ice. The man was a monster. She heard a cry as Hester flew at him, but it was quickly followed by a whimper of pain.

"Take care, my girl," Dacre warned. "Try that again and you will get the beating of your life."

Elinor was lifted to her feet and thrown like a sack across a pair of brawny shoulders. As the man ascended the cellar steps, she gave way to despair.

Dacre, she guessed, intended to spirit them away from London to some quiet hideaway and, once he did so, Marcus could have no hope of finding them.

Then her captor stopped, and she felt him stiffen.

"Stay exactly where you are," a familiar voice

advised. "You will place that lady, very gently, in the chair beside you. Then you will remove the blanket from her head."

With her heart in her eyes, Elinor looked up into Rokeby's face. His quick glance took in her blood-stained appearance, and his fingers tightened upon the pistol in his hand. His expression terrified her. At that moment he looked capable of murder.

"Tobias, you may call in the Runners." His voice was not his own and he did not look round as the Bow Street men led Dacre's bully-boys away. His eyes were fixed upon Lord Dacre's face, and there was no mistaking his intent.

"Marcus, please don't!" Elinor spoke in little more than a whisper. "Let him be tried in a court of law."

He did not seem to have heard her.

"Elinor, can you walk?" he asked quietly.

"I...I think so...but I beg of you..."

"Take Hester into another room. Tobias will go with you."

The boy started towards him with a plea for his father's life upon his lips, but he stopped at Rokeby's quick command.

"Back! I have no wish to harm you, but a single shot will break your leg. Elinor, you will do as I say."

Elinor stood up, knowing that further argument was useless. She reached out a hand to Hester, and then she was seized from behind.

"Fire away!" Dacre was holding her as a shield before him. "At this range you cannot miss." He began to sidle across the hall to the outer courtyard, dragging Elinor with him. She began to struggle wildly, but he held her fast. She bent her head and bit down into his wrist. She heard a curse, but he did not release her.

Then his grip seemed to slacken, and she heard a choking sound. She spun round to find that he was clutching at his upper arm. Then his hand moved to his breast, and his eyes began to roll. She could not understand it. Marcus could not have fired. There had been no sound of a shot.

She gazed in horror at Lord Dacre. A little foam was coming from his lips and his purple face was hideously contorted.

Marcus seized her arm and pulled her away. Then he was on his knees beside the stricken man.

"A seizure," he said briefly. He turned to Tobias. "You had best fetch the surgeon."

Even as he spoke the stertorous breathing stopped.

"Too late, I fear. He is gone... Tobias, I am sorry..."

The boy blinked away a tear. "It is for the best, my lord. I could not have watched you kill him, nor could I have borne to see him standing trial..."

Elinor found that her legs would not support her. She sank into a chair, but Hester had walked towards Tobias.

"Try not to think ill of him," she said. "He was your father, after all, and circumstances were against him."

"You have forgiven him?" Tobias looked at her in disbelief.

"I believe I shall do so in time, and so will Elinor."

"You are generous." Tobias raised her hand to his lips. "This is no sight for you. Allow me to take you to the salon. Miss Temple?"

Elinor was stiff with shock. To be swept from the

face of the earth in a few moments? It was a solemn thought. She stumbled towards Rokeby.

"Go with them." he said gently. "I will see to matters here."

She could only obey. Averting her eyes from the still figure on the ground, she followed the others out of the room.

Tobias seemed to have grown in stature. He was quick to summon the servants to bring wine, and was solicitous for their comfort.

"You will wish to return to Berkeley Square as soon as possible, I imagine," he told them. "But first the housekeeper shall show you to a room where you may wash."

Bor the first time Elinor became aware of the spectacle she must present. Her gown was rent in several places, and not only was it soiled from her sojourn in the cellar, but it bore the traces of bloodstains. The wound above her eye had closed, but even so, she could not show herself in public in her present condition.

Sadly, it was impossible to hide all traces of her ordeal. She had hoped to avoid Lady Hartfield at least until she had changed her gown, but at the sound of their carriage her ladyship had rushed into the hall.

"My dears!" The tears were rolling down the older woman's face. "Marcus promised that he would bring you back to me."

"We are quite safe." Elinor managed a crooked smile. "Ma'am, no harm has come to us."

"And Dacre?"

"He is dead." The curt reply brought horror to lady Hartfield's eyes.

"Oh, Marcus, you did not...?"

"No, I did not kill him, though I meant to. Dacre suffered a seizure."

"Divine retribution?"

"Possibly! Aunt, will you excuse me? I must go back to Tobias. The lad has borne up well, but he is much in need of support."

"Then go to him. Elinor and Hester are exhausted. You may see them in the morning."

Marcus took Elinor's hand. Then he looked deep into her eyes. "Until tomorrow?" It was at once a question and a promise, but she did not look away. Suddenly she felt breathless as the darkness of that swarthy countenance was lit by an inner glow. His lips rested lightly on her fingers, and then he bowed and left them.

Elinor looked at Lady Hartfield. She had expected to find the older woman prostrate with anxiety, but her ladyship's face was unaccountably serene. She had neither questioned Elinor and Hester, nor heaped reproaches upon their heads. There was even the trace of a smile about her mouth. It was a mystery which Elinor felt much too tired to solve.

Summoning the last of her strength, she made her way to her room. There, still swaying with exhaustion, she allowed herself to be stripped of her soiled and tattered garments, bathed in scented water, and helped into a clean bedrobe. As her head touched her pillow she fell into a deep sleep.

It was after noon on the following day when she awoke, and with returning consciousness came an overwhelming surge of joy. Hester was safe, but there was something more. She could remember little of the journey back to Berkeley Square after their ordeal. She had a vague recollection of being carried to Rokeby's coach. His arms had closed about her as if he would never let her go, but no words of love had passed between them. None were needed. Now she was sure of her love for him, and his for her.

She longed to see his beloved face, but it was Lady Hartfield who came to her.

"Are you feeling better, Elinor?" she asked. "Your head? We thought at first that the wound must needs be sewn together, but after the blood was washed away it did not seem so deep."

"My flesh heals quickly, ma'am." Elinor reached up a hand to explore the tender place. "I fear it will leave a scar."

"Your hair will hide it, my love, but I believe that you should rest today…"

"And Hester? How is she?"

"Still sleeping… She was badly shocked, you know. I don't think it wise to wake her yet."

Elinor's eyes met hers. "Ma'am, you must wonder at the events of yesterday. I should explain…"

"There is no need. Marcus has told me the whole. He questioned the men who took you and learned how Dacre planned to spirit you away."

"His wickedness was repaid in full," Elinor told her in a low voice. "I shall never forget his face as he fell to the ground."

"You must try to put it from your mind. The memory will fade in time, and, my dear, you will admit that his sudden death was for the best."

"I suppose so. Marcus was about to kill him… Lady Hartfield, if you please, I should like to see his lordship." A delicate flush of colour rose to her cheeks. "I feel quite well. With your permission I shall dress and come downstairs."

"There is no immediate hurry," her ladyship ob-

served calmly. "Marcus was here at first light to enquire about you, but I sent him about his business.
He will return in time to dine with us."

"Oh, I see!" Elinor's eyes were upon the coverlet.
"I wished to thank him, and...and..."

Lady Hartfield began to smile, but she did not pursue the subject. "Let me send a tray to you," she
said. "You may dress later, at your leisure."

For the first time in weeks, Elinor found that she
was ravenously hungry. Eagerly she devoured a dish
of asparagus tips accompanied by a sauce which was
known only to Lady Hartfield's chef. It was followed
by an omelette filled with mushrooms. Chicken
breasts were to follow, but by this time her appetite
was flagging. She refused them in favour of a com-
pôte of summer fruits, the whole accompanied by a
glass of chilled white wine.

As the tray was removed, Elinor stretched luxu-
riously. Now all that need concern her was a choice
of gown. How frivolous she had become. Must it be
the sea-green gauze or the pale blue embroidered
muslin? She settled at last upon a bergère gown in
white, which fitted her to perfection. The design was
charming, and it became her well.

As the maid brushed her hair she studied her own
face in the mirror. She was still pale, but the straying
curls upon her brow had served to conceal the ugly
wound. She had to admit, even to herself, that her
recent ordeal had left few traces. She threw a lacy
shawl about her shoulders and gathered up her reticule, striving to ignore the odd little sensation of excitement in the pit of her stomach.

Rather to her surprise there were no signs of life
within the household as she made her way downstairs. Even the servants seemed to have disappeared.

She wandered from the salon to the study, but all the rooms were empty. The day was warm. Her ladyship must be resting, she decided. It was disappointing. She felt invigorated, longing to share her feeling of exultation with another. Her heart told her who that must be.

She made her way into the garden. As she walked along the path to the fountain her skirts brushed against the low hedge of lavender which formed an edging. The scent was mingled with that of the white lilies which stood in regal beauty in their pots. Beneath it all she detected the perfume of mignonette.

She sank down upon the wall beside the fountain. The stone was still warm from the heat of the summer sun. Elinor dipped her fingers in the pool as she dreamt of her love. They had wasted so much time in misunderstandings. If only that time might be restored to them.

"Elinor!"

Startled, she looked up to find Marcus standing by her side. She had been too lost in thought to notice his approach. Now his tender smile lured her heart from her breast, and blindly she reached out to him.

Suddenly he was on his knees before her, showering kisses upon her hands.

"Is it true?" he murmured. "I had scarce dared to hope, but yesterday, when all was over and I brought you home, I sensed the bonds of love between us. Tell me I was not mistaken…"

For answer she bent forward and rested her cheek against his dark head. "Could you doubt it?" she asked in a whisper.

Then she was in his arms, and his lips found hers. She yielded to his kiss without reserve, unfolding like a flower beneath the sun. Her very soul went out to him, powerless to resist his passionate embrace. When he released her, she was breathless.

Marcus looked deep into her eyes, and his expression was one of wonder.

"My dearest love! My heart! I have been a fool. I don't deserve that you should care for me."

"But I do!" Elinor found her voice at last. "I tried to hide my feelings even from myself. I would not trust my heart."

"Nor mine," he told her ruefully. "Confess it. You believed me when I said that our marriage was to be for Hester's sake alone."

"You did not say you loved me," she said in a small voice. Her eyes were fixed upon the ground.

"Look at me!" he commanded. "Must I convince you further?" He made as if to seek her lips again, but, laughing, she protested.

"Marcus...we are in full view of the house. Someone will see us."

"Let them! May I not salute my promised bride? Oh, my dear, I have loved you from the moment of our first meeting, but you gave me no encouragement. I was desperate, knowing how you despised me..."

"I...I changed my mind quite soon, my lord."

"You did not tell me so, and I should not have guessed. With Dacre's threats, I saw the chance to offer you a bargain. I must have been mad, but it seemed to be my only chance of winning you. I knew you did not love me, but I could not bear to lose you."

Elinor assumed a stern expression. "And how were you to go on, sir, with a wife who hated you so much?"

"I don't know." Marcus ran his fingers through his hair. "But you had refused me once. I could not take the risk again. I hoped that in time, perhaps, you might come to think more kindly of me when you were my wife."

"Marcus! When did I refuse to marry you?"

"Have you forgotten so soon? It was the night when Talworth overheard our conversation."

"I...I misunderstood you." Elinor felt her face grow warm. "I thought you intended...something other than marriage."

"Indeed!" His eyes began to twinkle. "So you were to be a victim of my ravening lust? It is a tempting thought, my darling, but there is more to my love than a wish to have you in my bed. You must believe me."

"I do." She hid her face against his coat. "Oh, Marcus, I had not believed such happiness could exist."

There was but one answer to that. He kissed her so fiercely that her head began to spin. She clung to him with a passion that matched his own until at last he released her.

"Will you tempt me into folly?" he said unsteadily. "Come, my lovely witch, let us share our joy with my aunt and Hester. I am becoming importunate."

He reached out gently to brush the hair back from her brow, revealing the unhealed scar.

"I would that I could have spared you that," he murmured. "Does it trouble you still?"

Elinor shook her head. "I fear I shall always bear the mark though," she admitted. "It is a disfigurement."

"Not in my eyes." He rested his lips close to the

injury. "It will remind us of the day we found each other at last. Elinor, how soon shall we be wed? I am not a patient man…"

"Do I not know it?" she teased. "You must consider your high state, my lord. The ceremony must befit your rank. I doubt that it can be arranged before next year."

He stared at her in horror. "You cannot mean it? Is that what you wish?"

She was laughing as she hurried away from him, but he caught her before she had taken more than a few paces.

"Elinor, tell me the truth. Do you wish to celebrate our marriage here in London? I cannot rob you of your heart's desire, but I had hoped…'

"You have other plans, my lord?" Her expression was demure as she stood before him with lowered eyelids.

Marcus hesitated. "John mentioned a double wedding down at Merton…"

"Yes? Shall you prefer that, sir?"

He gave her a suspicious look. Then he slipped a hand beneath her chin and raised her head. "Cruel creature. You are laughing at me." He reached into his pocket and brought out a piece of paper, which he handed to her with a grin.

"A special licence? Marcus, when did you…?"

"This morning, my dear love. If you wish it, we may be wed today." He took her in his arms again, and made as if to seek her lips. "Will you agree?" he murmured.

"But it is too soon. Your aunt—?" The rest of her protest was lost as he gathered her to his breast. His mouth came down on hers, and she was lost to the world about them.

Then he took her hand and led her into the house. A look at their glowing faces told Lady Hartfield all that she had hoped to hear. Her eyes sparkled with unshed tears as she held out her arms to Elinor.

"You have all my good wishes for your future happiness, my dears." She felt about her for a hand-kerchief, and then she blew her nose. "Marcus, I congratulate you. You are a lucky man to have won Elinor for your bride."

"I know it, my dear." Marcus bent down and kissed her. "Aunt, we are to be wed today. I have the licence..."

A shriek of protest drowned his words. "Are you quite mad? Elinor, you have not allowed my nephew to persuade you into such a havey-cavey thing? Your parents will wish to see you wed—I cannot counte-nance such folly. There can be no reason for this unseemly haste."

Her ladyship might have offered a challenge. Beside her Elinor felt her lover tense. She glanced up at him to see that the firm, full-lipped mouth had hardened.

"We cannot marry today," she said quickly. "Marcus, you have forgot the time. It is evening. We should be too late."

There was a long silence. Then he smiled, and it was like sunlight breaking through the clouds.

"You are right, my darling. Aunt, you must for-give me. Am I quite sunk beneath reproach? I cannot yet believe in my good fortune. Suppose that Elinor should change her mind?"

The two women exchanged a look. Then Lady Hartfield spoke.

"Let us go into dinner," she said, half in amuse-ment and half in exasperation. "Otherwise, Marcus, you will provoke me into banishing you from my table. Have you no eyes, man? Look at Elinor! Does she seem about to cast you off?"

Obediently her erring nephew gazed at his love. Her heart was in her tender expression, and he could not doubt her further.

"Let us have no more of such nonsense," her ladyship said briskly. "Here is Hester. You shall tell her your good news."

"Hester, you will be surprised with what I have to say," Elinor began hesitantly. "Marcus and I intend to marry."

Hester beamed upon her. "I am not in the least surprised," she said. "It is I who have been blind. Oh, Elinor, I am so happy for you, and you too, my lord."

"But, Hester...?" Elinor looked at her friend in wonder. "You would not believe me when I told you of my love."

"John made me see that I was wrong...and her ladyship too. Are we to have a double wedding after all?"

Elinor looked at Marcus, and then at Lady Hartfield.

"I should like that above anything," she said at last.

"But, my dear, it is a bare three weeks away," her ladyship protested. "How can we possibly make the arrangements? Elinor must buy her bride-clothes, and..."

"She looks like a bride already," Marcus announced to the company at large. "Whatever she wore, she could not look lovelier than at this moment... My love, three weeks will seem like an eternity. Will you keep me waiting longer?"

Elinor blushed. "Let us agree to the double wedding down at Merton," she said firmly. "Your ladyship, I do not wish to disappoint you, but Marcus and I...well, we have no wish for an elaborate ceremony. Three weeks will be long enough to enable my parents to attend...and it must please the tenantry..."

"That is thoughtful of you, Elinor. I suppose I must agree. Marcus?"

"It shall be as you wish." His eyes were hungry as he looked at Elinor, but he made no further demur.

"Give us but a week or so. Then we shall go to Merton. You will write to Elinor's parents?" Her ladyship was clearly abstracted as she nibbled at an oyster patty. Her mind was elsewhere as she considered the serious matter of Elinor's trousseau.

Elinor herself was lost in a daze of happiness as she was borne to mantua-makers and milliners. Lace-trimmed underclothes were ordered by the dozen, until she was moved to protest.

"We shall visit London again, I make no doubt," she told Lady Hartfield shyly. "Ma'am, there is sufficient..."

"Nonsense, Elinor! You can have no idea! From now on you will have a place in society to consider...that is...unless my nephew intends to keep you hidden in the country."

"He has not said so, ma'am."

"I should not put it past him. Now, my dear, what do you think of this lilac silk? It has a demi-train, and the violet ribbons are a charming contrast." She looked at Elinor's face and sighed. "The Lord preserve me from young lovers! You have not understood a word."

Recalled to herself, Elinor tried to apply attention, but her heart was with her love. What did it matter what she wore? Marcus did not care. He longed, as she did, for the day when they were one.

It came at last, though later her memories were but a blur. As she walked towards him on her father's arm, she heard the voices raised in reverent song within the village church, but her recollection was only of his beloved face as he stood still and straight, waiting to claim her for his own.

Later, well-wishers came and went, and the feasting continued long into the evening. Beside her, Hester's face was radiant, her hand clasped tightly in that of her new husband. Elinor thought only of Marcus.

At last the revellers departed, and she felt a twinge of fear. Would she disappoint him? She was so inexperienced.

She made her way to their room, and there she suffered herself to be undressed and bathed. Her bedrobe was but a wisp of gauze, and her attendants smiled as they drew it over her head. Then they left her.

Lost in the downy comfort of the massive bed, Elinor looked about her. The last time she had seen this room was when Marcus had been in danger of his life.

That time seemed long ago, as did the first day of their meeting. How she had hated him...his arrogance...his lack of feeling! Now it seemed that she had never known him for the man he was. Yet today she had become his wife. She pinched herself to make sure that she was not dreaming.

As the door opened, her heart began to pound. As

Marcus came towards her, his eyes alight with love, she held out her arms to him.

"My dearest love." He took her hands and kissed them. "This is the happiest day of my life, and yet I can't believe that you are mine at last...here at Merton as my bride...I must be the luckiest man alive."

Shyly, she reached out and touched his cheek. "I have loved you for so long," she whispered. "Oh, Marcus, we have been so foolish...there were so many misunderstandings."

"I know." He gave her a rueful smile. "I had begun to despair of winning you. You gave me no encouragement, you know."

She coloured a little. "I dared not, lest I betray myself. I...well...I believed that there could be no question of our marriage."

"Do I not know it?" he said with feeling. "In the end I had to resort to underhand methods to persuade you."

"Oh, no!" She blushed prettily. "It was not underhand to think of Hester's happiness."

Marcus dropped a kiss upon her nose. "I was thinking also of my own. I hoped in time that you would learn to care for me, that is, if I behaved myself." He was smiling as he looked into her eyes.

"And shall you do so, sir?" she teased. "You made your conditions clear. You were to enjoy a certain freedom to lead your own way of life, and I was to be allowed a circle of admirers..."

He threw off his robe and slipped into bed beside her. "Come here, my lady Rokeby. Let me assure you now that I will kill any man who looks at you."

"And what of yourself, my lord? Have you changed your mind already?"

"There was no need to change it, Elinor. I spoke in anger and frustration. What other woman could compare with you? You are my only love."

He turned her face to his and kissed her tenderly. "I shall guard you with my life," he murmured as the world was lost to them.

Elinor held him close as his hands caressed her.

"You are not afraid of me?" he whispered.

Elinor pressed her lips into the hollow of his neck.

"I shall never be afraid of anything again, my love. I cannot live without you. I knew it on that dreadful day when Hester disappeared. As you walked into the room I wanted to run to you, to hold you in my arms, and to beg you to forget the past, but I thought it was too late for a new beginning."

"This is our beginning, Elinor." His caresses grew more urgent. "I worship you, my beloved wife, and to know that you love me in return is a constant wonder to me."

"Believe it, my darling." Suddenly Elinor lost her shyness. With a cry of passion she threw her arms about his neck, and held his head against her breast.

Her body was aflame as he led her gently through the rituals of love, and she was amazed by her own response to his passion.

When she lay at last content within the shelter of his arm, she prayed that he had not been disappointed in her. She was inexperienced, after all. Yet for her own part she had not thought such happiness existed.

His cheek was against her hair. Then he lifted his head to look down at her, and her misgivings vanished. His face was radiant, and she could not mistake the ardour in his eyes.

"Now we are one," he told her simply. "Long ago we spoke of the bonds of friendship, but now we are held together by a stronger tie...the bonds of love."

* * * * *

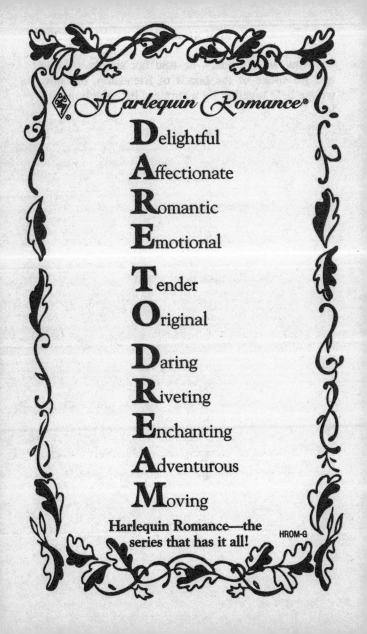

Harlequin Romance®

Delightful
Affectionate
Romantic
Emotional

Tender
Original

Daring
Riveting
Enchanting
Adventurous
Moving

Harlequin Romance—the
series that has it all!

HROM-G

HARLEQUIN PRESENTS®

HARLEQUIN PRESENTS
men you won't be able to resist
falling in love with...

HARLEQUIN PRESENTS
women who have feelings
just like your own...

HARLEQUIN PRESENTS
powerful passion in
exotic international settings...

HARLEQUIN PRESENTS
intense, dramatic stories that will keep you
turning to the very last page...

HARLEQUIN PRESENTS
The world's bestselling romance series!

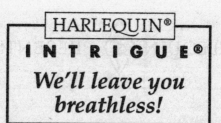

LOOK FOR OUR FOUR FABULOUS MEN!

Each month some of today's bestselling authors bring
four new fabulous men to Harlequin American Romance.
Whether they're rebel ranchers, millionaire power brokers
or sexy single dads, they're all gallant princes—and
they're all ready to sweep you into lighthearted fantasies
and contemporary fairy tales where anything is possible
and where all your dreams come true!

You don't even have to make a wish...
Harlequin American Romance will grant your every desire!

Look for Harlequin American Romance
wherever Harlequin books are sold!

∫ HARLEQUIN SUPERROMANCE®

...there's more to the story!

Superromance. A *big* satisfying read about unforget-
table characters. Each month we offer
four very different stories that range from family
drama to adventure and mystery, from highly emo-
tional stories to romantic comedies—and
much more! Stories about people you'll
believe in and care about. Stories too
compelling to put down....

Our authors are among today's *best* romance writ-
ers. You'll find familiar names and
talented newcomers. Many of them are
award winners—and you'll see why!

If you want the biggest and best
in romance fiction, you'll get it
from Superromance!

Available wherever Harlequin books are sold.

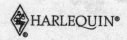

Not The Same Old Story!

Exciting, glamorous romance stories that take readers around the world.

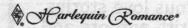
Sparkling, fresh and tender love stories that bring you pure romance.

Bold and adventurous—Temptation is strong women, bad boys, great sex!

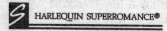
Provocative and realistic stories that celebrate life and love.

Contemporary fairy tales—where anything is possible and where dreams come true.

Heart-stopping, suspenseful adventures that combine the best of romance and mystery.

Humorous and romantic stories that capture the lighter side of love.